Praise for Lisa Whitefern's
Wicked Elementals Series

"I totally loved the characters. It was fun to read the sex scenes and all the use of the sex toys. I also enjoyed that the heroine had curves. The writing is easy and the romance and sex are really good. So of course I recommend it."

~ *Mary's Ménage Reviews on* Wicked Wonderland

Look for these titles by
Lisa Whitefern

Now Available:

Wicked Elementals
Wicked Wonderland
Wicked Safari

Wicked Safari

Lisa Whitefern

Samhain Publishing, Ltd.
11821 Mason Montgomery Road, 4B
Cincinnati, OH 45249
www.samhainpublishing.com

Editing by Linda Ingmanson
Cover by Gabrielle Prendergast

First Samhain Publishing, Ltd. electronic publication: March 2015
First Samhain Publishing, Ltd. print publication: March 2015

Dedication

To my amazing Samhain editor, Linda Ingmanson, and to Samhain author Renee Wildes, who writes marvelous fantasy romance and had the patience to proofread and give me advice on this book when others did not.

Prologue

Zimbabwe, Africa

Please let me keep this baby, Nhamo prayed as she pushed. *Please let me keep this little one.*

The heat hummed with the buzz of cicadas, the sky above a rich cobalt blue, the sun on her head warm as a hot paw.

Her mother, Chenai, knelt before her. Nhamo clutched the old woman's shoulders, bearing down as hard as she could, bending her knees with the effort.

The pain...will end...soon. Oh God, the burning.

She gritted her teeth as the shoulders broke through, and at long last, her second baby slid into its grandma's hands.

Nhamo dropped to the ground, breathing fast. She'd carried this baby so long that she had already grown to love it, sight unseen. Every kick had been a bonding experience. This labor had been as fast as her first. Maybe an hour.

Between her legs, the grass was sticky with blood.

Please. Don't give them reason to take another one.

"A boy. A boy, Nhamo."

Another boy.

Her mother seemed happy. Nhamo smiled. It was going to be all right.

God, he was so sweet, so adorable.

Mama Chenai had some muslin to wrap the baby in. But before her mother had even begun to wrap him, the humming began. Her newborn seemed to be humming, and he began to glow until he was incandescent with a silvery light.

It struck Nhamo as a blow to the chest, a powerful wrongness. Tears welled. She *knew*. Oh, she *knew* what would happen to him. She knew she couldn't stop it, and yet he was so beautiful.

The emptiness in her soul from losing her first son, Pili, would be magnified tenfold by this second loss.

Nhamo remained on the ground until the rest had been delivered, and her aunt had taken the afterbirth away.

The little one squalled, and beat his fists against his grandma's body. The vibrations of the witch doctors' drums pulsed through the ground. Their rhythm matched the beating of her heart, and filled her with pain and fear.

This can't happen again. Not a second time. Not a second boy.

She reached out to touch him again, brushing fingers over skin as smooth as the soft petals of the river lily. She took the baby from her mother's arms and held him close. But when she turned toward the faces of her tribe, she saw their features harden.

Three quick gasps burst from her like hiccups, and she let out a strangled sob.

The strangers were already gathered here. These were not the witch doctors who had tended to her as a child, who had helped her when she was ill. These were a new sort. These were strangers, a gang of money-hungry men.

Mukuru's humming meant *these* witch doctors would claim her son.

Her throat constricted so it was difficult to talk. "He's healthy. He's beautiful. Help me keep him."

Her mother stared at her. Finally, she whispered, "He's not natural."

Nhamo bit the inside of her cheek. "I'll hide him."

"You can't hide that." Chenai pointed at the glow.

"His name is Mukuru."

"Why bother to name him, child? He's *unnatural.* A changeling. Not of our blood "

"He *is* of our blood. He's ours."

"Shhh. Don't talk like that." Her mother lowered her voice. "You must accept his fate or be killed yourself. Remember, he is not one of us. He is a *changeling.*"

Clutching the glowing baby to her chest, Nhamo stood and followed her mother through the long grass, her heart thumping louder than the cursed drums as she wished for a miracle.

She approached the thorn enclosure surrounding her family's hut. Her mother pushed her toward the waiting men.

The witch doctors sat at the back of the hut. Some were white men from South Africa, and some were BaTonga like herself. Some wore wooden masks. Some wore Levis, Rolex watches and Nikes.

The smell of their magic was like matches, sulfur and eggs gone bad. By the light of the lantern, the men made music, faking the old tribal ways. Terror clenched in her chest. Her mouth and throat went dry.

The male members of her tribe sat with the other men, her uncle, father and husband among them.

The stolen teenage assassins, dressed in their lion skins, stood in the background, their faces impassive, waiting to see if another would join their brood.

Her father, Bomani, stepped forward and held out his hands. When Nhamo did not give the baby to him, he glared at her but set about inspecting the baby without comment.

Nhamo saw the traitorous glint in her father's eyes; he knew the humming meant money. Her lip curled when she glanced down at his expensive sneakers.

Finally, he spoke. "This baby must go with the others. He'll go with the witch doctors. Yes, this one must go. He's a changeling."

"Please." Her voice cracked on the word. "I'll do anything to keep him."

Bomani sneered. "We will pay our debts with this child."

She held Mukuru tightly against her body, but suddenly her uncle grabbed her, holding her still, while her father snatched the baby from her arms. Bomani handed Mukuru to a man in a wooden mask. The witch doctor clasped the child and headed out of the hut. Two of his friends followed him. Her shock at the suddenness of their combined actions gave way to screaming. She struggled against her uncle's grip, but the big man would not release her.

"Be silent. This will help your family. It is the only way to be rid of our debts. We don't want an unnatural child in our midst."

"Runo, that's your son! Stop that man," she screamed at her husband.

Runo only stared at the ground.

Her uncle tried to reason with her. "The witch doctors pay good money for the babies who are not normal. Your son will wear lion skins, be trained as an assassin to kill those who do not pay their debts. You must be proud."

"We gave them Pili. Don't let them take my second son." Tears streamed down her cheeks.

Nhamo pulled at Bomani's shirt, shaking him. Her father's face contorted with rage. He lifted a large wooden spear and held it above her. Though she was terrified, she almost welcomed death.

But another noise startled her father. He jerked around to stare at the entrance to the hut. Nhamo followed his gaze.

Every member of the tribe could sense the lion's magic as he entered the dwelling. Of that, she was sure.

Even as she feared the beast, Nhamo's heart leapt with hope. She had heard tales of a great lion who hated the witch doctors. A beast who was also a man.

The air around the lion sizzled with an electric charge, and golden sparks flew around him in a crazy whirlwind dance.

His great gold mane was streaked with brown and framed a massive head and fierce face. The lion's roar threatened like rolling thunder. The lion made eye contact with her. When she looked into his large golden eyes, her anxiety abated. Something in his gaze told her not to be afraid.

A young tribesman was the first to break the silence. He rushed at the lion with spear in hand, trying to be a hero, and Nhamo tripped him with her foot. Cursing, he fell to the dirt floor.

The lion stalked toward Bomani as though he were prey. Bomani's face went pale. He handed the baby back to Chenai. As much as Nhamo hated her father right then, she didn't want to see him dead.

"No, stop. Don't *kill* him."

The lion cuffed the man's head. Bomani fell, screaming. Blood flowed from claw marks on his scalp.

The scent of this lion's magic wasn't foul and tainted like that of the witch doctors. No, she sensed the creature's magic as heavy, golden, sensuous. Yes. She was sure now. This was the were-lion she had heard tales of. A were-lion who was part fae and part human, a Warrior of the Light, sworn to do as little harm as possible.

The maned lion growled deep and menacing, showing his fangs, then it surged out of the hut after the man in the wooden mask who had taken her baby.

Most of the medicine men stayed the whole night of the full moon, tending to Bomani's wounds. There would be a very high price for so many hours of the doctors' time. Nhamo lay in bed, hugging her legs to her chest, silent tears still streaming down her face. Her husband, Runo, tried to comfort her as best he could.

Then, it was there again, that sense of something powerful about to happen creeping up her spine. She turned to look at the entrance to the hut. The lion padded into view. From the lion's mouth hung a white muslin diaper with a sleeping baby hanging below.

Nhamo's heart sang. He'd done it. The lion had caught up with the witch doctors and their assassins before they got to the Storm Tower.

The lion padded up to her and laid the baby on her bed. Mukuru cried. Nhamo picked him up and inhaled his newborn scent. She kissed his exquisitely soft cheek before bringing him to her breast. They would never make her give him up again. Not now the were-lion had intervened. They were afraid of him.

Nhamo had her own baby back, but she wondered how many more children would be taken from the village. What would it take to save them?

She looked up at the lion, wanting to make eye contact with him again and thank him. But he was already leaving the hut, stalking out into the night.

Chapter One

Long Island, New York. Five years later.

"Are you interested in the sex life of lions?"

August frowned and tugged up the top of her vee-neck T-shirt. Professor Hendrik Kruger always seemed to address her cleavage rather than her face.

But her former advisor, Professor Buis, had a job at Harvard now. She'd *had* to put up with *this* guy supervising her PhD instead.

"Of course. I'm interested in everything about lions. My master's thesis was on lions' mating habits in captivity."

Dr. Kruger smiled and crossed his office to sit in his leather chair. The morning sun filtered through the blinds, catching the silver in his hair. August had heard other students in her dorm giggling about how hot Kruger was, calling him a "silver fox". It was true that Kruger was tall, tanned and strong jawed, but his eyes were dark, cold, wet stones.

August shuddered and folded her arms in front of her breasts.

Kruger pushed his glasses up the bridge of his nose and picked up some papers from his desk, scanning them. "I see all your research was done at Bronx Zoo. Have you ever studied lions in a purely natural habitat?"

She shook her head. The professor was *still* addressing her chest. *Creepy pervert.* Some men fooled themselves into thinking that women didn't notice these things. *Hello? We always notice, asshole.*

Kruger pushed his hands against his desk and stood. He put his finger on a poster on his wall. It was one August had noticed earlier, a blown-up photo of a magnificent male lion. The rich golden hues of his mane seemed so real, she imagined she could reach out and touch its softness.

"Africa is the best place to study lions," Kruger said.

"Oh, are you from there? You have a very strong New York accent, but your name—"

"My name is Afrikaners, yes. A lot of my relatives live in southern Africa, but I was born here."

"So you've studied lions over there yourself?"

"I had a personal relationship with a lioness in Zimbabwe once. The leader of her pride looked very much like this male."

August laughed. What a bizarre thing to say. "What do you mean, 'a personal relationship'?"

"She was a were-lion."

August stared at him, waiting for the punch line. Her stomach clenched. Surely he didn't believe in weres? Most people she knew at college didn't believe in anything paranormal, and she liked it that way. She didn't even believe in weres herself. In her twenty-three years on this planet she'd never encountered any. "I'm sorry. I don't understand your joke, Professor."

"I wasn't joking. And this brings me to another subject. You're a fine scientist. I've actually read some of your master's thesis. But if you want a job in this department beyond entry level, you need to do more field research."

She blinked, not understanding his casual change of subject. "I realize that."

"Good. Well, a wonderful opportunity has opened up for a student to do research in Zimbabwe. It would be a perfect fit for you."

It was the last thing she'd expected him to say. She imagined acacia trees, the sky an azure blue, the baked-yellow veldt and all the incredible wildlife.

Mom was mad enough when I moved out of her house and cut ties with all her crazy friends. Would she tolerate my leaving the country?

"That's an amazing offer, but I'll need some time to consider. It's pretty far out of my comfort zone." She tried a self-depreciating smile. "I lead a pretty boring, normal life."

Kruger lifted a brow. "Little half-fae don't get normal lives do they?"

His words were like the shock of a gut punch.

"Y...you believe in the half-fae? Seriously?" Most people she knew thought the Half-Fae Conferences her mother attended were just a bunch of kooky people fooling around. She tried a little humor. "Professor, I don't know anyone who believes in the half-fae except the half-fae themselves. And I'm not part of that crowd anymore."

Kruger grinned at her. The nervous flutter in August's stomach became a desperation to make him understand. "My passion is science. That's why I became a zoologist and an academic. I have no time for the half-fae and their...their nonsense."

"Well, it's unlikely your academic contract will be renewed. There's simply not enough money for us to take you on as a regular tutor this year. The zoology department is putting more money into overseas research programs."

A lump formed in her throat, and she clenched her fists. If she lost her teaching job, she couldn't afford her apartment, and then where could she go? Back to Mother's mansion? No way in hell. She tried to stop her lips from trembling. "I hadn't heard that there were money problems in the department. I...I need this job." She realized she was begging and clenched her jaw.

Kruger's smile was so smug she wanted to punch him. His gaze skimmed over her body, her black skirt, her legs, and back up to her breasts. Temper and anxiety knotted up inside her, but she kept silent.

"Of course you need this job," he said. "Or, rather, you need money. I'm offering you a scholarship, an apartment to live in, a marvelous adventure to go on. The department will even pay your airfare." Dr. Kruger walked around his desk to stand right next to her. He leaned close enough that she feared he might touch her. "You'll be working with trained professionals, August. You'll be working with *this* man, Arlan Leonard." He turned around a photo that had been sitting on his desk so it faced her. It was a photo of a man.

An Adonis of a man.

Desire glinted in the depths of his green-gold eyes. He wore a khaki tank, revealing muscular tanned shoulders and hints of his well-defined pecs. August itched to slip her hands beneath the cotton, and run her fingers over what she knew would be perfect abs. Blind hunger rose within her. She didn't know this man, not even his name. But she could almost feel his strong body covering hers, her nipples mashed beneath his chest. His rough tongue licking along her neck, grazing it, making her whimper.

A jolt of liquid heat shot between her legs, making her clench her thighs.

"Handsome, isn't he?"

Heat flamed across her cheeks. "Um, yeah, sure. He's gorgeous. Your son?" *Celibacy is making you lose your mind. You need to get laid, girl.*

"No, he's not my son, just one of my correspondence students. He works with lions in Africa."

She looked at the photo again a little nervously, interested despite herself. "Is he an American? Or is he from there?"

"Actually, he spent most of his childhood and teens in boarding schools in Australia and New Zealand. He has quite the accent. It's typical of rich white kids in Africa. Their parents ship them out to boarding schools in other countries, because life in Africa has many dangers, even for the rich."

"Sounds like an interesting guy."

"Oh, he is. Some people call him the Lion Whisperer. He can help you get up close and personal with them."

August didn't like how up close and personal Dr. Kruger was getting.

"Arlan's part sylph. He's a part fae like you. Like me." Kruger waved his hand to indicate both of them, then leaned closer to her. "You know, August, in the Fae Realm, sylphs live in ménage relationships. Have you tried mating with other half-fae yet? Have you been searching for your fated mates?"

He reached out to stroke her cheek, and she grabbed his wrist to stop him. She bit her lip. She'd never even suspected he was fae. The tension in the air was electric as, for half a minute, as each wondered how the other would respond. She itched to slap his face, but she didn't want to lose her chance at a job. Kruger had her academic career by the balls.

She let go of his wrist and thought of her dad's last words when he was suffering the week before he died. *"Don't let fear of your mother or the Half-Fae Network stop you from living your life."*

Her mind flashed back to the blood, all over that white lace, all over the rug, in that white, white room.

With a brutal mental shove, she pushed the memories from her mind and sat up straighter in her chair, shoulders back. She wasn't going to lose her job. "I'll take your offer of paid research work in Africa, but don't touch me again. I've no interest in you other than as a teacher."

Kruger sneered and waved his hand. "Fine. Your flight's already booked. I'll pick you up at seven o'clock this coming Saturday." He pulled open a drawer in his desk, retrieved a folder and opened it to hand her an airline ticket.

She jumped out of her chair. "You must be crazy. You expect me to just up and leave for Zimbabwe in three nights' time, with nothing prepared?"

"Things *are* prepared. I took the liberty of making an appointment for you with my own personal doctor. He's a good friend of mine and has made time in his busy schedule tomorrow to give you all the necessary vaccines and whatnot."

"I can't do this. It's all far too sudden."

"Don't you have a strong interest in protecting lions as a vulnerable species?"

August bit the inside of her cheek. "Yes, that's my dream."

A sly smile spread across his face. "Then why on earth would you turn down this kind of opportunity?"

He was right, in a way. It was something she'd dreamed about, but still...

"Why all the haste? It's very unusual." She backed away from him. "I'm sorry I really can't do this."

Kruger's smile faded. "It's best you do as I say, daughter of the dark fae. I know all your secrets. I know who and what you are, August Peak."

August clenched her teeth. She hated her last name. *Memories from school. August the Freak.* Everyone in her little 'burb knew her mother was one of those crazies who considered herself half-fae and went to those Half-Fae Network Conferences, dragging August and her sisters along. Always being the smallest child in the class hadn't helped either. Bookish, neglected midget freak.

"You're a friend of my mother's." She didn't pose it as a question. The answer was obvious.

"Yes, I'm friends with Duvessa. You mother is amazing."

August rolled her eyes.

"Everything Duvessa's done for the Half-Fae Network is incredible. She owns that huge casino. Crown Casino, that's the name, isn't it?"

"Yes," August whispered through clenched teeth.

"And she's the daughter of a fae princess."

"Listen, my Mom never even so much as met her own mother, you know that? She might talk a lot about being the daughter of the dark fae Princess Zenia, but she's never even been to the Fae Realm. She's only a half-fae. Her father was mortal."

Kruger shrugged. "Fae abandoning children they have with mortals is par for the course, especially among sylphs. You can't blame full-blooded fae for that. Why would they want to be burdened with a half-human child?"

"The fae should use protection, use condoms, and not be deadbeat dads and neglectful mothers."

Kruger laughed. "Mortal concepts. They don't apply to the fae. Dark fae are not tied to the tedious path of virtue. They just want to make love, have sex, have fun. Really, I can hardly believe Duvessa's daughter is so prim."

When she made a disgusted face, Kruger grinned. "Not even all mortals abide by those rules of yours, now do they? Lots of deadbeat dads and neglectful moms among humans too."

Frustration with his bullshit made her want to kick him, but she took a deep breath instead, thinking of her academic career. "Listen, Professor, you have to understand, if your primary interest in me is in my magical connections, I don't have any magic to speak of. I don't attend those conferences, now and—"

He pointed a finger at her. "*Both* your parents were half-fae. That makes you quite extraordinary in this day and age. "

August glared at him, her jaw tight.

Again Kruger's mouth eased into a smug smile. "Poor self-esteem in half-fae can inhibit magic powers. Is that your problem, August? We can work on that."

"My self-esteem is just fine." She bit the inside of her cheek at the partial lie, but her self-esteem was none of his business. "I choose not to use my powers. I don't have to use them. My magic, my right."

Contempt flashed across Kruger's face, then his eyes began to change turning from gray to amber. His pupils narrowed to slits. August's hands started to shake. She grabbed her books off his desk and turned toward the doorway.

21

"See you tonight, Ms. Peak." Kruger laughed after her.

As she ran down the corridor, she nearly tripped over a book some careless student had left on the floor. But she put her hand on the wall and managed to regain her balance. Anxiety bubbled in her stomach until it became a painful cramp. Kruger's eye change had struck a deep well of horror within her. Reptile eyes, like her mother's own serpent-like eyes when she became enraged.

August's pulse began to climb. If Kruger was Duvessa's friend, then he'd probably already discussed all this stuff with her mother. Maybe Mom even wanted her to go to Zimbabwe for some deranged reason of her own. Who knew with Duvessa?

She could hear her mother's past ranting in her mind. *"August, how stupid are you? How many times have I told you? Do you still not understand that the portals to the Fae Realm are closing up? There are only a few cities left in the world where the Half-Fae Conferences can be held, because these are the only places where a modicum of magic still exists.*

"I am descended from royal dark-fae blood. I am the daughter of Princess Zenia, granddaughter of Queen Zenobia. What is wrong with you? Why can't you respect your mother the way everyone else respects me?"

August had taken a deep breath and spoken the truth. *"There are some things I can never respect."*

She'd expected her mother to retaliate, had expected to be physically hurt in some way, but instead, a condescending smirk had crossed Duvessa's face.

"Dark fae are not tied like lesser creatures to petty morality and the tedious path of virtue. Dark fae are creatures of genius, so intelligent, so powerful that we are above the common horde. But I've never even been to the Fae Realm. Because of the stupidity of my mortal father's side of the family, I was bound to the mortal world. Mind-blowingly boring idiot humans."

Duvessa's voice had become a screech. *"The only mistake my royal mother ever made was mating with a stupid mortal. You wouldn't exist if she hadn't."*

Then, at last, August had been hurt. She'd paid for those words. August cringed, not wanting to let other memories back in. It was pathetic to be afraid of your own mother. But the unwanted memories hit her hard. The images stole her breath. Her knees weakened. and she leaned back against the wall of the corridor. She thought about going to the dean, but she knew the dean and Kruger were the best of friends. The thought that this man could destroy her career made her panic.

She pressed her forehead against the cool brick of the wall. If she wanted to keep her career, she would have to go to Africa. Somehow, she could see her life path shifting and changing before her now, like a high bridge twisting in an earthquake.

So much for her plans to have a quiet, scientific life.

23

Chapter Two

Zimbabwe, Africa

Zoologist Arlan Leonard clenched and unclenched his fists. As long as he was in control of his emotions, he was in control of the curse. But seeing the lioness Manyara in a pool of her own blood made his vision darken and anger course through his veins. They'd skinned part of her, but he'd know Manyara anywhere. They'd taken her skin so they could use her pelt for their assassin's costumes.

The new witch doctors in this area liked their assassins to be dressed in lion pelts. They gave their assassins weapons shaped like claws.

Some sick bullshit.

He got it. Arlan understood what it was about. It was about creating an image. They were all about appearances, these people. The lion skins and the clawlike weapons were meant to intimidate and threaten their victims. Leave an impression of magic. Make the villagers pay their so-called debts. Ironic that they tried to turn these children, these adolescents, into figurative monsters, pretend were-lions, when Arlan himself was the real thing.

Arlan bent down and used his pliers to unfasten the radio collar he had fitted on her himself. He'd known every inch of Manyara's tawny coat, and now she was just a mess of blood and gore.

The urgency of the curse seemed fueled by his rage over the death of Manyara, and he had to fight it.

Control, control. Deep, calming breaths. He would not shift. He would not give in to the velvet sensuousness of his were-form. The desire to feel a warm luxurious coat covering his body again. Sun on his silky fur. Arlan's fingernails extended and retracted, sharpened into claws and then flattened again into human fingers as he willed them back.

Scents became stronger. He could smell the smoke curling over the parched land and the sweat dripping off cattle. He could taste the hot dry air and the black tea and cut tobacco in the villagers' huts. He could hear the laugh of spotted hyenas in the distance, and the sound of vultures' wings.

Breathe deep. Control.

But Arlan wouldn't give in to the temptation, except when it was necessary to save the children. He'd never met any weres other than his ex-lover, Silvara, and he didn't believe she was even a real were-lion.

The bitch just used her dark-fae magic to turn me into one.

Silvara's cruel joke had been to turn him into the animal he loved, her revenge when Arlan told her he didn't love her the way she wanted, when he told her that he was sure she wasn't one of his fated mates.

He clenched his teeth, willing the golden fur sprouting on his arms to go down. He always wore clothes made of natural materials, as these would shift seamlessly with him if necessary. But he never shifted if he could help it. If he could stop it, he did. Slowly, the fur receded back into his body. His cotton T-shirt returned in full.

Arlan sighed and gave himself a figurative pat on the back for not shifting. He leaned back against the rough bark of an acacia tree. Behind him, he heard the high-pitched yips of zebras frolicking on the open plains, and listened to them while he tried to calm down.

He pulled out his wallet and flipped to a photo Kruger had given him. August was lifting weights. She wore skimpy gym shorts and a tank that showed off her flat stomach. Her sexy legs were short but very shapely. A flash of lust sent instant heat to his groin. Cursing his raging hormones, he scrutinized the picture. She was very petite, maybe five feet if that, feminine, curvy, yet trim. Her tiny size appealed to the dominant side of his nature.

The woman's profile from the side was classic, with delicate features, so serenely beautiful that it made him blink. A thick, shiny, chestnut braid, glowing with red highlights, hung down her back.

Visions flashed through Arlan's mind. He imagined fisting that thick braid in his hands as she knelt to suck his cock, or positioning her on her knees facedown on his mattress, cupping her tight ass, getting ready to drive into her.

Bloody hell!

Arlan slapped his wallet closed and slipped it into his back pocket, glancing down in some consternation at his tented shorts. August's mother was rumored to be a powerful dark fae. Could this August be using some kind of magic to ensnare him from afar?

Is that why I'm so turned on by a mere photo?

He shook his head. No, surely not. Having had a dark-fae ex-lover like Silvara had made him paranoid and distrustful of his own kind. Besides, Kruger had warned him of the powerful attraction between air and fire. Apparently, this girl had fire-fae magic in her blood and was a true half-fae, a breed becoming harder and harder to find.

Once he got home, he'd reread Kruger's instructions about sex magic and try to get his head around it some more.

Arlan scanned the dense thicket of thorn trees and, looked for the best path back to his work trailer, so he wouldn't frighten any of the wildlife. In the distance, a pair of giraffes browsed on leaves from the acacia tree. Sweat stung his eyes. He could taste the dust that hung like red paprika in the air. He had to step into the thicket, crunching branches as he went and cursing at each snap of a branch that might disrupt the animals' feeding. Two bush flies made persistent buzzing darts around his neck, and he brushed at them in annoyance.

Many miles away lay Arlan's sprawling stucco home, but while working with the lions in this part of the National Park, he slept in the work trailer. His friend and sometimes lover, Jay, slept there too, when his work took him out this way. Pride filled his soul when he thought of Jay in his cop's uniform. His childhood friend had finally fulfilled his dream to protect and serve.

A whoosh of wings over his head made Arlan glance up. A flock of egrets sailed above him. He followed their path for a while until he reached his work trailer, where he headed straight for the fridge and pulled out a Castle Lager. He tipped the beer to his lips and took a small sip. The ice-cold beverage was like ambrosia to his parched throat. He pulled a clean handkerchief out of his pocket, wiped the sweat from his brow and chugged more of his beer.

After setting the half-full bottle on the sink bench, he pulled the wallet full of photos out again to have another peek at this August. Her face had a delicate beauty, with the wide cheekbones of an old-fashioned film goddess. She also had one hell of a sexy body, he'd give her that. But even the thought of trusting another woman with dark-fae blood running through her veins was unpalatable. It should make him feel sick inside, not crazy aroused.

He took another sip and shrugged. Either August would take an interest in him, or she wouldn't. She'd either help him and Jay find the abducted children, or she wouldn't. He sure wasn't going to kiss her ass or let her manipulate him with dark-fae charm.

Given how hot she was, Jay would be interested. Jay was always interested in women. It seemed to take Jay's mind off the fact he was also attracted to men, a fact that, at age twenty-one, Jay wasn't mature enough to handle yet and found disturbing.

Lisa Whitefern

The beast within Arlan snarled at the thought. His cock was hard enough to cut diamonds just from looking at August. It made him want to seek out Jay.

Maybe, just maybe, he'll be willing to take a break from work.

Maybe today would be one of those rare days the dominant policeman put aside his issues about being bisexual. Arlan pushed open the door of his work trailer and stepped out into the blazing heat again.

The sound of cicadas grew in volume with each rising degree of heat from the sun. Paradise fly catchers flitted around the acacia trees that stood off in the distance, and the dried ground around them seemed to waver in the heat. Arlan kept walking in search of his lover's post.

At last he came to the observation post nestled among a cluster of granite boulders that afforded Jay a broad view of the main dirt road. From this vantage point, he could also take in any action on the many little dirt roads that forked off to the side.

Jay had stretched a canvas tarp across two boulders to protect himself from the heat. He'd lived here the past five days, coming back to the work trailer only to grab food and showers. Arlan bit his lip. Jay risked his life every day here to fight the men who threatened the wildlife in this area. It was something Arlan tried not to think too much about.

As he neared the observation point, he watched Jay bend to put a thermos back in his backpack lying on the ground. The action gave Arlan a good view of Jay's muscular butt in tight shorts. "Hey, Jay."

Jay straightened and stood up. A little sound of pleasure escaped Arlan's throat at the sight of his lover. Taller than Arlan by several inches, his best friend was built like a tank, with muscular arms and darker skin that bespoke a touch of Shona blood. His real fae mother must have been very fair-skinned, or Jay's skin might have been somewhere closer to the blue-black

28

of the Shona tribe so prevalent in this area. Instead, it was a luscious caramel color, his facial features strong and sculpted.

Jay lowered his sunglasses. Cynical dark eyes caught Arlan and pinned him to the spot, glittering fae eyes that had haunted Arlan's dreams since that day in boarding school when his best friend had become something more.

Where was Jay's head at today? What mood was he in? His lover had issues. Arlan's life mate was a cop, and in this country, things could be deadly dangerous, but they had magic on their side. At last, Jay spoke. "Why don't you come on over and say hello?" There was a definite edge to the word "hello".

He'd half expected to be sworn at and told to bugger off, but Jay appeared to be in a good mood, a horny mood. Arlan didn't need to be asked twice. He stepped toward his —on-again-off-again lover.

Jay began humming one of his protection spells. Arlan had just enough fae blood in his veins to see the faintest pale blue light surrounding them. Jay could make strange lights appear, but he was probably fooling himself about how strong his magic was. Jay was only half-fae, after all.

As soon as Arlan was within reach, Jay grabbed his shoulders and bent in for a kiss. Arlan moaned into his mouth. Jay pulled back, nipped quickly at his ear, blew softly on his exposed neck, then bit down. Arlan yelped, but his dick swelled in response. Hell! The way Jay blew hot and cold was going to drive him crazy.

What the fuck was with all this sudden passion after denying him for months, after all the bullshit arguments about not being bisexual?

I shouldn't do this. I'm going to end up angry again.

Aggression, testosterone and lust surged through his veins as Arlan gripped Jay's firm, muscled ass and pulled him closer until his younger lover's body was flush against his groin. The lion within Arlan rode him hard, wanting to take control. Jay's tongue, tasting of burnt coffee, thrust into Arlan's mouth. He pulled harder on Arlan's hair, yanking his head back and forcing his lips apart for more.

The battle for who is the Alpha is always between us.

But today Arlan could feel himself yielding, submitting as the velvet smoothness of Jay's lips slid against his, coaxing, teasing and demanding a reaction. Jay shoved his tongue deeper into Arlan's mouth, smiling a little as his lover gagged from the depth. Arlan choked, but his cock was completely rigid, straining against his khaki shorts.

Jay relented and pulled back. Arlan moaned, panting, trying to recover his breath. Jay's massive biceps bunched as he pulled his T-shirt over his head. Arlan had the urge to bend and lick the slope of Jay's broad chest. To lick down the exposed stomach muscles and kiss each one. Jay had perfect abs. But as soon as Arlan began, Jay held him still and glanced nervously around. "Just hold up. I need to put a stronger circle of magic protection around us." Jay pushed on Arlan's head in an obvious effort to make him kneel and hummed more magic until the violet circle of light around them stood sharp and bright.

Then he pulled his thick, heavy cock from his khaki trousers. Its dark, curving length reared up before Arlan, the mushroom head gleaming purple-black in the sunshine.

Maybe this is one battle I don't mind losing. Arlan dropped to his knees on the baked yellow grass.

Jay must have showered in the trailer not that long ago. He still smelled of citrus shower gel combined with the raw scent of the land and Jay's own delicious musky male scent underneath. Arlan's cock strained painfully against the cotton of his shorts. Part of him still expected Jay to reject him at the last possible minute, as he had sometimes done in the past. Tentatively, he brushed the base of Jay's cock with his lips.

The hot-straw smell of lion grass mixed with the intense scent of the younger man's arousal. Arlan took one long lick across his lover's skin and waited. Today, Jay didn't seem about to change his mind. Relaxing at last, Arlan licked up and down the shaft, dipping his tongue occasionally into the little slit. He took some of Jay's pre-come and worked it down the silky skin of his shaft. He stopped and looked up into Jay's dark brown eyes that flashed with glints of onyx. Slowly, Arlan worked his hand up and down. Jay moaned and gripped his lover's hair, jerking Arlan's head up a little.

"Don't do that so slowly, you little tease. Speed up before I slam your face into my crotch and make you gag on it."

Arlan moaned at the thick lust in Jay's voice, the harsh words inspiring him to pick up the pace. Quickly, he closed his lips around the head, sinking down as far as he could, sucking up and down the length again and again, increasing the pressure. Arlan's cock became even harder, and his balls drew up. He started to really get into it, using the tongue work he knew Jay loved. Jay growled and arched his back, his moans mingling with the hum of cicadas.

Suddenly, Jay gasped, pushing roughly at Arlan's head, wrenching his dick from Arlan's mouth. He bent and pulled up his khakis.

Arlan clenched his fists and gritted his teeth, red-hot fury warring with the humiliation of rejection. The lion pressed against the inside of his skin. He growled low in his throat, his fingers changing, his claws unsheathing in his rage. "What the *fuck*? Jay what the *hell* is wrong with you?"

Jay yanked Arlan up and slammed his hand over his friend's mouth, gripping it tight. He felt Jay's warm breath on his ear as he whispered, "No, mate. It's not about that."

Arlan turned and followed Jay's gaze to see the dust plume of a moving vehicle, and swore softly. *Dammit to hell!* They both ducked down. Jay gave Arlan's hair a momentary caress, an unspoken apology.

A silver Hummer slowed, and the driver stopped near a giant baobab tree. Arlan clenched his jaw tight. When the door opened, golden lion pelts lay visible on the backseat. One of them was probably Manyara's. Not all poachers were greedy. Some men were desperate to feed their families. But this lot, with their expensive car... They were obviously part of the crime racket run by the witch doctors. Who else wanted lion skins?

Two burly men in khaki trousers climbed awkwardly out of the car. One wore no shirt, only a mesh vest, and one of the wooden masks the witch doctors favored. Around his waist was a canvas webbing belt heavy with fat brass cartridges. On the other side, a bottle filled with some dark substance hung from his belt. The poachers slung rifles over their shoulders.

The men headed on foot in the direction of the watering hole, where, from his vantage point, Arlan could clearly see a black rhino taking a drink.

"Look at how heavy she is, her belly low to the ground. She's with calf." Jay was particularly fond of rhinos.

Arlan nodded. "They want her horn."

"Fucking greedy bastards. They have money. They don't need it." Jay's feelings matched his own. The men had a nice car. These men weren't starving. This was purely about greed.

Jay trained his gun on the men, who were still some distance from the mother rhino. One of the men turned to face Arlan, and he thought he saw a fae gleam in the man's eyes, but he turned away too quickly for Arlan to be sure. The man didn't seem to notice him. Was Jay's magic really powerful enough to hide them? It seemed so.

"They won't get her." Jay's voice was deep and raw with anger. His hands shook as he aimed his gun. If Jay wanted to shoot the poachers, it was his legal right here in Zimbabwe to do so. Arlan almost hoped he would.

Chapter Three

It was late in the day, the sun mellowing to an orange red through the hazy dust that always hung over the savannah during the dry season, by the time Arlan got back to the work trailer. He'd spent the rest of the day "calling" lions, playing tapes of other lions and dying prey to try to lure the animals to him so he could study them.

Now back at the trailer, he pushed open the door. Jay sat on a fold-out couch, polishing his boots. He glanced up and raised one eyebrow in greeting, then went back to polishing.

"How did the arrest go?"

After they'd spotted the poachers, Arlan had stepped back to let Jay go after the men. It drove Arlan crazy to think of his friend in danger, but it was Jay's job and one he was very good at.

Jay didn't glance up. "I took them down to the station after you went home. Bastards are in the cells. Rhino's alive. That's what counts."

"It was brave of you not to shoot them."

Jay still didn't look up at him. The frown on Jay's face set Arlan's teeth on edge. At last Jay spoke. "I'd never take a life I didn't have to. You know that."

The tension between them was like a taut rubber band ready to snap. To Arlan, Jay's foul mood was no real mystery. A heavy weight lay in his chest. He had long been patient with Jay.

Three years older, Arlan had protected Jay, his father's business partner's son, from bullies in the days before Jay surprised everyone with a mammoth growth spurt and hours spent in the gym. Jay's ambition had always been to become a policeman. He'd wanted to right the wrongs he'd seen in Africa. Now he was a fine cop, but massively fucked up about his bisexuality. Arlan had once gone through some of the same kind of angst, but his patience with Jay's bullshit was wearing thin.

Arlan tried to make eye contact with his friend again, but Jay turned away. Well, hell. Arlan wasn't going to play this game.

"We got a package from Kris and Nick's Toy Emporium today. It contained fae condoms. The kinds that are so fairy thin, you can't even feel them."

Jay was silent a moment longer. Then he shrugged. "Maybe one of us will go into town tomorrow night and get lucky with a *girl.*"

"Maybe." *Yeah, right, asshole.*

Arlan shook his head and opened up his laptop. "I'm gonna log online and read that email Kruger sent us. The one about sex magic. "

Jay dropped into the chair opposite and twisted the top off a bottle of Castle Lager. "Yeah, read *that* to me."

After opening up the laptop sitting on the makeshift desk, Arlan logged on, typing in his email address and password. "Here it is." He took a deep breath before reading aloud and trying to imitate Professor Kruger's New York accent. "The practice of sex magic in its most basic form involves using the energy of sexual arousal by intense visualization of the desired object in the seconds after orgasm." Arlan paused as he was rewarded by Jay's snorting laugh at his imitation.

Once Jay was silent again, he continued. "In the moments after orgasm is achieved, one must visualize the desired result. In this case, Mr. Leonard, you, your friend Jay Nandoro and Ms. August Peak will be visualizing the enchanted storm tower that is the secret hideout of the witch doctors. We need to find their tower before we can hope to defeat their magic. "

Jay rolled his eyes. "Obviously."

Arlan smiled at Jay's sarcasm. He put on the fake New York accent again.

"Though you claim, Mr. Leonard, that you are only a quarter fae, you must not believe that that means you are without power. The fae blood that runs through your veins means that you can still tap into the ancient power source if only you put the work in. Sex magic is one way for a man with only a small amount of fae blood in his veins to do just that."

Arlan stopped to take another pull on his beer before continuing. "Success at achieving sex magic requires two men of fae blood and a willing female of a superior nature forming a ménage. Elements of power exchange, submission and domination between the parties involved may also increase the chance of success. All participants engaged in sex magic must be pure of heart."

"Pure of heart? What does that mean?"

Arlan scratched his head. "I dunno. I guess it just means you're not an asshole?" He clicked the little x in the corner of the screen to close the browser and glanced over at Jay.

"And what does 'a female of a superior nature' mean?

Arlan shrugged. "Who knows. The guy's a bit of a snob, but he's an excellent zoologist, and pretty knowledgeable about magic too."

Jay's lip curled in a sneer. "Sex magic." He spat out the words. "That's the kind of thing witch doctors do, witches in general or sorcerers. Humans with no fae blood in them at all. My mother would have been disgusted."

"Well, your mother was at least half-fae and able to visit the Fae Realm, right? She was never in our situation of being totally trapped in the mortal realm with almost no understanding of how to use magic."

Jay glared at him.

Arlan sighed. "You've never actually told me everything that happened with your mother, mate. You can't get pissed with me for getting stuff wrong when I don't know any details. All you ever say is she's not around."

"She basically died when I was six, okay?"

"Basically died?"

"Died, fell into a permanent coma, whatever." He waved his hand in a dismissive gesture. "She tried to use magic to heal my dad after he was shanked in prison."

A lump of sympathy rose in Arlan's throat. *Jay's as much of an orphan as I am. No wonder he's so fucked up.* "I'm sorry."

Jay took another deep pull of beer. "Anyway, the thought of doing sex magic like some witch or sorcerer goes against the grain. My mother despised mortal's attempts at magic. She used to talk about that." He sniffed. "But I was too little when we lost her. She never had time to teach me more than some dumb party tricks."

"I didn't even know full-blooded fae like your mother could fall into a coma trying to use healing magic. I thought that only happened to half-fae."

"Yeah, well, there's been so much interbreeding between fae and half-fae, my mother must have some human blood in her somewhere. I don't know that there are any real full-blooded fae living in the mortal realm, Arlan. She was powerful, so people just called her that. She didn't manage to survive trying to heal my dad anyway. She's been in a coma since I was six. I'm twenty-one. She's not coming out of it." He took another sip of beer before he changed the subject again. "You know this professor of yours seems like a total wanker."

Arlan laughed. "Say what you really feel, Jay."

He raised one eyebrow. "I always do." He put his beer down on the coffee table. "Listen, the guy is pushing his agenda on you, on me, trying to make it seem easy. But from everything I've heard among the half-fae, sex magic is difficult to conduct and often doesn't work. Even if August agrees to it, it's not necessarily going to do us any good at all."

Arlan sighed.

"Also, you and the professor are making a lot of assumptions about August. Why would she want to be involved in sex magic? And why would she be willing to do it with us?"

Arlan used his fingernail to scratch some of the label off his bottle. "Well, we have to do *something*. We have to try. The witch doctors are getting stronger and stronger."

"We both have fae blood. You'd think we could beat a bunch of humans messing around with powders and drums."

"I think the witch doctors probably have some magic blood. I've scented it. It's like..." He paused to think for a second. "It smells like sulfur. It's up to you and me to find out where it comes from."

A muscle twitched in Jay's jaw. "Yeah, you're right. I guess we have to try any means available, because this shit has been going on for, what? Ten years now?"

"Any of those kids who are still alive are losing their childhoods year after year. Being trained as assassins... It's sick, Jay."

Jay nodded. Arlan rubbed his hands over his face." I also hate that from what Kruger's told me, it sounds like August's mother is some world-famous dark fae. So this could be some kind of trick. I'm not unaware of that."

Jay shrugged. "Relax, she's not your ex."

"Mate, Silvara was the most manipulative creature I've ever met. She sure had me fooled. I never would have believed she was dark fae."

"Exactly my point."

"Give me that photo you got."

Arlan fished his wallet out of his pocket again and flipped to the picture of August.

Jay whistled. "She's super hot. But has an innocent face."

"Looks can be deceiving."

Jay laughed. "Aren't you the one who wanted to do this sex magic thing? We don't try it, the children don't get saved. It's that simple."

Arlan thought of Mukuru. That sweet baby had grabbed his heart more than any other. And that was one he'd saved, when there were so many others he had not. "You're right."

Jay laughed. "Okay, mate, well, let's do this thing. Let's meet August."

"I'm meeting her tomorrow at noon."

"Crap, I have to work. You and your flexible job."

Arlan took the wallet back from his friend and put in his pocket. "Don't worry, you'll see her soon enough."

"You don't sound that happy about meeting her."

Arlan sighed and rubbed his hands over his face. "She's of dark-fae blood. I don't think she's the right person to do this thing with."

Jay gave Arlan one of his sexy, cynical smiles. "Right or wrong, I'm pretty sure we'll have fun trying."

Chapter Four

"So you've come to help save our lions?"

Runo, the junior game warden, smiled at August and Professor Kruger, his perfect white teeth contrasting sharply against his ebony skin. His hair hung in thin braids, bright with shiny red ochre.

August smiled at the guide. "I can't wait to see them."

It was early morning, and the glow of the rising sun sent pink and orange rays knifing skyward. The spiky yellow flowers of the spiny acacia trees shimmered against the dawn sky.

They headed for Hwange National Park. August followed the junior game warden through the grass. It was prickly on her bare legs. Now and then, stickers and burrs punctured her feet, but it wasn't an unpleasant kind of pain. Certainly, a little pain was worth it to be here, in this land where lions still ran free.

Runo opened the door to his Land Cruiser, and she buckled herself in, then gasped when he took off at breakneck speed with seemingly no concern about the many potholes they encountered. August grasped the handle on the side of the door and screamed. Runo's only response was laugher. He slowed and parked within viewing distance of some lion cubs.

Runo climbed into the backseat and brought out a thermos. He poured tea for Professor Kruger and gave her a mug as well. The three sat in the Land Cruiser drinking and watched the lioness with her cubs.

Panthera Leo.

Their sleek golden coats blended beautifully with the dry grass. The mischievous, bouncy cubs leaped around their mother, who took little notice of their antics except to swipe an occasional paw at them. One little one yawned, showing its sharp fangs and its long, curling tongue. They were cute now, but would soon be lethal.

Suddenly, the pride froze. All eyes turned, staring into the distance. August followed their gaze.

The morning light revealed a broad-shouldered man. She shivered—not from the dawn chill, but from the realization she was the subject of his stare.

The man's golden brown hair was tied back with a strip of leather, his face tan, with high cheekbones. She could feel the tension in the air, her nipples tightening beneath her thin khaki shirt. Sweet Jesus, the man was more stunning than in his photo. The mysterious Arlan Leonard.

For a moment more, he continued to stare at her like a beast watching its prey, but his gaze left hers when he noticed the lioness. The mother rose to meet him and pressed her face against his chest in a typical feline cheek-rub greeting. The cubs tumbled around his feet.

In all her time working with the big cats, she'd never seen a person interact with them so effortlessly. It was almost as if Arlan were one of the pride. He obviously had an amazing knack with them.

Arlan turned and headed back to his vehicle to get something.

Runo's calm voice interrupted the riot of erotic and inappropriate thoughts her brain tossed up. "This is Chido. She's one of only two remaining lionesses in this area. The electronic collar she wears lets us monitor her whereabouts."

Her breath caught when she realized Arlan was heading back toward them. Stubble peppered his jaw. She imagined touching it, finding it as rough as sandpaper. He wore what once might have been a khaki shirt but was now sun bleached to near white. The short sleeves were rolled up to reveal powerful biceps. The muscles in his arms were roped and seemed to ripple with power as he dragged a large animal carcass across the grass.

Kruger placed a hand on her shoulder. "That's a dead impala."

"Where did that come from?"

"A cheetah killed it and left most of the carcass when a car scared him off. We sometimes feed the cubs, because not all those cubs are Chido's. She can't be expected to feed them all. The mother of some of those cubs is dead."

"Because of poachers?"

"Yes. Almost all the lions that used to be in this area have been killed by poachers. That's why you're needed here. We need to find ways to encourage the remaining lions and lionesses to breed so they don't become extinct in this region."

August sighed inwardly. She hadn't realized poaching was a problem to this extent.

Arlan approached the Land Cruiser. Runo and Professor Kruger climbed out of the vehicle. She stayed nervously where she was.

"Come out, August. Arlan won't let the female hurt you," Runo coaxed.

But it wasn't the lions that frightened her. It was their tamer and her reaction to him. And there was something so familiar about his face...

Professor Kruger took her hand to help her out of the Land Cruiser. To calm her nerves, she reached back in the car for her cup of tea. Even as she turned from Arlan to get the drink, she could feel his gaze on her back, and a shot of liquid heat sizzled between her legs.

Good God. A handsome face and a good body didn't usually fry her connection to the rational part of her brain. He was all muscle, from his pecs to the washboard abs she could see beneath the thin material of his shirt. Good Lord, but he made her mouth water.

41

Obviously, she needed a good session with her vibrator to straighten herself out. Pity she forgot to pack it.

It's been five years since you last got laid, loser.

Fuck off, I was studying.

She leaned against the Land Cruiser, sipping the cooling tea. An image of her high school lover, Ryan, came into her head.

Nothing could be worse than losing her virginity to Ryan and the public humiliation he'd put her through. Not to mention she didn't need any man commenting on her scars, which was bound to happen.

"August, this is zoologist Arlan Leonard." Kruger nearly stuttered with excitement as he managed to introduce her. The thought crossed her mind that Kruger was sexually attracted to Arlan too.

August managed a weak smile.

"Arlan, this is the woman I've been so eager for you to meet. August."

Arlan looked her over. "Hey there, August."

His accent was to die for. Was he British? No, Australian? She passed her cup of tea to Runo when Arlan extended his hand so she could take it. Arlan's grip was strong and firm. Maybe her panties were just wet from the heat of the day?

"August. That's an unusual name. Were you born that month?"

"Um, yes. Yes, I was."

"Same here. Both Leos, huh?"

She nodded. "I've always been told I'm nothing like a Leo, since I have Virgo rising and a lot of planets in Virgo." Oh God, she was babbling.

He stared at her without responding.

She managed a smile. "I can't place your accent, Arlan. Where are you from?"

He took a step back. "I'm from here."

Kruger smirked and gave Arlan a slap on the shoulder. "Arlan's parents were Kiwis, New Zealanders. His mother's a half-fae. They came here for business reasons when he was a toddler, but Arlan went to boarding school and college in New Zealand, hence the accent. It's the standard thing, Europeans sending their kids away from Africa during their school years."

"Oh, how interesting. Yes, I remember now." She gestured to Kruger. "You mentioned that before didn't you, Professor?" More silence stretched between them that she felt compelled to fill. "How old were you when you went to boarding school? Were they strict there?"

Arlan's sexy lips set in a line, and his eyes went cold. "I was seven, and yes."

August swallowed and shoved her hands in the pockets of her cotton shorts. Maybe she shouldn't have said anything. But how horrible to be a little child and be sent away from your parents to a boarding school in another country. Getting away from her own mother would have been a blessing, sure, but she would have missed her dad like crazy. She couldn't imagine being as young as seven and not having anyone to hug.

She glanced back up at Arlan to find him glaring at her like she was something he'd scraped off the bottom of his shoe.

Talk about awkward.

She felt the color rise in her cheeks and tried to change the subject. "What kind of business do your parents run, Arlan?"

His lip curled, and he seemed to grit his teeth.

Kruger laughed. "That's kind of a sensitive subject with Arlan. He hates his parents' business. You seem to have a talent for finding his sore spots."

Arlan slapped Kruger's shoulder. "Nonsense. Nothing's a drama, mate, but why don't you take August back into town, find her somewhere to sleep? I've told you before I only want people at camp who have a real commitment to the lions. It messes up their routine to have random people around. It's disturbing for them."

For a second, she was too stunned by his rudeness to react. Then she steeled herself to glance up into the intensity of his gaze, determined not to let him know how intimidating she found him. Before she could even answer, Kruger spoke. "We'll discuss that later. Listen, Arlan, Runo and I have to leave now. I have a class to teach. Show August around a bit, will you?"

"Um, I'm a zoologist same as you," she said. "I have a lot of training working with lions. It's what I'm here for. Didn't Kruger tell you that?"

Arlan ignored her completely, turning from her and directing his comments to Kruger. "If the dark fae is staying out here, I don't know where she'll sleep."

Kruger smirked. "She's staying here. Don't flake out on me. We need this woman."

Outrage made August light-headed and at a loss for words.

Kruger lifted his hand in a good-bye gesture and headed toward the Land Cruiser. Runo glanced at August uncertainly and gave an apologetic smile before following Kruger.

She should call out to them, run to catch up, but the combination of her attraction to Arlan and her fury at the rudeness of the two men had made her thoughts freeze. Plumes of dust flew up as the Land Cruiser hit the dirt road. Anger built in August like a white heat. Finally, she found her tongue and turned to Arlan. "Is this how you always treat women here? I'm not putting up with this."

There was an air of casual dominance about Arlan that made her shiver. His gaze raked over her body, taking in every curve. He made her self-conscious, but his blatant appraisal had her nipples stiffening beneath her shirt. "I'm sorry. I have every respect for *women* and other zoologists. It's just the dark fae I have a problem with. Especially ones that are sexy as hell."

Blood pooled in her cheeks. As much as she wanted to slide her glance away, she refused to submit to his intimidation tactics. The words hung heavy in the air between them. August swore and kicked herself for not running to catch up with

Kruger. "Listen, I'm staying in an apartment Kruger owns in Hwange. You don't need to show me around or anything else. Just drive me back to his place. We don't need to speak to each other again."

"Why are you here, little dark fae? What's your plan?"

"I'm not dark fae."

"When Kruger told me about you, I did some digging around, some research. Your mother's a VIP in the Half-Fae Network. She has her finger in a lot of pies."

August felt a nerve twitch in her jaw. "I don't know about much of any of that. My mother and I are estranged. I can't stand her."

He reached out and grabbed her. She managed one short scream as he pulled her close and tossed her onto the dry grass. Strobes of light exploded behind her eyes as she hit the ground, sending shards of pain through her limbs. His solid, muscular body landed on top of her.

"Are you all right? Are you hurt?" he muttered.

"What the hell? Get *off* me, you insane Neanderthal."

She pushed again, wriggling to get out from under him, but Arlan pinned her to the ground.

A sudden noise like a car backfiring made her flinch and clutch his biceps with both hands. Arlan gripped her tight and rolled her over twice until they were both behind a tree and he was covering her body again.

Despite the pain, his masculine weight poured lust into her brain. Her nipples poked through her bra and thin shirt against his rock-hard chest. Strong arms encircled her, and she caught a whiff of cedar wood and musky male that made every part of her tingle. Something pressed against her hip, throbbing through the soft material of his shorts. A curl of desire wrapped in her stomach. Liquid arousal seeped from her core.

"Are you okay? Are you hurt, baby?"

"Don't call me baby. Let me go. I don't like you."

Arlan's nostrils flared. He took a deep sniff. His mouth quirked in an infuriating grin. "Oh, you like me, all right. I can smell your heat on the open air."

A shiver ran through her. If her arms hadn't been trapped by his, she would have slapped his face.

But the force with which he held her, the coarseness of his words, the rough edge that had betrayed his own arousal from the minute they met... *Damn!* He was obnoxious, and still he turned her on.

You're a pervert, Peak.

Something slammed into an anthill and whip-cracked the air around them. Lead scythed across the grass above their heads.

"Oh my God! Someone's shooting at us?" She let loose a scream as more bullets ripped through the grass, spraying dirt at her feet.

The back windscreen of the Land Cruiser shattered.

"You catch on fast, kid."

She glanced around frantically and finally saw the three men hiding behind an acacia tree.

Arlan clasped her shoulder. "My gun's in the damn car. Keep down."

One of the men was reloading his weapon. The other two hurled some kind of black powder with flecks of red into the air and chanted something she couldn't make out. For a second, she thought the language might be the national language, Shona, but then she knew it wasn't. "That's not Shona?"

Arlan raised his eyebrows. "That's not Shona, or BaTonga or any tribal language. It's a magic language. And if I know these people. Guns won't be all they're using. They'll use magic as well."

"What are they throwing? Oh God, that's not...?"

"Get down!"

A fat pillar of jet-colored powder billowed upward from behind the trees.

As they crouched on the ground, his hand covering her mouth, Arlan whispered in her ear, "Dark dust. The very opposite of your Tinkerbelle fairy dust. The evil stuff."

Arlan pressed his mouth against her hair and neck. She guessed that was his way of protecting himself as he sheltered her with his body and hands.

A man wearing an elaborate feathered headdress rushed forward and hurled the substance from a glass bottle right in her face. Arlan's hand stopped the dust from getting in her mouth but not her eyes and nose. August spluttered against his hand. She couldn't help but inhale. Her nasal passages stung like fire, and the substance got in her mouth despite Arlan's protection. As it slid down the back of her throat, choking pain grasped her esophagus. She rubbed at her stinging eyes. The world around her vibrated and buzzed. Her vision dimmed, and she drifted into darkness.

Chapter Five

Two sets of warm hands skimmed along her body, making her moan. Arlan Leonard kissed down her stomach, while the tall, handsome part-African man eased her thighs apart.

Who was he, this other beautiful man? Her body refused to let her mind care, as his fingers skimmed over the skimpy lace of her panties.

Meanwhile, Arlan flicked his tongue into her belly button, causing wild sensations to skitter through her, until she gripped his hair.

The mysterious man, whose darkish skin indicated some African blood, paddled his fingers against the gusset of her panties until they were soaked through. He grinned at the power he had over her. He was a natural Dom. This man would own her. His eyes never left hers as he scraped a fingernail over the lace right at her center, across her clit, through her panties. She whimpered, her legs too weak to hold her up, so he bent to force her legs apart, holding her steady against the wall as he teased the crease of her thigh with his tongue. Her panties were so soaked, they weren't much of a barrier between his insistent fingers and her snatch. Her desire pulsed hot when his callused fingers strayed near her center again, tormenting her.

"Damn, baby. So slick, so eager."

Every part of her burned with need. She could hardly breathe from the lust coursing through her veins. He tormented her with his fingers a moment longer, then slid his tongue under the lace to lick her swollen slit.

Arlan's lips found one nipple, and he flicked his tongue over it while tweaking the other nipple with his thumb and forefinger.

The mystery man forced his rolled tongue under her panties, fucking her with it, making her cream against his face.

"Do you love it, August?" The combination of Arlan's accent and the dark lust in his voice sent a thrill straight to her already tormented pussy. "Do you love that bastard eating you out?"

"Yes," she whispered. "Oh yes." She lifted her hips, writhing against the mystery Dom's face, trying to catch it, trying to reach that peak.

"Sleeping Beauty?"

What?

Her mind fought to catch the dream. She hadn't come, she needed to come, but the dream was like a distant mirage fading and melting. She groaned, desolate at the loss of her almost-orgasm. Slowly, she rose to consciousness.

"I was wondering when you'd stir."

She opened her eyes. There was a man in the room with her, and he wasn't Arlan or Professor Kruger. He was a huge, dark-skinned man she didn't know. She jerked her hand from between her legs, relieved that she was well covered up by a sheet and blanket.

The man moved toward her. Blood pumping, she struggled to sit up, then scooted backward until her back pressed against the headboard.

"Hey. Hey, sweetheart. Come on now, I'm not going to hurt you." He held out a hand containing an indigo-blue mug. "You really need to drink this. That dark dust is putrid stuff. Fucking dark-fae psychos."

The memory of the shooting and the dark dust jumped back to the forefront of her mind, wiping out the pleasant, nebulous remnants of whatever she'd been dreaming. Icy fear tightened in her lungs.

Dark dust.

49

It could stop pureblood humans' breathing, cause internal bleeding, make tumors grow or other medical mischief on the wishes and strength of power of the dark fae using it. It could seriously harm half-fae too. Why hadn't she died? Her eyes widened as a thought struck her.

Jay held a blue mug toward here, along with some pills. "Here, you took a bit of a whack to the head. You might want some Ibuprofen for it."

Reluctantly, she took the mug and pills from his hands. Her mouth was too dry not to accept a gift of water.

He had an elegant, sculpted face. A truly beautiful face. Mostly European features, despite his coloring. His hair had been shaved down to barely more than stubble, and more of the same shadowed his jaw. He appeared to be younger than she was, with a glow to his caramel skin that those in their late teens and very early twenties have. A glint in his eye instantly warned of his fae heritage. God, he was half-fae for sure.

Can I never get away from them?

Gulping her water down too fast, she choked and started to splutter. A firm whack on the back from a massive hand set her right but pissed her off.

"Aren't you going to take those?" He gestured to the supposed painkillers she'd left lying on the bed.

"Who *are* you?" Her voice sounded shrill to her own ears. "Where is *Arlan*? Where's Professor Kruger? Do you know Kruger?"

The man ran a hand over his shaved head. "I'm Jay. And, yeah, I know Kruger." Jay made a face.

"I'm staying in an apartment he owns in Hwange for a while. I need to get—"

"Hang on a second, mate, there's something I really have to do. I'll be right back." He walked out of the bedroom, leaving her sitting there alone.

Outside the bedroom, she heard a low rumble and then a roar. She scrambled up to pull back the blue curtains just enough to see a portion of the veldt. Yes, a lion. He was right outside the trailer, and he was magnificent. Big, even for a male. Hearing Jay return, she dropped the curtain and turned to face him. When she glanced over at him, he was holding a metal bowl in his hand, full of chunks of meat. The smell of the raw beef made her queasy.

"I don't know how long he'll stay like this. That shooting was quite a shock for both of you, I'm sure." He opened the door and step out of the trailer.

"Wait! I have training with lions. You don't want to just go out there."

He shut the door behind him and she heard the lock turn on the outside. He'd locked her in. She swore.

August jumped out of the bed, ran to the door and tugged on the inside handle. She swore again.

Why has he locked me in?

Memories of being shot at came back, and she started to shake, bile rising in her throat. Was he one of those men? Why had he kidnapped her? Who was he? Where was Arlan?

Her heart thumping against her ribs, she made for the kitchen and found the knife he'd used to chop up the beef. She rinsed it under the tap and hid it in the pocket of her shorts, gripping it tightly.

She returned to the bedroom and sat on the bed. She needed a car and a way to get back to the apartment in Hwange.

In a moment, the key turned in the lock again. Jay stepped back into the room. She squinted as bright sunlight flooded the trailer. The tiny scar she'd seen on his shoulder was more apparent now in the sunlight, revealed by his sleeveless T-shirt. Seeing he had a scar to match some of her own made her a little less nervous, even if the scar was only from the removal of a mole or birthmark.

His impressive height and broad shoulders made him appear dangerous. A lump welled in her throat, but when she looked in his eyes, they seemed filled with only kindness and empathy.

She managed to speak. "Why are you holding me here?"

"I'm a friend of Arlan's. Sorry, I had to go feed Arlan just now. I don't know how long he'll be in this form."

"What?"

"He got upset about you being shot at and having dark dust thrown at you. He has trouble controlling his shifting ability when he gets emotional. I feed him when he turns into a lion so he doesn't end up killing any of the animals he loves, because that would be tragic."

O...kay, then. This man is completely, one hundred percent insane. I have to do something now or never.

Adrenaline roaring through her blood, she pulled the knife from her pocket and pointed it at him. "Just let me go, forget about me, and I won't tell anyone you kidnapped me."

"What? I didn't kidnap you."

She tried to make her voice as gentle and sympathetic as possible. "You're not well. You should see a doctor." She made a bolt for the door.

Jay lunged at her. His fingers closed around her wrist and slammed it against the windowsill, pushing her body between him and the side of the trailer. Her breath whooshed out of her lungs, and she dropped the knife.

She stared down at it, the threat of tears burning. "Let me go." She struggled against his vise-like grip. "You're *crazy*. Just let me go." His hands only tightened around her waist, and he hauled her back onto the bed. A sob gathered in her throat.

"Listen, listen, sweetie, don't you remember being shot at? *I* didn't kidnap you. My friend Arlan carried you here. You need protection." He pinned her to the bed with his body. "I'm sorry, August." He shook his head. "I don't want to do this to you, but put your hands above your head."

She didn't move

"Now!"

His voice was such a dark command, she unthinkingly obeyed. He pushed her back against the pillows and straddled her. Reaching forward, he caught both her wrists, trapping them in his large hand, pinning her to the bed.

She tried to pull away, but he held her tight. She almost cried out, not from pain but from amazement at the sheer power of his hold. Deftly, he reached to take something from a side-table drawer, and she heard the clink of cuffs. The cuffs were attached to a chain, which he fixed to the bolt on the wall above the bed.

She was helpless.

Panic swirled in her belly, along with another sensation. God, what was wrong with her? She couldn't be aroused by this.

"Shh, shh, don't be afraid. Don't be afraid," Jay whispered, tucking a wisp of hair that had come loose from her braid behind her ear. "Shh, baby, I'm a police officer."

The way he touched her and spoke to her, the look in his eyes, all reminded her of the way she herself treated stray dogs and cats.

Maybe he really is a cop?

But the handcuffs were lined with something soft. Maybe velvet. They weren't policeman's handcuffs. His body pressed against hers, his rock-hard length against her pussy. Her panties were damp, and her nipples ached. Magic scented the air.

She looked into his eyes, and the last of her fear eased. Maybe she was crazy, but something told her this man would never hurt her. She was no stranger to leers from students at the university, considering her breasts were a little too big for her small frame. Jay's expression looked nothing like those leers.

He shifted the pillow underneath her head to make her more comfortable. "Sorry about the handcuffs, sweetness, but I can't have you trying to get out of here on your own. There are people who want to kill you."

"Why?" *Is that pathetic squeak really my voice?* "Why do they want to kill me? Who are they?"

He sighed. "It's a gang of people who call themselves witch doctors. Some of them are Shona, some are white men, some may have dark-fae blood, although the rumor is that most of them don't. They dress up as witch doctors and control everyone around here, taking money from them."

"But what would they want with me?"

"Babe, I can only guess they've heard about your mother. She's some kind of powerful half-fae, right? Plus you were hanging out with Arlan, and he's been trying to stop these people for a long time. They hate him."

"I never told Arlan about my mother. I don't understand any of this."

"This is a very greedy crowd, sweetness." He shrugged. "I can only guess they're worried you're some kind of threat to them. But anyway..." He laughed. "They're the ones that *tried* to kidnap you. Not me."

He fumbled in his pocket and pulled out his wallet. "I get that you're scared of me, but I'm a cop." He flashed his badge. "I work mostly in the anti-poaching unit, protecting our wildlife here in Hwange."

August let her head fall back against the pillows and let out a breath. The badge calmed her more than she would admit to him. Even while logic told her the badge might be a fake, her intuition said he was for real. And, sure, the handcuffs were still kind of kinky and crazy, but she had pulled a knife on him after all. "These aren't police handcuffs, though."

An ironic smile fluttered across his lips. "That's true."

"You've used these on other women?"

He frowned. "Sometimes."

Even with that badge, she wasn't sure she could trust him. There was a cynical twist to his mouth, the same expression in his eyes that made him seem almost...bad. But it was part of the appeal. Jay still sat astride her, his cock hard against her thigh, so close to her pussy that her body vibrated, wanting him to shift just slightly. The bulge in his shorts seemed impossibly large. She fought a shiver that washed over her body. When he moved, she whimpered.

"You feel it too, don't you, baby," he whispered. "The intense attraction between fire and air. Your mother was part fire fae, right?"

"And you're sylph born? Part air fae? I...I have heard about fire and air fae having an attraction, but I never thought it would be like this." She gulped.

His pupils appeared so large, it seemed they'd swallowed the rest of his eyes. Darkness. "Yes. I want inside you so bad, my cock is about to burst."

She drew in a ragged breath as her pussy clenched involuntarily. Her mother had spoken of the powerful attraction between fire fae and air fae.

Jay shifted again, and his cock pressed harder against her wet crease, through their thin summer clothing. Her nipples were bullet hard. They hurt.

Embarrassed, she tried to wiggle a little so his cock wouldn't be flat up against her pussy, so he wouldn't feel how slick she was beneath her thin shorts and panties.

I have to remember this man is crazy. He thinks Arlan is a lion.

Fear throbbed in her, as fierce as her lust.

"Listen, Jay. No disrespect, but you're having delusions. You know I took some psychology classes as part of my science degree." One of Jay's eyebrows arched critically in a sexy way. She tried not to react to it. "I...I mean I minored in psychology. There is nothing to be ashamed of. What you have... It's an illness." She gulped at the amused twist of his mouth. "What I'm saying, Jay is... Well, you think *Arlan* is a *lion*. That's not normal. Uncuff me. We'll find Arlan and get you to a doctor."

Jay shook his head. His features crinkled in amusement, his smile too smoldering for her liking.

"Seriously? That's what this is all about? Your grandmother was some crazy dark-fae princess, your mother is a powerful half-fae, but you don't believe in were-lions?"

Her breath caught in her throat. "Are you saying Arlan's a were-lion?"

"Yes, sweetness." His words were a soft whisper against her ear, with the faintest hint of a laugh. Her snatch clenched at the sound of his voice.

This is so wrong.

This is not the plan. You should be surrounded by zoology textbooks right now. You should be working on your PhD, alone in your room.

She had to keep him talking.

"He's a were-lion? Is he half-fae as well?"

"No, baby. Arlan is only a quarter fae. He has no magic power other than shifting, and that's not really a power since it seems to happen against his will. A former lover of his put a curse on him. She was dark fae."

A chill ran through her. "Why would Arlan date a dark fae? He doesn't seem like an evil guy."

"Oh, hell no. He's the best dude you could ever meet. He didn't know what Silvara was when he first met her."

"Why did she put a curse on him?"

Jay sighed. "I don't really know. She shifted into a lion form and bit and clawed him when he tried to dump her. Something like that."

He must have seen the fear on her face. His hand stroked down her braid, over and over. His touch so gentle that she wanted to cry.

She needed to distract him and herself a bit more from the tension between them, and then talk him into unhandcuffing her. "Can't you tell me any more about what happened? Between Arlan and this dark fae, I mean."

He bent forward and touched his lips to her earlobe. "To be honest, all I care about right now is your skin on my skin, you know what I mean?"

Her heart slammed against her chest, her breath coming in little gasps. She shouldn't have just obeyed his command to put her hands above her head. But she hadn't obeyed from sheer fear. A part of her had wanted to play into his power, to be his docile submissive. That kind of power play with a gorgeous man had always been one of her secret dark fantasies. And now, here she was, handcuffed to a wall.

"Do you want me too, sweet thing?"

She swallowed, her face hot with emotion.

He tilted his head to one side, brushing the bulge in his shorts against her again. "Do you want me too, August?"

Oh hell!

Her heart thrummed. Her sex flared. But she couldn't give in yet. "Do you get off on this?"

"On what?"

"A woman being handcuffed to your wall? I mean, I know you did it because I pulled a knife on you, but..."

The very devil was in his smile. "Yes. I get off on this."

Out of pride, she tried to sound haughty. "So you're some kind of pervert? You get off on women being tied up?"

One eyebrow shot up, and an amused, cynical expression crossed his face. "You call me names even though your nipples are stiff beneath your shirt? You expect me to answer your questions, but you haven't answered mine."

In the heat, she could smell her own arousal, just as Arlan had said he could scent her when they were out in the veldt. Both men were right. She was a hypocrite. She needed release. "I d-don't... I don't normally do this kind of thing."

He put a finger to her lips. "Shh. I know. I don't judge a woman for her needs. Only cowards and losers do that. Men who can hardly call themselves men."

She nodded, her brain too overwhelmed with lust to speak. Still he waited. He began to grin, and his smile was wicked but not without mercy.

It was time to stop closing herself off to everything because of her ex, Ryan, and his asshole friends. Because of her mother. She was letting them win, letting the bullies wreck her self-esteem and close her off from life.

With Ryan, you were hoping for a boyfriend. This time, you won't hope. A little meaningless fling to get out of a rut.

"Yes," she finally managed. "Yeah. I'm interested. I can't help it." Her words came out thick, choked, as though her tongue were trying to move through honey. She nearly sobbed with embarrassment and arousal.

His answering groan lit a flame inside her. His mouth moved along her throat, pulsing damp heat as he licked and sucked.

"You're so petite, so tiny like a china doll, with that shiny hair, that tight braid. I love that." He brushed a hand over it, gave it a tug." Beautiful, rich auburn hair. I knew you were mine the minute I laid eyes on you, August."

She didn't know how to respond to his declaration of possession. Probably it was part of some Dom act and not meant to be taken seriously.

"Mmmm, you're a hot little thing. He ran his tongue over her shirt, over the nipples that pressed against the lace of her bra, and she lost the ability to think. Microscopic jolts of pleasure spiked in her brain, destroying rational thought.

His fingers moved to the buttons on her khaki shirt, and he quickly and efficiently unbuttoned each one until her shirt fell open, revealing her lacy forest-green bra. She gave a sigh of relief, pleased she had a collection of pretty underwear that she bought for herself, just for fun, even when she was too busy studying to expect anyone to see it.

She was glad her shirt still hung over her shoulders, hiding the scars there.

He murmured his appreciation, almost made her feel beautiful. Okay, she was tiny, but she kept her body taut with sessions at the gym.

Isn't it time you let go and actually start enjoying your body?

Jay scooped a hand in one cup, and the warmth of his fingers brushing a nipple made her shiver. He lifted one breast free, and then the other. Her breasts jutted awkwardly above underwire and rucked-down bra cups.

"Gorgeous," he whispered.

August was hyperaware of the leisurely track his gaze took strolling up and down her body. His final low growl of pure male need gave her a sweet bellyache. A yearning. He bent forward and kissed the top of each breast reverently.

"You are gorgeous."

Wow! For him to use the word gorgeous was amazing. He must have dated women much more attractive —and taller— than she was. He stopped to tug his sleeveless T-shirt over his head.

She gaped at the slabs of muscle revealed, at his six-pack, his luscious biceps and pectorals. The urge to lick every inch of his smooth caramel skin suffused her.

God.

She wasn't sure she'd ever even *talked* to someone this handsome before.

If his chest is that big, how big is his...?

Jay killed her train of thought by cupping her breast. Her nipple pushed into his palm, stiff and yearning. He pinched one nipple and then the other, making her arch as fresh arousal soaked her panties.

"You sure about this, babe?" He stopped and leaned back. "I won't take advantage of you."

August snorted. "You have me handcuffed and chained to a hook in your wall, and you don't want to take advantage of me?"

His eyes narrowed, but he didn't back down. "I know what *I* want. I want this so bad it's killing me. But this is *your* chance to back out. Say the word now, and we'll stop."

She swallowed a raw, painful lump in her throat. Her nerves were tingling, her pulse racing. Fear of the unknown and of his tremendous size reined her in. "You're right. We shouldn't. We only just met."

"The fact we just met means nothing to me. I don't care about society's sorry-ass rules. How do *you* feel about it? Do you want to stop?"

I want to drink you. I want to drown myself in you.

"Th-this attraction between air and fire. It's painful. Yes...I want—"

Jay groaned.

His firm lips slid across her skin. He dropped a trail of kisses down the valley between her breasts, making her writhe for more until her nipples were sharp bullets stabbing toward the sky. He covered her nipple with his mouth. His tongue stroked her gently, his mouth drawing her in tight. He pulled his mouth from her nipple and took the other, his hand on her waist.

He sucked on a nipple, and his thumb grazed the other. The shock of that sensation went straight between her legs. He was huge and heavy, but held his body so carefully above her, she felt no discomfort at all.

As much as being bound aroused her, she longed to clasp those firm brown muscles and feel his strength. Magic was being unleashed. Her half-fae power connected somehow with his. She gritted her teeth as the wild, flickering burn of lust increased.

"I think nature wants to right itself," he said. "Nature wants more fae to mate with fae. That explains this pressure, this fierce burn."

August managed a nod. She was glad her shorts and panties were on, so he couldn't see her scars or her...need. She was so wet already, it embarrassed her, but he wasn't going to let her have her privacy much longer. With confident efficiency, he unbuttoned her shorts and tugged them off, then tossed them to the ground.

Because of the heat, she wore just a lacy thong that matched the green of her bra. She hoped he understood they were so skimpy only because of the weather. She hoped he wouldn't notice her scars.

Silence. He's looking at them. She cringed, waiting for him to ask where she got them, like Ryan had.

Although the truth was, Ryan already knew.

She felt his shock at the sight of her thighs, his concern and compassion. Then his head dropped, and he kissed one. He was kissing her scars. One by one, his mouth traced the burn marks on her thighs.

Ryan said they were gross.

She gasped, her eyes filling with tears.

He finished kissing her thighs and came up to whisper in her ear again. "You know what I think, darling? I think you like being chained to my wall. A Dom can tell. This isn't just about fire and air, is it?" He pinched her nipple lightly, and she squealed. "Is it?"

She stared at him, her mind so drenched with lust that it felt almost blank. He'd been concerned about her scars but had had the decency not to invade her privacy about them. He'd even *kissed* them. This man might make her feel good, then reject her and make her feel bad, but good, bad, did it really matter? Her libido said no.

"Spread your legs, August."

She gasped as she obeyed, growing weak all over. Heat rose to her hairline as the command humiliated and thrilled her all at once.

Jay's pupils spread. His hands went to her breasts again to caress them. There was no longer any hesitation in him. He gave off the arrogant air of a man in complete control. If he were to touch her between her legs now, she would lose it. She'd humiliate herself by having an instant orgasm. Instead, he forced his hands beneath the cheeks of her ass and grinned at her. She gasped as he pinched her. The mild sting drove her pussy forward, so it pressed against his cock again.

"No." He smacked one butt cheek. "Wait." He pushed her panties to one side and trailed his fingers lightly up and down her inner thighs. She threw back her head and moaned. He was torturing her.

"Hold still."

Her body rebelled against her mind, her hips wanting to rise to press against him, but she obeyed. Then his fingers finally grazed her drenched opening. He angled his hand to shove two fingers in at once, sharp, insistent jabs in the tunnel that was so ready for them.

"Don't move."

A moan tore from her throat against her will. He stopped and sat all the way up so he could appraise her. She felt ridiculously vulnerable, shy and lewd, hands cuffed and chained above her, bra cups rucked down, two fingers spearing her pussy.

Finally he spoke. "You, August Peak, are so fucking beautiful."

She gasped at his unexpected praise. A voice in the back of her mind screeched in denial. She wasn't beautiful. But the negative thought slid away like silver mercury slipping through a crack in a rock.

Only lust and joy remained.

"Ah, you're so wet, so ready, babe." He pressed inside, hitting her G-spot, and she arched back on a moan. "A man could swim in there."

Warmth rose to her cheeks. His thumb grazed her clit while his fingers continued to press and thrust, and he added a third. He rubbed strong, firm fingers on her clit a moment more and then stopped, leaving her bereft. She couldn't stop herself from groaning long and loud, and he lightly slapped her ass cheek again, shutting her up.

Then he sat back to unbutton his shorts. She saw that his choice in the heat was to go commando.

She leaned back, closing her eyes, and heard the rip of a foil packet.

"Just say the word, August, and this goes no further."

The thought of him stopping now made her groan with frustration. This was magic lust, but it felt too good to fight. And sex with another man might wash Ryan from her mind. "I don't want you to stop."

Jay smiled. "I have to protect such a beautiful woman."

She watched him slide the condom on his length, enjoying the way he exhaled. Then he shifted his body until the head of him pressed against her sex, and she whimpered, feeling the enormity of him. The thrusts came deep and slow. She couldn't believe he was so hard, so huge. A laugh of disbelief escaped her.

"They're fae condoms," he whispered in her ear. Then he moved down her body. The feel of his mouth on her nipple made her head swim. It was like being plugged into some strong electrical current that charged her whole body.

His thumb again rubbed her clit while the width of him stretched her, burned at her opening. He body gushed in response, waves of pleasure surging over her, her body drenched in sensation as a thousand tiny sparks of pleasure sparked within. She cried out.

Jay looked stricken. "Am I hurting you, darling? You're so tight."

She shook her head. "No...please..."

"Please what?"

A flash of shame mingled with desire. She could say it if she had to. "I...I... Please, fuck me."

And then he was there inside her again, thick, hot and throbbing. He was so huge, she felt impaled like a kebab on a stick. It was heaven.

He forced himself up inside her, drawing back just slightly, only to shove himself in harder again. It was what she wanted, what she craved. His fingers worked relentlessly at her clit, demanding she find pleasure.

Her bondage became more frustrating as she longed to grip his biceps or his ass and force him still deeper, but at the same time, it heightened her arousal.

He let go, pounding, screwing up into her with all his fierce masculine force.

She came in sharp gasps, wailing at the deep stabs of pleasure, jerking and bucking off the bed, her braid and breasts bouncing, the chain clattering against the wall.

"That's it. That's it, sexy. Yes, fuck, yes, beautiful, come for me."

August glowed with the effect of the climax, and also with delight at his praise.

But that was dangerous, because while she might be ready to let another man have power over her body, no one was going to have power over her mind ever again. She lay there vibrating, overwhelmed with words she couldn't say. And part of her knew, knew that the unloved little girl inside her had given in too quickly to the touch of a beautiful man.

At least, unlike with Ryan, this was about pure lust. She didn't know Jay at all, and he didn't know her, so no ulterior motive could be involved.

Chapter Six

Jay stared into his coffee cup as he stirred it, losing himself in the swirling black liquid. A lump of guilt lodged in his throat, making it difficult to swallow. The headline that leaped out at him from the *Zimbabwe Herald* on the table made his stomach clench even tighter. *Sodomites earn seven-year jail term.*

He put a book of Arlan's on top of the newspaper so he wouldn't see the headline anymore.

August's face flashed into his mind again. But thinking of all that sweetness, all the innocence he'd seen in those soft blue-gray eyes as she gave herself to him made him feel even worse. Her face was so arresting, so serenely beautiful, that when he first saw her, it had made him blink in surprise.

Christ, I'm a bastard.

August had fallen asleep almost immediately after their lovemaking, obviously exhausted and worn down from the events of the day. She didn't even wake when he uncuffed her and laid her arms gently down on the bed. Nor had she stirred when he'd brought out the citrus-scented massage oil and worked it into her wrists to ease any possible stiffness. When he watched her sleeping, a fierce protective instinct had welled up inside him, making him regret having given in to the overwhelming chemistry between them.

He drew in a sharp breath. Fuck it. He needed to admit it to himself. Seducing August so quickly had been a stupid, selfish act. The woman had recently been attacked, shot at, had even had the poisonous dark-fae dust thrown at her. Why had he thought it was okay to seduce her? The timing had been wrong, wrong, wrong.

He glanced at the bowl of yogurt sitting next to his coffee cup. Good sex had first made him crave food, then guilt had stolen his appetite.

And yet guilt couldn't stop his cock springing up again at the thought of everything about her. That smile. Those large, full breasts on that tiny frame. That curvy ass.

Jay groaned at the memory. So what if he kept comparing it to Arlan's tight butt? So what if both shapes could make him hard? That just made him a regular super-horny young guy. It didn't make him bi. His hands clenched into fists. A delicate woman like August would probably be grossed out if she knew what he did with Arlan.

He didn't know what would be worse, the guys down at the station discovering his secret, or a chick like August discovering it. She was some sort of bookish academic, but however intellectual she was, she'd still be pissed if she found out she'd slept with a guy who slept with guys.

The bullshit between him and Arlan needed to stop.

Arlan had tried to get him to read books about the fae and half-fae history. But he wasn't a big reader like Arlan. Jay preferred to use his body, lift weights, run, work out. He liked being a cop because it was physical. He read the odd thriller or some Stephen King—horror, guy stuff.

Jay took another long sip of coffee. Arlan said he shouldn't be ashamed, that the two of them were fated mates. As far as Jay was concerned, the two of them were best friends because their dads had been business partners. The other stuff that happened between them was...well, these things happened at all-boys boarding schools. Teenage boys were fiercely horny. Men in their early twenties the same. And now it had become a habit. A bad one.

He swallowed another spoonful of yogurt.

He'd had a birthday in January. He was twenty-one now. Time to take stock of his life. He'd become a policeman to protect and serve. Protecting the wildlife he and Arlan loved meant everything. And when it came to catching poachers, he was successful, but in every other area of his life, he was a fuckup.

The sound of Arlan opening the door broke his train of thought. He set his coffee down and went to greet him. "You look like shit."

"Thanks, mate." Arlan ran his hand through his hair, and clumps of dirt and dry leaves fell at his feet.

There was blood on his hands and around his mouth, a cut on his face. Jay's gut clenched at the sight of the blood. Not because he cared if Arlan's lion had killed an animal for food, but because Arlan, in human form, was so devoted to protecting Zimbabwe's wildlife.

"I left you some food. Did you kill something?"

Arlan shoved past him and headed for the sink. He washed his hands with the cedarwood-scented soap he favored, grabbing a dishcloth to get rid of the blood. "Nothing's dead. Got in a fight." He paused and shot Jay a wry grin. "You should see the other lion."

Jay smiled.

"So where's August?"

"She's asleep."

Concern flickered across Arlan's features. "Still?"

Jay swallowed. "She was awake for a little while."

"She's been through a lot."

A pang of regret squeezed Jay's stomach, and he nodded his agreement. Arlan leaned back on the heels of his Safari sandals, his back pressed against the wall. He crossed his muscular arms over his chest. Jay turned his head, trying not to notice the way Arlan's biceps bulged.

Arlan waited another beat, and then his eyes narrowed. "Jay…"

"What?"

"There's something you're not telling me"

"We'll talk about it later."

"We'll talk about it now."

Jay put his head in his hands. Arlan waited a beat and then headed for the bedroom. Jay thought about running after him and grabbing him, trying to haul him back, but thought better of it. He held his breath and closed his eyes.

It wasn't long before he heard a small thunk on the glass coffee table. He opened his eyes to see the velvet-lined handcuffs. The damn things almost seemed to pulse with accusation all on their own.

"You want to tell me about these?" Arlan stabbed a finger toward the handcuffs. "They weren't in the bedside table. They were lying on the floor."

A muscle twitched in Jay's jaw, but he stayed silent. Arlan wasn't his minder. He didn't have to answer to him.

"Seriously, what is this shit, Jay? You jumped the gun on this? You've risked the whole goddamn plan? You think I don't know why?"

Jay opened his eyes, his nostrils flaring. "Because she's *hot*, that's why. That's all."

"Because you and I nearly had sex today. Because you always have to prove you're not gay."

Jay walked away from him, heading back for his coffee. "Because I'm not fucking gay. I *like* girls. I like women."

"You know I like women too, Jay. All fae are—"

Jay slapped a hand on the table,

"I *hate* that word bi too. Stupid fucking word. Why do people have to be shoved in stupid little boxes?"

"In the Fae Realm, everyone lives in ménage rela—"

"We're not in the Fae fucking Realm, get that through your thick fucking head. I have to go to work every day. Plain ordinary work. I work with cops who would *loathe* me if they knew I—"

"Jay..."

He hated the way Arlan's voice got now, too kind and almost condescending just because he was three years older. "You and I have known each other forever, and I think that we're—"

Jay raised a hand. He sat down. He could guess what Arlan was about to say, something soft and romantic that he didn't want to hear. "Listen, mate we're friends, but the shit that sometimes happens between you and me..." He took a sip of coffee. "For me, it's just... It's a bit of tension relief. Being a cop is stressful. Life is stressful. That's it. That's *all.*" He felt momentary guilt, but it was better this way.

"Tension relief?" Arlan's voice fell to a bare whisper.

Adrenaline, guilt and rage surged through Jay's bloodstream. Before he knew what he was doing, he gave the whole table a violent push.

Bowl and coffee cup spun across the surface, shattering against the wall, yogurt and coffee splattering them both. Arlan took a quick step backward, brushing yogurt off his arms, his eyes full of pain and anger.

"What's going on?" They both turned. August stood in the doorway, mussed and sleepy, her tiny body draped in one of Jay's shirts. She stared at the broken table and the rest of the mess.

Arlan stepped toward her. "August, beautiful, how are you feeling?"

Jay angled around the smashed table. "Don't be fake, Arlan."

Arlan whipped his head around, shock on his face. "What? What's your problem *now*, asshole?"

"You. Acting so concerned about her when we planned to use her."

"What?" August looked confused, wary...stricken.

Jay strode over to the laptop and switched it on, quickly finding the email Kruger had CCed him on.

"What do you mean, use me?" Her voice shook.

Arlan stood up. "Jay, don't do this. Not this way."

Something inside him told him to stop, but rage and adrenaline pushed those thoughts aside. Besides, she had a right to know. He spun the laptop in August's direction.

"Read it."

Arlan could have pushed Jay away from the laptop and forced him against the wall to stop this, but what would that have achieved? The damage was done. August wouldn't have trusted him if he'd tried to stop her reading the email.

He was still smarting from Jay's stupid words about "tension relief", even though he knew Jay didn't mean it. His chest constricted as he waited for August's reaction.

The children, the lions, the possibility of using sex magic to find the storm tower were all hanging in the balance, ready to be shattered like the coffee cup and the cereal bowl. Worse, this sweet, beautiful, oddly familiar woman was not going to understand. She was going to be offended they needed her for sex magic.

She'd blanched when Jay had said they were using her. Her face still appeared unusually pale and milky in the dim light of the trailer, but her chin jutted up with determination. This woman was fragile, but strong in her own way.

He watched her now as she read the email.

The red highlights in her chestnut braid caught the sunlight coming in through the window. Arlan wondered what it would be like to feel that glossy hair in his hands, warm, rich and thick. He wondered what it would look like loose, hanging around her pretty face.

When he'd knocked her to the ground to save her from the bullets, her scent had been sweet and exciting, like jasmine, orange blossom and musk. Her cheekbones were wide and high, like a movie starlet's from the fifties. All her facial features were delicate, but her lips had a unique quirk to them that made him long to taste them. Made him wonder how they'd move beneath his own. He imagined her under him again, imagined her hips lifting, her pretty legs twining around his waist.

Hello? Moron? She doesn't exactly seem to even like you. And once she finishes reading the letter, she's going to hate you more. Your libido is way ahead of reality.

He glanced at her lips again. He knew that quirk; it was more than familiar.

Oh Jesus. August... Gus for short, because her three-year-old sister, May, couldn't pronounce August. No... No!

Pictures flashed in his mind. Dark dust in bottles on a shelf above an oven. A beautiful, clever eleven-year-old girl with a bruise blooming violently on her upper cheek, more bruises of varying shades of yellow, purple, black on her legs; fresh cigarette burns on her shoulders. God, no!

Guilt hollowed his belly, and he drew a ragged breath. He'd been a twelve-year-old boy surrounded by adults impressed by Mrs. Peak's astonishing fae powers. He hadn't saved August or her father. Fate was bringing her back into his life to teach him a lesson for his failure and cowardice.

The few times he'd actually spoken to her as a child, her soft, scared voice had ripped at his heart.

She didn't remember him. That was no surprise.

"Gus." He whispered it. But she heard him. August's swallow was so loud, he could hear it.

She turned and fled into the bathroom, slamming the door. He wanted to punch the wall as he listened to her dry heave.

Lisa Whitefern

Was it because of the remaining effects of the dark dust, or was it because of remembering her mother's abuse? He didn't know.

He bent down to haul up the glass table. But it was ruined. The table now had a huge crack in which he could see a split image of himself. One side of his face ascended; the other descended. His image was warped. And nothing could be done to set it right.

Chapter Seven

The trailer only had two single bedrooms, so Jay slept in one and Arlan set up an old army cot across from August's bed next to the opposite wall.

Guilt pressed down on Arlan until it threatened to suffocate him. August seemed to have no idea he'd been one of the kids who had once witnessed her humiliation when she was eleven.

By moonlight, Arlan could see the lush curves of August's breasts and thighs as she lay beneath the thin sheet on his old army cot. Her hair was still done up in that long chestnut braid. Her skin glowed with health. Her complexion was pale as ivory. Recognition had jolted his every nerve. He knew her.

A muscle worked in his jaw as he fought to control his dick, which wanted to harden at the sight of her. Despite his guilt, he wanted her with a bone-deep yearning he'd never felt for a woman before.

Was he a fool to think something had happened between them in such a short time? He'd thought she was seriously attracted to him, but then he'd come home to find she'd been fooling around with Jay. It had been a shock. He'd thought she was more reserved than that.

But the connection between her and Jay was as electric as it had been between her and Arlan. There was no denying it.

And when he inhaled, the beast in him could scent her intoxicating jasmine-and-orange-blossom perfume, the musk underneath, even from across the room. Could that mean...?

Yes. You're scenting one of your fated mates. Your other fated mate.

Was it possible? Could she really be his other fated mate, or was his mind playing tricks on him? Either way, he didn't deserve her. He'd failed her when she was only a child. Why should she forgive him for that?

August moaned softly in her sleep and turned over with a wiggle that stirred his cock to a full erection. With a sigh, he turned around and pulled off his T-shirt. He unzipped his shorts before his cock could burst through the fabric, and raised his butt enough so he could draw them down to his knees. Carefully, he pulled his boxers down over his erection.

His cock continued to swell as he remembered what she looked like when she'd first climbed out of the Land Cruiser. Her hair appeared brown in the moonlight now, but outside it had been alive with red highlights. She'd been nervous about getting out of the Land Cruiser with the lions there, and her small teeth had tugged at her lower lip, calling attention to the lush, sexy curve of it.

And then he'd been rude to her, made her mad.

Fuck, that had been hot.

He pictured her large breasts hanging loosely inside her cotton shirt, and his hand fastened around his cock as he started a slow, pumping action.

But then he took a peek back at August in the nearby cot. Thank God. She was still asleep.

His cock didn't care about her unhappy past or his failure to save her.

What the hell? Fantasy was harmless and free.

He went to the bathroom and grabbed a towel, then headed back and climbed into the cot, pulling the sheets over himself. Turning away from her, he returned his hand to his cock and began the pumping motion again while he imagined kissing down her neck to her breasts and burying his head between them, licking and kissing the soft, round mounds.

He pictured her small body wriggling beneath his own while his hands ranged over her fine curves and between her thighs.

He couldn't help imagining a gold collar of ownership around her pretty neck. A feral purr rose within him. He imagined her on her knees, sucking Jay's cock while he slapped her little heart-shaped ass.

Oh God!

He didn't know if she'd be into that, and yet something...something in her eyes made him think she would be.

Jay would come in her mouth, and once her cute little ass was hot and red, Arlan would reach around stroke her soft wet folds, rub her clit until she shattered and screamed both their names.

Arlan's balls, heavy and tight, contracted. The first spurt shot from his cock. He came in sharp, violent, bursts of sensation that fired through him like electricity as he emitted four more rapid-fire jets into his towel.

August lay as still as she could, feigning sleep. She still felt a little groggy and disoriented, but good Lord, Arlan was every bit as gorgeous as Jay. She'd watched him pull off his tank, watched the flex of muscles beneath his tan skin, licked her lips as the moonlight slanted across that taut six-pack stomach.

When she closed her eyes, she could still see him hooking his thumbs into his khaki shorts and easing them from his hips, slowly exposing his firm ass and muscular back.

He'd turned and, she'd seen how stiff his cock was in his underwear.

Arlan had rolled on his side underneath the sheet, but she'd still seen the outline of his buttocks beneath as they pumped slowly back and forth. What would it be like to grip that gorgeous ass with both hands as he pumped into her?

She let her hand creep slowly to her pussy, not wanting to make any sudden movements that might lead him to realize she wasn't asleep.

Lisa Whitefern

Her fingers brushed her swollen wetness, and she moved them back and forth as she pictured Arlan in her mind. Sexual inexperience had never stopped her from having a creative imagination and intense desires.

First she conjured up her usual fantasies of being taken, dominated, controlled, but this time, instead of faceless men, she imagined Arlan and Jay as her masters.

August called up a montage of images to push her over the edge. Arlan tying her hands behind her back. Jay commanding her to get down on all fours so he could spank her and take her from behind. Arlan wielding a paddle.

Then she thought of the way the two men had looked when they stood over that coffee table. She knew the intensity and aggression between them was more than just anger. And she'd thought these two alpha males could rip each other's throats out...or rip each other's clothes off.

Her blood sped up more than a little at the thought. She had a number of man-love books on her e-book reader. Another one of her fantasies leapt to mind, only this time instead of characters in a story, she saw Arlan and Jay, their washboard abs and sculpted pecs bathed in sunlight, their hands on each other.

Golden and caramel skin glistened; muscular arms embraced. In her imagination, Arlan licked a path down Jay's stomach to the thin ribbon of hair that led to the policeman's beautiful cock.

Her fingers moved faster and faster over her clit, and she struggled to suppress her moans of pleasure as she slid over the slope of orgasm. Then that groggy sickness enveloped her again, and she drifted into darkness.

Arlan awoke bathed in sweat. The nightmare was still so real, so vivid. He pushed up into a sitting position and leaned against the headboard.

76

How could he fall asleep after a blissful orgasm and be awakened by nightmares? Ugh.

He had no choice. He had to try to remember everything, had to confront the memories of what he *really* saw back when he was twelve, had to actually confront the memory instead of just letting it brush the surface, then pushing the horror back from his mind.

Who was Gus Peak? What had Arlan seen? What had his life been like back when he met her that one time when he was twelve?

He spent every school term far away from his parents at boarding school in New Zealand. But school holidays were spent either in Zimbabwe or traveling to half-fae conferences around the world with them and his nanny.

That one summer, they'd stayed at a hotel on Long Island. His parents and nanny had left him to the babysitting care of Duvessa Peak while they went sightseeing with the other half-fae conference attendees, who were tourists in New York.

He forced himself to remember it now. His one pathetic, sad attempt to get his parents involved, to get some kind of help for Gus had failed.

"Dad, I need to talk to you about something." Arlan's stomach churned. He'd had his thirteenth birthday only yesterday, and he'd never faced such an adult task in his life before.

Marshall Leonard set down his newspaper and scrutinized his son.

Arlan swallowed and took a deep breath." I don't want to go to Mrs. Peak's house again. Duvessa bullies her own kid, Dad. We need to help Gus. We have to do something. We need to stop Duvessa."

Marshall took a sip of his coffee. "Duvessa Peak is a very influential member of the Half-Fae Network. That woman has more genuine magical ability than possibly anyone you or I will ever meet again in this lifetime. She owns Crown Casino and a large hotel that provides much funding support to the Network.

Then there are the magic diaries from the Fae Realm, proof she's the daughter of a full-blooded fae princess." He glared at his son. "I'm sorry you don't enjoy her as a babysitter. That's a pity."

Arlan gulped. "Um... She makes fun of Gus in front of all the kids. Gus was tied to some pipes in the basement and the kids...the kids practiced magic on her. They hurt her."

Marshall Leonard looked startled. "Duvessa tied her to pipes?"

Arlan drummed his fingers nervously on the dining room table. He had to get this right. He had to say the right thing... "Well, no, the other kids did. And they put a gag in her mouth, an old rag."

"The other children tied her to some pipes. So it was a game?"

Arlan ran his fingers through his hair. "Well, yes. No. I mean... I don't know."

"It sounds like a game." Marshall laughed and ruffled Arlan's hair. "You worry too much, kid. You worry about the animals, about conservation, about hunting. You worry about people and magic. Just relax and enjoy life."

"Dad, the way Duvessa treats Gus is wrong. She calls her horrible names. She hurts her with magic. It leaves burn marks and..."

His father's eyes hardened. He pointed a finger at Arlan. "Listen, young man, if you don't like seeing this girl punished by her mother when she's misbehaving, you don't have to go there. But no more crazy stories. I don't want to hear them." He patted Arlan's knee. "Duvessa's promised to teach your mother and me some very powerful magic, and even to help us find our third."

"Your third?"

"Our missing fated mate."

"Why is that so important, Dad? This is important, what I'm trying to tell you. Duvessa's an abuser. She hurts her daughter."

"Having connections in the Half-Fae Network are what's important. I will not have you mess things up for your mother and me with your nonsense."

Arlan flinched at his father's anger, but Marshall's next words were less harsh. *"It's something you'll understand when you're older. Why don't you go watch something on TV?"*

"Dad? Are you a Warrior of the Light? I mean, you and Mum, you've chosen the light path, right?"

Marshall Leonard curled his lip. *"I'm not having this discussion with a twelve-year-old."*

Arlan felt a muscle twitch in his jaw as he remembered. His dad had been no Warrior of the Light. All Marshall Leonard cared about was hunting and money, and connections in the half-fae network that could help him make more money.

It was the only time he'd tried to do something about what he'd seen Duvessa do to Gus. His parents never left him with Duvessa again. They left New York. Gradually, over the years, he'd almost forgotten about that one horrible day in the basement. She was just some little girl he met one day of his life and had eventually forgotten about.

He remembered August's voice down in that basement. When she'd spoken, her words had been strong and dignified, a sharp contrast to Duvessa's crazy ranting. He'd admired her then as he did now.

But what else had happened to her? If her mother had done that to her that one day, what else did she do?

Arlan's stomach tightened like a clay brick in the hot sun. He couldn't give in to the sudden infatuation and lust he felt for August now. He didn't deserve to get to know the adult woman she'd become.

But what if she's your fated mate? What if she's your third?

It was difficult to get the possibility out of his mind when he was so attracted to her, and Jay was too. He had to force himself to remember the whole day. The day he'd first met her.

A dim orange light bled in to the room from a street lamp outside. Everything was strangely fluid and ghostlike. Arlan wished he was at home watching TV or curled up reading in his own bed.

Earlier today, the kids had been left in the large, dark basement with a wide variety of board games. Duvessa had popped in and out from time to time with lemonade and trays of snacks. The half-fae adults were on some kind of sightseeing tour. Being shut in a room to play board games sucked, but he was starting to enjoy himself.

It was fun playing Scrabble with Duvessa's daughter, Gus. She was witty, and the first kid he'd met who could beat him at the game. He couldn't understand why the other half-fae kids seemed to shun her. He guessed she was just too smart for them.

And then Duvessa had come in the room again. "Hey kids. How about we do something a little more fun than board games?"

Bizarrely, she suggested the kids tie Gus to some old pipes sticking out of the wall. At Duvessa's instructions, they'd even put a gag in her mouth.

It was supposed to be game.

It was basically a game.

Gus was "It". Apparently Gus was always "It".

Arlan's mouth went dry. He licked his lips and tried to swallow. This was a mean game. Duvessa shouldn't be here. She was August's mother.

Duvessa smiled. Her eyes looked weird in the gloom like the eyes of a snake, amber colored, too much iris not enough pupil. He could almost taste the fear in the room, sharp and tangy with a biting edge. But there was excitement too. Some kids were giggling.

His gaze landed on her wrists, which were red where the rope was pulling on her. "I think the rope is hurting Gus. That rope is too rough."

A taller boy gave him a shove into the wall. "Shut up, dumbass."

Duvessa leaned against the wall smoking. "This should be a fun game." There was an eerie, jittery excitement among the kids.

The boy who'd pushed him stepped forward. "I'm going first." The tall boy started humming. And then the screams began.

That was what had made him wake drenched in sweat.

He'd heard her scream in his dreams. He took some deep, strong breaths to calm himself. As his pulse rate finally began to slow, he managed to latch on to one miserable thought.

Eventually I'll have to tell her that I was there.

He thought about the feel of her in his arms. Everything about her was soft and silky, that rich, thick chestnut hair, that delicate, satiny skin.

Arlan imagined the radiant, powerful, magical half-fae woman that August might have been had she been brought up in a loving home, and he made a vow to himself. All his reading told him low self-esteem inhibited power in half-fae. Had that been her mother's motive? But why? Why inhibit magic power in your own child?

One day, Jay and I will make someone pay for the damage that's been done to her.

But for now, they needed her. They need her to help them save other abused children.

Chapter Eight

Jay walked into the lengthening afternoon shadows carrying August, who was still fast asleep. He scanned his surroundings and headed toward Arlan and the Land Cruiser.

Arlan had been ready to get in the car, but he rushed around to open the back door so Jay could place August in the backseat and do up her seat belt. Then Jay climbed into the driver's seat, and Arlan was soon beside him in the passenger's.

"What did you say to August before she ran into the bathroom? You whispered something, some word that upset her?"

Arlan flinched and his smile faded. He took a long sip from his Coca-Cola, then finally set it in the cup holder on the side door. "I met her once when I was a kid, okay? She used to go by a nickname. Gus. I said that name."

Jay stared at him. "What? Where did you meet her?"

"I just remembered she attended some of the Half-Fae Network's biannual conferences that I went to in different countries as a child. My parents went, her parents went, families mixed, kids played together." Arlan's eyes looked pained and haunted. "Bad things happened, Jay. There were a lot of dark fae at those gatherings."

"So you're saying her parents were involved in dark magic?"

"Yeah. Well, her mother was, at least. And she used it against her."

"And now you and I are pulling her into our fight against more dark magic?"

Arlan put his face in his hands. "It's for the..."

"Yeah, yeah, I know it's for the children. It's always about the children, or the animals or whatever with you."

"Jay, for fuck's sake, it's all important."

Jay was quiet for a second. "Yeah, mate, you're right." He rubbed his temples. "Of course, it's all important. I'm just fucking worried about *her* right now, you know?" He stroked a strand of August's hair. "It seems like dark dust really knocks people the fuck out."

"Yup. The smaller you are, the less body weight, the more it's likely to affect you, and even if you recover the way she did, it can still knock you out again at random. It might take her a couple more days to recover."

"Fuck, I hope it doesn't take that long. Is she going to be all right?"

Arlan nodded. "I think so."

At first, they drove on a good tar road, but as they neared town, the road became full of potholes that Jay had to negotiate. They had had to stop twice, once for a herd of elephants and then for some black rhinos who wouldn't move from the path.

Finally they reached the gateway to their seven thousand acres of private land. The luxury hunting lodge they'd inherited from their business-partner fathers was a sprawling cream-colored stucco mansion backing onto a cliff face with staggering views of sunsets over the veldt, and distant glimpses of the Zambezi river.

Arlan stopped and used the remote for the electric gates, and they drove on down the long driveway lined by purple Jacaranda trees.

When Arlan stopped the car again, Jay went to get August from the backseat.

Now a pang of regret tightened in his chest. Her petite body had felt so soft and warm in his arms. She was so tiny and easy to carry. Her silky skin, even now, was giving him half a hard-on, and he cursed himself.

Arlan got out of the car and strode ahead. Massive pillars playing sentry to elegant gold-inlaid double front doors, which Arlan opened for them.

August had passed out after vomiting and then slept the entire trip home. It enraged Jay that the dark dust had made her so sick. He supposed when she woke up, she was going to get a shock finding herself in the lounge of the Leonard Hunting Lodge instead of in the trailer. They walked through the entranceway and into the one of the large lounge areas, where the entertainment center and bar were.

Arlan seemed equally agitated. He put some Bach on at a very low volume on the stereo so as not to wake up August. Then Arlan paced back and forth in front of the wood-paneled bar, finally stopping to grab himself a Castle from the fridge. "She's definitely an immortal, Jay. One of the immortal half-fae, or that dark dust would have just killed her. She's inherited the fae gene for immortality. That means she's even more valuable as a half-fae who could help us with the sex magic. She's full of untapped potential."

Jay's lips tightened. "You mean full of magical potential."

"Yes."

Jay said nothing more but laid August down on the white leather couch as gently as possible. Then he shot Arlan a glance he hoped expressed his disgust.

Arlan ran a hand over his face. "Fuck, Jay. I get that you think I'm using her. But this isn't about *me*. It's not about us. It's for the *kids*."

Arlan motioned to the set of photographs sitting on the mantel. Photos of kids he'd managed to save from the witch doctors. There were no photos of the ones who'd been stolen. The ones he hadn't managed to get back.

"Yeah, I get it, mate. But I don't want her to feel used. You know?"

Arlan's shoulders slumped. "Yeah I understand."

August shifted and sighed in her sleep. The summer dress he'd put on her when she was asleep was soft and faded, feminine and alluring in its cut, hugging her body in all the right places.

The faint musky scent of her perfume jump-started several of his nerve endings. He wanted her to wake with lust slick between her thighs, aching for him to make love to her again. He shook his head. "I don't understand why she was fine for a while when she first woke up from the dark-dust attack."

More than fine.

"She's strong but she's had a number of shocks, Jay. Dark dust is very draining, even for an immortal half-fae. In mortals, it can damage internal organs if it's inhaled."

"How do you know all this shit?"

"I read up on it in Dad's library. If an immortal half-fae inhales dark dust, it can affect them periodically for months, causing sudden sleep attacks. We're really going to have to protect her and watch her every hour of the day, because she could fall asleep at any time."

Jay stroked a hand over her braid. Her hair was so shiny and pretty. He didn't want to think about her being in danger any more than he had to. He glanced back up at Arlan. "Right now, what August needs most is nourishment."

Jay began to hum, fae humming from the back of his throat. Indigo light rose from the palm of his outstretched hand, and soon a bowl of chicken soup appeared on the table, along with a bottle of some type of liquid

"What's that?" Arlan pointed to the bottle.

"It's a drink like Lucozade with a blast of fae magic in it. Should replace electrolytes, help her get her energy back."

August rolled over on the couch. Her eyes opened.

"Hey, beautiful." Arlan sounded sincere, Jay couldn't deny it. He should try to stop judging Arlan so harshly. His friend's motivations were in truth pure and unselfish. It was just the fact that this situation could end up hurting August that bothered Jay.

Arlan's touch on August's shoulder was so gentle. He obviously liked her as much as Jay did. Jay didn't know whether to be jealous or turned on. His cock did, though, rising a little in his shorts.

To distract himself, he glanced over at the pictures of the children Arlan had saved. Even as a policeman, he'd had no luck saving any of those kids. Only Arlan's lion-shifting magic had saved them. While Arlan might have only a quarter fae blood, his friend was a true Warrior of the Light. Powerful light-fae magic guided Arlan in his were form. The curse that Arlan hated so much seemed to Jay to have a positive side, to be almost preordained, although he'd never said that to Arlan. Not worth pissing him off.

August sat up and glanced around the room. Jay stifled a laugh when her mouth dropped open. Whatever she'd been expecting to see, it wasn't zebra heads on the walls.

Arlan's face crinkled in disgust and embarrassment. "Yeah we'll be getting rid of those soon."

"Where the hell am I?" She didn't sound amused. Realizing the sight of the zebra heads probably wasn't the least bit funny to an animal-loving zoologist, Jay stopped grinning.

He opened his mouth to explain, but Arlan spoke before he did. "August you remember Kruger told you I didn't like my father's business? Well, that's because my father and Jay's father became extremely wealthy running a string of hunting lodges across southern Africa. We've recently inherited all of them. I'm sorry you had to see this." He waved a hand at the zebra heads.

"Inherited? Oh. I'm sorry for your loss. The loss of your father, I mean."

Arlan nodded. "Jay's father was taken to prison for political reasons and lost his life in a fight."

"I'm so sorry."

Jay guessed Arlan didn't want to explain the complicated circumstances of his mother's coma and that she wasn't strictly dead. "Don't be sorry. It was a long time ago."

"A long time ago? But, how old are you, Jay?"

"I'm twenty-one. Yeah, I was six when I lost them both, so yeah it was a long time ago. My parents had a third, their fated mate. I called him uncle. He looked after me. He's still alive. Anyway, Arlan lost his parents fairly recently, and it just didn't feel right to take all his father's stuff down."

"Oh, I see. Of course. I'm sorry Arlan."

Jay saw kindness and compassion in her gray-blue eyes. Despite the mistakes he and Arlan had made with her since she'd arrived, and despite getting over the attack, she still cared that they'd lost their parents. She was a good person.

Arlan sat down. "Anyway, yeah, my parents drove down to Johannesburg to visit relatives a couple of months ago. They were both shot at a traffic light. Carjacking."

August's hand flew to her mouth.

Arlan shrugged. "Truthfully, I very rarely saw them when they were alive. I was usually at boarding school or with a nanny, and then I was working and living elsewhere."

"Still, that's awful."

"Well, anyway, Jay and I moved in here right after they died. It just felt wrong to take Dad's things down immediately, as much as I hate those damn zebra heads."

"I get it."

"Stupid, really. I'll have them taken down tomorrow."

The kind concern in August's gaze touched Jay's soul. "You two have been through so much."

"Yeah, we're big guys. Stop worrying about us. How are you feeling?"

August rubbed her temples. "Well, I guess I passed out again, huh? I don't know what's wrong with me."

"It's the dark dust." Jay motioned to the soup and drink. "Eat, drink, sweetness. Get your strength back up."

August stared at the soup, then shrugged and pulled the bowl across the table and started eating.

"That email I showed you, it's not an insult to you, August. It's just that we need help. If you don't want to do it, we completely understand," Jay explained.

He watched a blush creep up her cheeks, just as it had when he'd first shown her Kruger's email. Even though he'd made love to her already, Jay felt his own cheeks heat at what they were asking her to do.

She stopped spooning soup into her mouth and picked up the bottle. She drank and pulled a face at the taste. "For some prisoners in a tower? For some children."

Arlan walked over to the mantelpiece. "Yes. Here are pictures of some children we managed to rescue." There was a kind of raw desperation in Arlan's voice whenever he spoke of the children he'd saved and those he hadn't.

Jay's heart swelled with love and admiration for his friend. Arlan picked up one of the photographs brought it back to the coffee table and set it down beside her. It was the photo of a laughing five-year-old. Jay had peeked at it many times, knowing Arlan had saved this adorable child from evil.

"That's Mukuru of the BaTonga tribe," Arlan whispered. "He's one of the lucky ones. But we're racing against the clock to find the others. They're losing their childhood. We don't know what horrors they have to endure."

August picked up the photograph. The little boy had been caught in the middle of a full-belly laugh. "He's adorable."

"That's one of the children I was able to save. There are dozens more I wasn't."

"I suppose the woman standing behind him is his mother?"

Arlan took the photo from her. "Yes, that's Nhamo." He set the photo back down.

"Why is it called the storm tower?"

Jay shrugged. "Named after some dark fae, an air fae, no doubt."

"What's it made out of?"

"Magic stones," Arlan said.

Jay put his hands in his pockets. "It's a gray tower too. Gray as a stormy sky."

"Wow! What an odd thing. You know you probably saved my life, from flying bullets, from the dark dust that day."

"August..."

"You saved me. I mean, even if I have the immortal gene, you saved me from—"

Arlan shook his head. "Listen, that has nothing to do with any of this. You don't owe us anything. You have to make this decision on your own."

Arlan nodded at Jay's words. "And I acted like a jerk before any of them started shooting at us anyway."

"You did, actually." The words were spoken with no wrath.

Soft blue-gray eyes locked with his. Arlan brushed a lock of hair back from her face. "I'm sorry, sweetness. The thing is, I'd heard your mother was a dark fae. I have a lot of issues with them."

"So Jay told me. He said you dated one of them, and she cursed you?"

"It was a very brief relationship I had with a woman. But, yeah, she was dark fae, and she put the were-lion curse on me."

August shrugged. "Well, I forgive you. And as I said, you saved my life, so of course, I'll help you."

Arlan stilled and shook his head. "Like I said, you owe me nothing. Please don't base this decision on that."

Pride in his friend made Jay smile, and he gave Arlan's shoulder a squeeze. Jay's cock twitched as she scrutinized them both.

She gave an adorable little shrug that stiffened his cock to a full erection, then she said, "I kind of doubt having sex with either of you will be a hardship."

Arlan's heart did a little flip. The blue-gray eyes of the child she'd been were the same.

Occasionally, he saw the glitter in them that gave away her fae blood, but it didn't appear often. Guilt as fresh as it had been fourteen years ago welled up in him. He mourned the life she might have had, an attractive, intelligent woman like that. No wonder she came across as somewhat uptight.

And now that he remembered, he had to wonder... He'd seen dark dust on her mother's shelves. He'd wondered if it had had anything to do with... But no, he couldn't think about that.

He'd tried to help her, he'd tried to stop them, but none of the adults had listened to the thirteen-year-old boy he'd been. The bizarre things that had happened might have gone even beyond a parent abusing her child. She'd said her father had shot himself.

She turned around to face them, her expression steely now. "I suppose these children are beaten? Starved? Do they practice magic on them? Do they punish them using magic?" August's voice was as cool as ice clinking in a glass.

A hard lump formed in Arlan's throat, making it difficult to speak. "We don't know what's happening in that tower. No one does. We know they train some of these children to kill, to be assassins for them. Those are the only ones we've seen since they've been abducted."

August bit her lip. "And the government and police do nothing?"

"The government doesn't believe in magic. They don't have an understanding of what's going on at all."

Jay leaned forward. "When a child is stolen we, the police launch a search party. But, to be honest, we've never found a single child. Only magic can combat magic. And I'm the only half-fae policeman I know of around here."

"Can't you use your fae powers to do something?"

Jay gave a cynical snort. He gestured to her soup and drink. "Eat your soup, and drink up. Culinary magic is about the best anyone will get from me." He looked down at his shoes for a second, then looked up at her again. "The gifts I have aren't the kind that could help those kids anyway."

"You don't think you're powerful enough?"

"I know I'm not."

August spooned up some more soup.

Arlan touched her lightly on the shoulder. "These are the reasons why I believe the only way we can find the witch doctors' storm tower is to try Kruger's suggestions. If we find the tower, we find the children."

"I might help you, Arlan, for the sake of those children." She lifted her chin and shot Jay an angry stare. "But you could have told me about all this before we... You should have just told me. Now I feel you used me. You tried to manipulate me. I don't appreciate that."

Jay grabbed her arm, his eyes flashing dark. "What are you talking about? I didn't use you. Why would you even think that?"

August set the bottle down on the table with a firm thwack. "I found out the first lover I ever had used me for a bet, for a dare, a joke." Her anxious chuckle was completely without mirth, her expression defensive, as though she feared they might laugh with her.

Arlan couldn't comprehend what she was saying. "A joke?"

"Ryan Garrison told me he and his friends remembered me from elementary and middle school, and he knew I'd be an easy mark. He and his friends thought the whole thing about being half-fae was funny, some crazy nonsense. They paid him a hundred dollars for seducing the midget freak whose mother thought she was magic."

Arlan inhaled, struggling to keep his claws from snapping out. Red rage tinged his vision. "That's crazy. Tell me where he lives. I'll rip my claws into him."

August flinched. Then a small smile quirked her lips. "He lives in New York, Arlan, a little far away for you to pay him a visit. But thanks."

Jay seemed calm, but from his brooding expression, Arlan knew a storm was just below the surface. "Fucking idiot bullies. They called you a midget? You're what, five foot?"

She gave a faint rueful smile. "Not quite. Almost. I'm almost five foot. My mother, she was..." August stopped and gulped.

"Crazy." Jay shook his head.

A vision of Duvessa filled Arlan's mind. He'd almost forgotten what she looked like, but it came back to him. A tall, terrifying creature. Even when August was eleven, she'd been very small for her age. And her mother had made fun of her height.

Arlan had wondered how a mother could be so cruel, could treat her own flesh and blood that way. Of course, she'd never done it when other adults were around. But Duvessa did like to babysit all the kids of the other half-fae during the conference period.

"Well, anyway, that was my freshman experience. I transferred campus and...well, whatever, there's no reason you should care about any of this. I don't know why I'm even telling you." Her cheeks brightened to pink.

Arlan wondered what exactly she'd been about to say about her mother. God knew he'd had enough nightmares about that woman. He wanted to tell August that she would never be with another man like Ryan again. The part of his mind that cried out that she was his fated mate, that she was their third, wanted to tell her she'd never be with anyone but him and Jay again.

But what right did he have to claim her when he hadn't saved her all those years ago? And what if his instincts about her being his fated mate were completely wrong? He leaned against the wall, pressed his wrists against his eye sockets. "August tell me what you were going to say, just now about your mother. Just spit it out."

August chewed on the nail of her little finger and shrugged. "I think she might have put Ryan and those boys up to the whole thing."

Jay's face dulled with shock. "What? What the fuck? Why on earth would a mother do that?"

August shook her hair back from her face. "She's dark fae. We don't get along. You know what, guys? This is not something I ever wanted to discuss with you. I only told you so you'll understand why I was so pissed off you didn't tell me right away about the whole sex-magic thing. Call me an idiot, but I was really starting to trust the two of you."

Crap. She seemed ready to cry.

Jay didn't hesitate. He sat down on the couch next to her and took her in his arms. At first, she stiffened and resisted. But then she relaxed and allowed him to pull her close.

Jay cradled her in his strong embrace. "I made love to you because you're beautiful. That's all."

Buried in Jay's chest, she let out a ragged sigh that made Arlan's stomach hollow.

Jay kissed the top of her head. "Listen to me, August. You don't need to do anything you don't want to do. Our fight with the witch doctors is not your fight. We can find someone else."

She took a deep breath. "These witch doctors have already made it about me, though. Haven't they? They tried to kill me. I think I want to do this. Just let me think about it a little more."

Jay put his arm around her waist and gave her a quick squeeze. "You take as much time to think about this as you want, sweetie."

The beast in Arlan wanted to roar. Jay was making him feel like a villain. But his focus was saving the children as soon as possible, getting the babies back to their mothers. They needed

August. And the way his body hungered for her was more animal than man. He needed to get more control of himself before he shifted.

August tipped her head back. "Thanks. "I don't want to talk about this anymore. Can we talk about something else?"

Jay stood. "Well, I'm sick of this air-conditioning, baby. How about we go out and have a swim? Would you like that? We have a big pool outside. You'll love it."

"I have nothing to wear in the pool."

"Did you pack a bikini when you flew over here? Kruger came by the trailer when you were asleep, gave us your suitcase. Arlan texted him saying we were going to be your bodyguards."

August's smile lit up her face, but she couldn't quite erase the sadness from her eyes.

The world seemed to tilt on its axis as Arlan remembered that smile. The smile of the little girl she'd been, the eleven-year-old girl whose smiles had charmed him, and whose screams still filled his nightmares.

Leonard Hunting Lodge was even more impressive and imposing than her mother's mansion, all high-arched ceilings, white and cognac leather, and zebra-print detailing. Arlan's parents had certainly had a thing for zebras. Her lips twisted in disgust. Pity they killed them. She would have loved the safari-chic décor otherwise.

Arlan led her into a sumptuous guest bedroom decorated in white and black. Again with the zebra-print accents, but tastefully done.

When she turned to face him, she noticed his eyes were a pale green surrounded by a circle of gold.

Gorgeous.

The blessed heat meant he still wore only his tank and shorts. His body was hard and defined, all rippling muscle beneath his golden tan as he braced himself against the wall

Make small talk, idiot.

"Um... Your father's lodge, seems like he hunted a lot of zebras?"

"My father and Jay's father ran all kinds of animal hunts, but I guess the zebra hunts were his favorite." Sadness crossed his face. "Unfortunately, my father had a point when he said hunting is essential to the economy in Zimbabwe right now. He also had this twisted idea that hunting helped conserve the wildlife population. It's a popular opinion amongst those involved in trophy hunting out here."

Moral outrage made her lose air in her lungs. "I can't believe you believe any of *that*."

Arlan sighed. "My dad and Jay's dad, Mr. Nandoro, sustained and paid for the breeding of animals so that they could make money holding hunting safaris. So their business, in a twisted way, kept the population going. They claimed it was humane and a strong justification for trophy hunting."

"That's just outrageous. And trophy hunting means the biggest and strongest get taken out of circulation, which is counterproductive to species sustainability."

Arlan gave her a sad smile. "I know."

You've ended the hunting tours, I presume?"

He leaned against the wall, brushing his hair off his face. "I've shut down some of them, yes. But a lot of people will lose their jobs. Our parents have lodges across southern Africa. I've actually closed down over half of them, but..." He gave a deep sigh, "...not all. Not yet."

August glared at him in outrage.

"Look, I just don't want anyone to end up impoverished by my shutting all the lodges down too fast. I need time to work it out."

"It must be very ironic for you, being as you're a were."

His body stilled. "So Jay told you about that?"

She nodded. "I saw you in your lion form."

Arlan shrugged. "In Africa, you either hunt or you're hunted, predator or prey."

There was a dark edge to his voice that made her shudder. His words brought back the memory of being shot at. Anxiety made her stomach knot. "Arlan, do you think I should fly back to New York because these men want to kill me? I want to help you out but..."

He walked toward her and touched her shoulder. "I don't think it would even be safe for you to try to go back to New York right now."

He stared into her eyes, and for a weird breathless moment, she thought he might kiss her. The idea filled her with confused emotions. She'd already been with his friend Jay, and something about his face disturbed her, something familiar.

A valley of silence stretched between them.

Finally, Arlan cleared his throat. "When I first met you, before the shooting started, well... I was a complete ass. I admit that."

"You were, actually."

Arlan shrugged. "I guess I was judging you on the fact you have dark-fae connections, and that was bullshit."

August raised a brow in answer. "I get it. It's all right, Jay told me about all that too. I mean, he told me a dark fae put a curse on you."

Arlan shoved his hands in the pockets of his shorts and rocked back on his heels. "Seems you two got very close, very fast."

Heat rose in her cheeks. She didn't regret her impulsive little fling with Jay. It had been damn fun and hot, but she wished it hadn't been drawn to Arlan's attention. She sat down on the bed.

He motioned to her suitcase that lay on the zebra-print ottoman. "How about you find that swimsuit?"

She unzipped the case and rummaged through until she found her bright yellow bikini. She liked its happy daffodil color. "Most of the clothes I've got are khaki. I know it's really the only color choice out here if you don't want to be charged by an elephant. So a yellow swimsuit makes a nice change." She held it out for Arlan's approval.

Arlan groaned. "I can only imagine how good that's going to look when it's actually on you." She pulled a face at him, laughing, and waved him away.

"I'll wait outside the door and then take you to the pool area." Arlan started to go out of the room. Then he swung back in. "August, what do you usually drink?"

"Drink?"

"At a bar?"

"Oh, a merlot, or a gin and tonic."

He nodded and headed out the door.

August stretched and began to take off her clothes. Her body was tight with stress. Having a swim was going to be lovely. In the bright sunshine, the two hunks would clearly see the scars on her shoulders and thighs, but oh well. If she was going to do this sex-magic thing with them, that had to happen at some point.

Hell, her mind was so addled from the heat and the dark dust, she'd imagined Arlan had called her Gus back in the trailer. She hadn't been called that in ten years. She doubted he would suddenly have come up with the nickname on his own.

August bit the inside of her cheek as she pulled off her skirt.

Why did you tell those two Greek gods that embarrassing story about losing your virginity because of a bet? What on earth were you thinking?

Because when they asked her questions, they both seemed so kind. She wasn't used to that kind of concern. It made her feel as if she could tell them anything. That was dangerous.

She did up the bikini top in the back and opened the door to find Arlan waiting for her. His eyes darkened, and he gave a low wolf whistle.

She waved a hand at him in embarrassment. "Show me the pool."

His gaze drifted over the faint scars on her shoulders, then slid farther to alight on the worst ones on her upper thighs. He paled. Shame, anger and defensiveness rose in her. But before she could say a word, he took her hand. Shivers shot across her skin, sizzling through her veins and firing up her body.

You don't get touched often enough. That's what's making you overreact to these gorgeous men. Get a grip.

His lips quirked in a small smile. "Your fingers feel good, soft but strong." He gave her hand a gentle squeeze.

Kruger had said that Arlan had sylph blood in him. He was part air fae, same as Jay. Was that why the attraction to both these men was so intense? She'd already made love to Jay. She shouldn't be flirting with his best friend. Or maybe this wasn't flirting. Maybe this was only being friendly.

God, I know nothing about men.

She enjoyed entwining her fingers with his. They were so thick that they stretched her own fingers wide so they almost hurt, but a woman could draw a lot of comfort from such a big, safe hand.

"Come on." Arlan tugged at her and started leading her down the hall.

When she passed a wall cabinet, she gave a little yelp of surprise as a ball of ginger fur jumped off. She let go of Arlan's hand and caught it in her arms. She held the kitten up and had a look at it. It had an adorable face. She cuddled it close. It was so nice to feel its soft warm fur and hear its purring. She glanced up to see Arlan smiling at her.

"That's Mambava. He's a little OCD. He has some weird thing about not liking to walk on the floor, so he stays up high and waits for people to pass so he can jump into their arms and be carried around."

August laughed. "Aw, he's adorable. How old is he?"

"About three months."

"Is he part Persian? He's pretty fluffy."

"Maybe. Not sure. He was a rescue kitten."

"My cats were all rescue kittens too." She frowned. "He makes me realize how much I miss them."

She held Mambava to her cheek, enjoying his softness and purring some more, her stomach hollowing with a surprise wave of homesickness for her pets.

Arlan asked, "How many cats do you have at home."

August looked away. "Um...five."

Arlan's lips quirked.

"Just call me the crazy cat lady."

He squeezed her hand. "You're far too beautiful to be a crazy cat lady. You're a zoologist. You love animals. It doesn't surprise me. Have any other pets?"

"I almost took in a bird, then decided that would be a bad idea."

Arlan laughed. "So who's taking care of your cats?"

"My sister April. It's okay. She loves them too." When they got to the lounge, Mambava started scrambling in her arms. She let him go, and he sprang onto a bookcase and curled up for a nap. She laughed and then peered out the glass doors and gasped when she saw the gigantic pool.

Arlan pulled open the sliding glass doors. "It's an infinity pool."

Holy hell! How rich are these dudes?

She stepped outside, the heat of the African sun warming her instantly, the sky a bright enameled blue. She could see now that their home was built among sandstone rocks and the pool itself was vast and breathtaking, surrounded by beautiful glass mosaic tiles. What was really impressive were the perimeter pools. Water flowed over several gradient edges into overflow spas. The overall effect was of water flowing into the horizon extending out in front of her like a vanishing edge.

Arlan laughed, and she realized she'd been gaping openmouthed at everything. "I guess you inherited a fortune."

"I guess we did."

"My mother has always been very focused on using fae power to increase wealth, but...she hasn't achieved anything like this."

A muscle twitched in Arlan's jaw. "Yeah, well, they earned a lot of money in the regular way through building a huge business." He put a hand on her shoulder. "I'm going to go get us some drinks and some nibbles. You still want a gin and tonic?"

August nodded, and he left to get the refreshments.

She crossed the tiles to view the lavishly crafted gates. Through the gaps in its pattern, she could see hundreds of stone steps leading down to the veldt.

In the distance, there was a view of rows of lavender jacaranda trees, and she could even see the Zambezi River. She spotted a family of elephants drinking their fill. The baby elephant was slipping and sliding in the mud, trying to be close to his mother.

The simple beauty of the family drinking together made a sudden lump form in her throat. She gripped the gate until her hands ached. August turned around and walked back to the pool.

Jay swam a smooth freestyle toward her until he stood in the shallow end. There weren't many men who could pull off a brief-style bathing suit, but Jay's body was hot enough to wear the sleek black style. She'd truly never seen men with bodies as ripped and perfect as these two, outside of ads and movies.

Water droplets shone on the flawless caramel skin of those broad shoulders and perfect abs. Jay's smile at seeing her lit up his whole face. "Hey, sweetness. Wow! You look gorgeous in that little thing."

She averted her eyes, still not used to taking compliments. "Hi, Jay."

After crossing to the edge of the pool, she sat and dangled her toes in the water. Jay waded over to where she was, then, without warning, he grabbed both her ankles.

"I love your sexy legs."

"Oh yeah, a leggy super model, that's me." She struck a mock pose.

He gave her ankles a firm yank. She let him pull her into water, screaming and laughing as she splashed into depth. Water flooded her nose and mouth, making her splutter, then he was pulling her upright, drawing her against him.

The cool water felt amazing in contrast to the burning sun, but not as amazing as being pressed against Jay's rock-hard chest. He put his palms on the edge of the pool on either side of her, caging her in. The all-male scent of him hit her system like a drug.

"I love how petite you are. It's part of your beauty. Don't insult yourself again."

Heat spread across her cheeks. She was still unused to compliments, still surprised he would act as though more had passed between them than a one-night stand.

He started tickling her. "Stop it. Stop." She laughed, warning him between breaths, "You'll drown me at this rate."

He stopped tickling and pushed her up against the side of the pool. He caressed her cheek with the tips of his calloused fingers, then put his hand under her chin, tipping her head back for a kiss. At the first touch of his tongue against hers, she dissolved, fell apart, something hot and delicious stirring in her gut.

Lisa Whitefern

His hungry mouth fused with hers. His touch fired her body with need, causing a sharp ache inside that needed to be filled. Her legs shook, and his hands moved to wrap around her waist, holding her firm.

Jay's kisses were very different from Ryan's. He seemed to kiss for kissing's sake, not just as some fast and furious prelude to getting clothes off. For all Jay's strength and sexual magnetism, there was a blissful quality to his kisses that made her swoon, made her open up and liquefy, made her forget where she was. Greedily, she met his mouth halfway, and they devoured and consumed each other.

His breath feathered across her skin as he whispered in her ear, "When you insult yourself, it pisses me off. We need to do something about it. Maybe I'll have to spank you for it later."

The rich, dark tone of his words sent chills up and down her spine, and her knees started to give way. She had nothing to grip but his hard forearms. Mesmerized by his heat and her own lustful, submissive reaction to his words, she couldn't speak, so she only returned his gaze. Her body reacted to him too strongly. Her nipples weren't tight just because of the cold water. Her vagina pulsed with need.

Movement to the side broke the moment for her, and she turned her head a little to see Arlan walking toward them carrying her gin and tonic and a little dish of something. He set them on a little table near the pool. She covered her mouth with her hand. How could she have let Jay make her forget Arlan was there? It seemed unpardonably rude.

She couldn't read the zoologist's expression. Was that actual pain she saw in his eyes? He turned around and headed back towards the bar. August let go of Jay. Squirming, she managed to duck under his arm. She pushed her legs hard against the wall of the pool to propel herself into a quick and powerful backstroke, swimming as fast as she could.

She thought back to when the crash of that glass coffee table and the arguing had woken her. She'd entered the trailer's

102

kitchen and had more than one shock. The air between the two men had been charged. Both had positively shimmered with sexual tension.

August picked up the pace of her swimming. Another one of her crazy, horny fantasies, two males together, all that rock-hard muscle, slick limbs and large dicks... One of her kinkier fantasies.

She knew enough gay and bi men back home on Long Island to know. She could tell Arlan and Jay had some kind of romantic bond as well as sizzling heat. And yet they were both apparently attracted to her, which was amazing. Apparently, they were bi.

August swam as hard as she could, trying to block out her thinking with physical activity, wondering when she'd reach the invisible edge of the pool. That one word from Kruger's email flashed before her eyes. *Ménage.* She swam even faster.

So much had happened since she'd arrived in Africa, she hadn't allowed herself to even think of the full implications of that email. Could her heart bear more casual, meaningless sex with one man, let alone two?

Jay chased after her with a strong breaststroke.

He caught her ankle, but his grip on her foot slipped. She righted herself and splashed him. Laughing, he splashed her back, and while she was still giggling, he maneuvered her until he'd pressed her up against the wall of the pool again. Her legs couldn't even reach the bottom here.

Every inch of him was aware of her, of her soft breasts rising and falling, of her sweet jasmine scent.

"Why did you have to catch me?"

He cocked his head to one side, smiling at her, and raised his brows. Her question needed no answer, and she must know it. He nuzzled her neck, tickling her, and she started to laugh again, the melodic sound reaching all the way down to his soul. Even in the short time since he'd met her he felt more focused and alive than he had in years. How good it would feel to have her for his own to care for and to love.

He had to have her again. The need for her burned in his gut. Was it really just the pull between fire and air? Was it really just lust? His rough, raw need for her blended with so many...feelings.

Mine.

August stilled almost as though she'd heard his ridiculously possessive unspoken thought. Her face grew serious; her soft blue-gray eyes darkened with passion as he tipped her head back. He brushed just a light kiss over her mouth, teasing her.

The blood from his brain was dropping so fast to his cock, he felt dizzy. This was dangerous. But she didn't pull away, and he let his fingertips lightly graze the outside of her bikini bottoms. The ragged change in her breathing was his reward.

"What about Arlan?" Her voice was a whisper. "Isn't this rude to him?"

"No. Why would it be?"

Confusion and uncertainty flickered in her eyes. His own conflicting emotions made his head ache. He buried his face against her neck, inhaling her clean, womanly scent. She turned her head, searching around. "Where *is* Arlan anyway?"

"Pretty sure he's back at the bar."

When he brought his mouth to hers, he relished the softening of her body against his, the delicious slow female yielding of it. He let his fingers lightly skim the satiny material of her bikini top and exhaled when he touched the silk of her cleavage.

"I do want to help you find the tower. I want to help you and Arlan."

"Shh."

"No, Jay. I'm going to help you and Arlan save those children. They won't suffer more abuse because I was too cowardly." Her mouth had taken on that stubborn set that meant she wouldn't back down.

As much as he wanted to protect her, she was part of this now, part of their fight against evil. And he was a self-centered bastard. All he wanted was to touch her. Unable to stop himself, Jay pushed down one of the cups of her bright yellow bikini so that her breast popped out into his hand.

It was so exquisite, elegantly rounded, milky white, with faint traces of blue underneath. Jay wanted to trace those veins with his tongue until he reached the pink tip of her nipple. He didn't know if she was a C cup or D cup or whatever, but they were surprisingly large on her petite frame,

Her breath came in fast pants against his neck.

"Jesus," he whispered.

Unable to wait another second, he palmed them both, the weight of his lower body holding her still against the wall. "Sweetness, you're driving me crazy. You're so fucking *hot.*" He moved his legs around to cage her with his body. Her limbs trembled. It warmed him to realize he had the same impact on her that she had on him.

He slid down to circle her freed breast with slow open-mouthed kisses. The press of the other swollen nipple, through its cup and against his palm made his cock ache like a raw wound. The springy, slick tenderness of her other nipple felt like heaven against his tongue.

Jay moved his hand down and skimmed the line of her bikini pants again. Slipping a finger under the fabric he moaned, pleased to feel plenty of her own viscous liquid there. He loved the sensation of wet, slippery pussy beneath his fingers. The water around added a new layer of sensation. Jay slid a thick finger inside her and groaned at her tightness. Her own soft moan delighted him. He imagined the scent of her pussy beneath the chlorine, though the smell of the pool obscured it. Arlan, with his feline powers, would be able to scent her even here.

Don't think about Arlan now.

In the back of his throat, he began to hum a fae tune to protect her pussy from the chlorine. She glanced up at him in surprise. But he shushed her, soothed her.

He drilled into her, adding a second finger, making her groan louder, deeper.

Oh yes.

He loved finger fucking, loved watching the pleasure build and her pretty eyes glaze over. He wanted to add a third digit but was afraid of hurting her, so he thrust into her harder and faster with his fingers. His balls were tight, his cock steel. At last, she came, gasping, her core milking his fingers.

He barely knew her, and yet, somehow, he could see a future with her that stretched out ahead of him, as if he'd come to a fork in the road that one way or another would change everything. How Arlan would fit into it, he couldn't say.

Chapter Nine

August tugged up the cup of her bra, closed her eyes and floated on her back, partly from embarrassment, partly to recover from her orgasm.

The attraction between her and Jay bewildered her in its intensity. Since Ryan, she'd avoided a lot of socializing and concentrated on her studies. With Jay, she felt overwhelmed by the combustible heat between them.

When she opened her eyes again and looked around, neither Jay nor Arlan were anywhere to be seen. She doggy paddled to the edge, spotted Arlan and decided to get out.

When she stepped out of the pool, Arlan wrapped her in a huge fluffy white towel and worked at drying her. The sun was so hot, she'd dry in minutes without his help, but it was clear he wanted to spoil her, to make her feel pampered. If he'd been bothered by her making out with Jay, he showed no sign of it now.

She finally took a handful of the cocktail mix he'd left on the little table for her and took a sip of her gin and tonic.

"What have you been doing, Arlan? You never even changed into your swim trunks."

His smile was apologetic. "I didn't feel in the mood. I have a good book on my e-book reader. I was enjoying it when I wasn't checking you out in that yellow bikini."

August smiled, finally getting used to the flirting. She supposed it was just their way with women.

He led her to outdoor dining furniture positioned near the house. She sipped her drink as she walked. Jay appeared in the doorway and came over to sit at the table with them. More food and drink were already waiting, laid out on the table. Some type of delicious meat on crisp noodles, and a bottle of merlot.

She smiled at him. "This smells divine. What is it? Who cooked it?" She took a bite and tasted ginger on the meat.

"Fried crocodile, caught fresh from the Zambezi River, on vegetable strips with noodles, garlic, ginger and Soya sauce."

Crocodile?

She held the food in her mouth for a moment, then chewed it down. It actually tasted really good. She laughed. "Wow, crocodile I never thought of eating such a thing."

"We have a lot of crocodile in the Zambezi. Jay takes them from there. It's a popular dish here. And to answer your other question, Jay used magic to prepare it while you swam."

"Culinary magic, wow!" She took a mouthful and started to chew. She couldn't decide if it tasted like fried chicken or crispy fried fish, but it was good. "My mom was actually pretty good at culinary magic herself. But as I grew older, she started employing cooks. I think she became more interested in making money, and it kind of took over all her other interests." August sighed and took a sip of her wine. "I was even able to do a little bit of culinary magic as a child, but not anymore."

"I can guess why."

Not now. Don't make me think about her now.

Her face heated at the pity and questions she saw in Arlan's green-gold eyes.

Don't tell. It could make them want you even less once the sex magic experiment is over. What man would want a woman with so much baggage?

His gaze locked with hers. She believed in emotional honesty. She was going to be making love with these men. She needed to be straight up and honest with them.

Don't be a coward. Just explain and get it over with.

She let her lips curve in a wry smile. "The self-esteem thing?"

Jay glared at Arlan.

"No. It's all right, Jay. He's right. Human low self-esteem damages fae power in a half-fae." She took another long sip of wine, avoiding their gaze. "Yeah, I have issues. My mother was dark fae, and I was a child abuse victim. So yeah I'm sure my low self-esteem killed any fae power I might have had."

Jay swore. He stood, gripping the table, his muscles clenching in tightly controlled fury. "Hang on. You mean your father abused you—is that what you mean?"

"*No.*" August pushed back her chair. She hated how many people assumed child abuse was done only by fathers, by men. It made her angry. "No. No. No. There was no sexual abuse. And no it was *not* my father. Never my father. What I went through wasn't the kind of thing you could talk to your school counselor about."

Jay reached across the table and took her hand, his thumb stroking across her fingers. "Let it out, August. Talk to us."

She shrugged, embarrassed. "I can't really say exactly how much it affected any fae power I had or might have, because as a teen and adult, I threw myself into schoolwork. I haven't even attempted to do any magic since I was ten or eleven. I didn't want magic in my life."

A muscle twitched in Jay's jaw. She could sense the rage rippling under his forced control. "I don't care about the fucking magic. Who abused you, August? Arlan and I will make the bastard pay."

"My *mother*, all right?"

"Your mother? Holy shit! What did she do?"

Arlan threw down his napkin. "Just shut up, Jay. When she wants to talk about it more, she will. Leave it be."

She gave Arlan a grateful smile and wondered why his gaze shifted away from hers. "It's okay, Jay," she said softly. "My mother has a lot of power in the Half-Fae Network. She had a lot of people working for her. There was this one awful guy called Willem, who…" She shook her head. "Well, actually, Arlan's right. I don't think I want to talk about this anymore."

She forced a smile so as not to make Jay feel any worse. Arlan didn't need to be so harsh with him.

Jay took her hand. "You deserve to be cherished and protected, August." He gave her fist a firm squeeze.

She nodded dumbly, too touched to speak. She realized how numb she'd been for so long. They two of them were making her feel so much emotion. Arlan smiled at her, filling her wineglass for the third time.

Finally, she found her voice again. "So I gather neither of you feels confident enough in your fae abilities to try to stop these kidnappings with your own magic? That's why you need my help?"

Jay sat and pushed back a little in his chair. "Basically, yeah, that's right."

Arlan nodded. "Fae power in the mortal world gets more and more diluted by the interbreeding of fae and humans with each passing generation. That's what the Half-Fae Network was invented to combat."

"You sound like my mother. That's one of her big issues. She's always ranting about the dilution of fae blood because of interbreeding. She's bitter she wasn't born a full-blooded fae. The funny thing is, she never blames her dark-fae mother for seducing her dad and then disappearing back to the Fae Realm. She doesn't care that her mother was a deadbeat who just abandoned her."

"Yeah the dark fae never seem to see things that way. They just idolize the fae." Arlan rolled his eyes. "I have to admit, though, I wish I had more fae blood myself. Magic calls me to be a Warrior of the Light, but I have fuck all control of any power." Arlan rubbed the bridge of his nose. "I can understand your mother's frustration, even if she and I have taken very different paths."

She clapped her hands as a sudden thought struck her. "Hey, you two are part sylph, right? Can either of you fly?" Arlan shook his head, and Jay glanced at his watch.

"It's getting late, Arlan." Some form of communication she didn't understand passed between them. Arlan got up from the table and went into the house for something.

Jay shifted his chair close to her and took her hand, lacing his fingers with hers. He curved his other hand around the nape of her neck. "Relax." He leaned forward and gave her the briefest kiss on the lips. Why did even this innocent kiss to reassure have to burn like flame? She could get lost in his kisses forever.

After a few moments, Arlan returned. Her held a large white cotton robe that was obviously his own. "Here, put this on before the night grows colder. Is your suit still wet?"

"No, it's fine. The heat's dried it. It's so warm in this country." She stood and allowed him to slip it on her. Once he'd wrapped her in the robe, he gave her a random hug, his beefy arms wrapping tight around her. August, pressed back against him and sighed, the massive strength of those arms made her feel utterly, blissfully safe and protected. There was a sweetness to his hug that brought tears to her eyes. No one had held her like this, since before her father died. No one had held her like this, since she was eleven.

Arlan finally let her go, guiding her back into her seat.

Jay swallowed a bite of crocodile, then shook his head. "You know, I think there's already some kind of magic messing with the three of us right now."

Arlan raised a brow. "The thought's crossed my mind as well. I think the reason the attraction between the three of us is so intense may be more than even the connection between fire and air, I think magic may be trying to right itself, trying to attract fae to fae to continue its own existence. The attraction between Silvara and me was intense, but what I feel for August is so much more."

Jay put his fork down. "You read too fucking much, mate, that's your problem. Let's just enjoy what the night brings."

She wasn't sure what either of them meant, but she felt tipsy and ready for anything, so she just smiled at them both, anticipation building in her like a white heat.

They finished their meals, and Jay began muttering in fae and humming. Once again a spray of indigo light shot from his palm. Dishes and cups danced in the air and landed smoothly on the table. They ate hot pudding with brandy, honey and dates, vanilla ice cream and Amarula coffee.

August finished a mouthful of ice cream and put down her spoon. "So can we talk about that email Kruger sent?" She hoped she wasn't blushing. "I mean...I think I gather from that email that sex magic works by using a process of intense visualization in the moments after orgasm. Is that right?" Had she stuttered? She bit her lip, hoping they couldn't see how self-conscious she felt.

Arlan had finished his ice cream and was drinking his Amarula. "That's right. Regular fae magic works by visualization while humming fae music, and sex magic uses the energy of sexual arousal to visualize the desired object after orgasm. The idea is that we can bring the storm tower to where we are. Then we can free the children. When I was a teen, I once heard adults at a half-fae conference talking about how sex magic doesn't always work."

Jay nodded. "You have to try different things and hope for success. I've read about ways you can try."

Arlan set down his drink. "I have some trinkets that are meant to possibly help. I hope you understand, sweetie. We just want to do everything we can to save those children. I'm friendly with some of their mothers and—"

"I actually have some understanding of how painful it must be to lose a child." August chewed on the nail of her little finger. "I mean, I'm not a mother, but I almost lost a younger sister to illness. She couldn't say my name, so she used to call me Gus,

112

and I had that nickname as a kid." August's face grew serious. "My sister May was in the hospital when she was four with some unknown illness, and she nearly died, so yeah, I can kind of imagine what it's like for all those mothers in the village. They must think about their loss every minute." A lump formed in her throat. "Every...single...minute."

Memories of May in the hospital clouded her mind. She'd been sick with the same mystery condition her father had. The doctors had said May wouldn't live. It was what had pushed her father over the edge, what had killed him.

"August—" Concern showed in Jay's eyes. "I won't let you do anything you don't want to do. You have to be certain about this."

She held up a hand. "No, Jay." She sat up straighter, put her shoulders back. "I'm sure now. I'm sure I want to do this. I want to help. I want to make love to both of you. I want to find that storm tower."

"Are you sure?" Jay's words were as sharp as the edge of a blade.

"After what I went through as a child, how could I not try to help these kids? I'm in this one hundred percent."

Jay gave her a searching look. "You'd need a safe word. You can use zebra."

August laughed. "Okay."

"And hard limits. Have you heard of those? You tell us anything you're not comfortable doing."

"I've read about them."

When Jay smiled, her cheeks burst into flames. He leaned forward and put his hand on her knee. "Hey, sweetness," he whispered in her ear. "Don't be afraid or embarrassed. Relax."

He took her hand and pulled her to her feet.

Arlan placed his cheek against hers, his stubble rubbing her skin. She was already losing her heart to Jay. It would be madness to lose it to Arlan as well, but she could feel it happening against logical thought.

113

Arlan's lips sought every inch of her neck. August stood on tiptoes, sinking her fingers into the muscles of his shoulders. As a scientist, she knew sex was just a biological function. She needed to focus on that part and guard her heart.

Slanting his mouth over hers, Arlan teased at her lips with his own. August grasped his upper arms, enjoying the bunching of his muscles beneath his skin. Her robe fell open, and the warmth of his body seemed to seep into hers, heating her from the inside out. Their tongues mated, slipping and sliding against each other.

This ecstasy, this swooning feels dangerously close to love.

No, you idiot, it's just infatuation. Get a hold of yourself.

August whimpered as her body alternated between thrills and chills. The knowledge that he was a were-lion, with all the power and strength that entailed, made blood pool in her groin. His masculine presence, like Jay's, was slowly overpowering and enveloping her.

He broke the kiss. "Come on. How about the three of us enjoy the sunset?" He took her hand, leading her to the large green canvas daybed that, like the outdoor dining furniture, was arranged against the house.

His gaze locked on hers. She swallowed, but the wine and Amarula had made her both light-headed and brave.

Arlan clasped her shoulder. "You just sit down, enjoy the sunset. There are some trinkets that are supposed to help. Jay and I'll go get them."

August nodded, rendered speechless by anticipation and lust that made her weak. She would relax; she would enjoy this for what it was. She would help them with the magic.

She lay back on the daybed, glanced up at the sky and gasped. It had transformed from azure into a breathtaking explosion of burnt orange, vivid tangerine, gold and sienna. In her mind's eye, she saw the two men with their shirts off, imagined what they would look like soon, the sunset on their healthy, perfect skin, light playing on every ripple of bronzed muscle. Arlan and Jay were intimidating when their shoulders were straining the seams of their shirts, but with their shirts off, they would loom much larger. Still, she trusted them. They might break her heart by not loving her, but they would never willingly or deliberately hurt her.

She heard Jay's and Arlan's footsteps and turned to see them making an altar on a little side table. They set down trinkets: a gleaming chalice, an ornately carved dagger, a mysterious coin, what appeared to be oil in an attractive curved glass bottle. A pale gold gleamed around each of these objects that spoke of fae magic, but not dark magic like the trinkets in Duvessa's mansion.

"I brought some of these." Arlan showed her the gold packets. "Ordered online from Kris and Nick's Toy Emporium."

"Magic condoms?"

Arlan nodded, smiling. "Fae condoms from Nick and Kris. You can't feel them at all."

"Oh yes. Nick and Kris, the toymakers." Heat rose to her cheeks. "I've heard of them."

Jay strode over to the daybed. His intense black gaze locked with her own. "Are you ready now, sweetness?"

She swallowed hard. "As I'll ever be." Jay chuckled and placed a tender kiss on her lips. She'd been drunk on wine, but now she was drunk on arousal, intoxicated by the effect they had on her. Arlan smiled down at her. She managed a nervous smile back. He laid his weight on top of her and parted her robe, pulling down her bikini cups, gently sliding his hand over one breast. She slid her fingers under the back of his tank. His skin was smooth and silky to her touch. Glancing down, she was surprised to see how engorged her nipples were. Arlan stared at them for a moment too, then he lowered his head and sucked one into his mouth, making her almost faint with pleasure. Her pussy contracted. She could feel the line that connected nipples to clit. Her other breast was crying out for attention, and Arlan didn't leave her hanging.

As he sucked, he shifted his weight off her, as if worried he was too heavy for her. The cooler air of evening brushing against her damp bikini bottom felt like a lover's touch, she was that sensitive and wet. Jay, sitting on the other side of the daybed, smiled at her and slid one finger under the edge of her bikini bottom.

She bit her lip as his finger began circling her clit, and whimpered as invisible lines shimmered from nipple to clit, from clit to brain. She spread her legs wider, aching as the rough pad of Jay's thumb scraped where it felt best.

But Arlan growled and shoved Jay's hand away. He stood and stepped back to unzip his fly.

Before Arlan could get his cock out, though, Jay pounced. There was no other word for it. He turned her over until she was on all fours on the daybed. The intensity of each man's desire for her mixed with the scent of them and had her feminine parts heated to a froth.

Jay brushed the hair from the back of her neck and kissed her there. "Are you comfortable, darling girl?"

She managed a nod.

Arlan sat on the other side of the bed. Gripping her hair, Arlan pulled her head back and brushed his lips over her own. The kiss started as a caress and built in intensity until it became a branding iron.

Arlan reached down and cupped her hanging breast, stroking a thumb over her taut nipple. She moaned, accepting the thrust of his tongue. The were-lion growled low in his throat. "I want you." His voice was thick with desire. "You're mine, August, mine and Jay's. Do you understand?" It was a rhetorical question that demanded understanding, demanded acceptance. She didn't know how to respond or what to think. The rational, philosophical zoologist had gone, replaced by the dominant were-beast. Arlan was all lust.

Jay had her bikini pants around her ankles and was tugging them off. What a rude image he must have of her from that angle. She closed her eyes and groaned. Part of her was embarrassed, but she couldn't protest. She'd fantasized about being in this position with a hot man too many times to count. She had alcohol as an excuse. She *wanted* this.

She could sense Jay angling back to get a good look at her. The heat in her face rose to her hairline.

"You have a very, very pretty pussy," Jay murmured.

"She's beautiful everywhere." Arlan's words made her smile. She was almost starting to believe their compliments. Neither of them seemed to care about her height at all. Maybe they even liked it. Jay's hot breath whispered across her sex.

Oh God.

He blew across her swollen clit, spread her lips gently. His tongue hit her clit with a quick flick.

Oh God, oh God.

This act, this exquisite pleasure wasn't something she'd expected or even thought about. The sensation of Jay rasping his tongue over her swollen bud had her shaking. He slurped her clit into his mouth, sucking on it mercilessly and lighting up all her nerve endings.

Arlan held her head against his broad chest so he could see around her. He made a low animal sound in his throat, whispering, "Yeah. Tongue-fuck that pussy. Give it to her. Make her come. Make her scream." Perhaps his dirty talk and guttural vocal tone should have offended her, but it only served to ratchet her arousal up another notch.

Jay suddenly stopped, and she whimpered with need.

How can he stop? The bastard. "Mmm. She smells and tastes so good, Arlan."

"I'll bet she does, mate." Arlan sounded faintly jealous. "How wet is she?"

"She's beyond wet. She soaking."

August gritted her teeth. They were discussing her like a plaything when all she wanted now was sensation, not words.

But the way they were discussing her like an object called to the submissive in her. She moaned, too overwhelmed with need to even beg.

A sudden press of warm, oily fingers on the curve of her ass gave her an erotic jolt. Jay's fingers tickled, sliding over her sphincter, pressing into her puckered flesh, while his mouth latched back on her clit until she was blind with pleasure.

In her mind's eye, she pictured Jay's tongue jabbing fiercely into Arlan's mouth while Arlan parried his thrusts with equal aggression. At last the images in her mind combined with all sensation, making her shatter and cry out their names.

Arlan smiled at her. With his hair tousled from bending to suck her breasts, he looked more boyish than he normally did.

Since she'd come, she tried to envision a tower made of gray stone as hard as she could. She even tried to remember how to hum like a fae.

She heard a packet rip open, then felt something rub at her entrance. It was the head of Jay's fat cock. At the same time, Arlan opened the fly of his shorts and brought out his shaft. His cock stood ramrod straight, bobbing against his flat egg-box abs, almost reaching his navel. The head of it was shiny and the color of a ripe plum. August was ready to take a bite. When he saw she was willing to take him in her mouth, he smiled.

She'd only done this once with Ryan, but Arlan's cock was so much bigger and a nicer shape than Ryan's. She felt confident from reading books that she wouldn't do it badly.

She leaned forward, kissing his golden balls and watching them tighten in response. Arlan took a handful of her hair, painting her mouth with the essence of his precome. The salty taste of it exploded on her taste buds. A thrill shot from her mouth to her nipples to her snatch. Tugging on her hair, he slid the head of his shaft between her lips. She groaned, trying to make her mouth into a toothless ball, drawing him in deeper.

She loved the noises he made, loved when the expression on his face changed to obvious fear that she might stop.

Jay, meanwhile, had not entered her pussy but was rubbing his shaft between her nether lips, stimulating her clit. His oil-covered finger still probed at her rosette. She gasped at the intrusion, the feel of that private place being stretched. Her clit thrummed as he rubbed his shaft against it. Male flesh melting into her, the sensation of it against her pussy delicious.

The thrust of Jay's finger had an edge to it, not quite pleasure, not quite pain, but the mere thought that he had penetrated such a secret place, that he was looking down and watching his finger go in and out, thrilled the submissive side of her.

Arlan's thigh was warm against her cheek. He still gripped her hair as he pistoned his cock in and out of her mouth. Jay's finger thrust in her ass, and her tender, swollen bud rubbed against his steel-hard dick. The only thing left out was her aching hole.

Jay continued thrusting his finger in her ass with fantastic dexterity. August's head spun. The two of them caused a fever inside her, one that spread and intensified until she wasn't sure where their bodies ended and hers began. Her snatch pulsed and ached for fulfillment.

Through the haze of painful aching lust in her head and pussy, she heard Jay laugh. Finally he pressed the huge head of his cock at her entrance. She backed against him, trying to swallow him up with her pussy.

His hand lay on her back, steadying her. "Easy, easy sweetness."

He drove the broad head of his cock inside. She tensed around the thickness. August bucked back against Jay, her whole body arching to get him in deeper, desperate for that second explosion, pleasure building inside her, the sensation of having her mouth full of Arlan's cock increasing the dark, dirty pleasure of it all. Her mind exploded with the realization she was servicing two men's cocks at once.

She opened her throat to take Arlan as deep as she could, even as she pressed back against Jay so her clit rubbed against the base of his shaft, giving each man equal pleasure simultaneously. Together, the three of them moved like one animal, finding a rhythm that satisfied.

Arlan was the first to climax, With a fierce growl, he pulled out, and the hot splash of come warmed her breasts in the now cooler evening. He zipped his shorts back up and, taking her head in his hands, kissed her so powerfully, her head swam.

With Arlan no longer in her throat, there was nothing to stop Jay from picking up the pace and jackhammering away, the wildness igniting all her nerve endings. She clenched her muscles and shifted position, trying to milk every last ounce of sensation from his massive cock.

The stroke of Jay's cock against her clit as he pistoned in and out drove her to a second climax. The muscles of her snatch contracted just as he groaned out his own climax. She fell forward on her forearms, her eyes closed. Her body felt completely relaxed, and everything around her had a shimmering, surreal quality to it. She was only vaguely aware of Jay carefully pulling out and dumping the fae condom into the wastepaper basket.

"You. Are. Amazing." Arlan's comment entered her mind's blissful haze, reminding her of what she had to do.

She smiled, fighting the drowsy, blissful feeling, and began to concentrate on envisioning the tower, humming low in her throat, trying to remember how to hum like a fae. But gloom cut through the bliss, plunging them into despair. She sensed it from Arlan stronger than from Jay. The storm tower hadn't appeared.

August opened her eyes. Everything appeared strange and new in the moonlight. The dagger, chalice and coin were gilded with fae light, mocking her with their unused power.

Above her, the moon hung huge and silver-white in an ink-black sky. It shimmered on the surface of the pool, the reflection trembling, wavering, spreading and contracting, and when she turned to gaze at Arlan, his body seemed to do the same. She blinked, then gasped as claws shot out of Arlan's...paws. A ragged growl ripped from his throat. She bit down on her fist to keep from screaming. She'd known he was a were. She shouldn't scream. What he was going through looked and sounded like agony, limbs cracking and stretching, skin transforming to luxurious fur. He fell on all fours but nearly retained his normal height. He was a huge lion, a gorgeous lion.

A magic lion.

Gold sparks of fae power shot off his skin. However powerless Arlan felt as a quarter-fae in his human form, this lion radiated magic.

Jay laid his hands on her waist, stroking her, soothing her. He obviously sensed her surprise. "It's okay, baby, it's okay. Let me deal with him now."

A little sob escaped her simply because of the momentary agony she'd seen on Arlan's face.

Jay walked over to the gates, unlocked and threw them open. August watched in silent amazement as the big lion padded across the courtyard. His magnificent tail swung as he descended the seemingly endless display of stone steps, down the cliff face and down to the veldt.

Chapter Ten

"I don't know why the floodlights didn't turn on automatically when the sun went down. Must be a malfunction." Jay fiddled with a switch, and they came on, lighting up the complex network of fountains and pools. The effect was breathtaking. "Let's hop in the Jacuzzi, baby girl."

"Aren't you worried about Arlan?"

He took her in his arms. "No. Not really." He glanced away from her for a second. "Maybe a little bit. But he's immortal, at least in his lion form. They've shot at him, thrown dark dust at him—he's survived it all. You haven't seen him with his tank top off yet, have you?"

Only in my dreams.

She shook her head.

He traced the pattern of the burn scars on her upper arm. "He has his own scar, a bullet wound."

She cuddled against his broad chest for comfort. "Why was there golden magic shooting from his fur?"

"It seems he's a Warrior of the Light. Despite his lack of control over his magic power, I guess he inherited that gene. It's like there's a compass inside him directing him to fight evil. The witch doctors are probably stealing another child right now. It tends to happen when the moon is full."

He took her hand and led her down to the Jacuzzi. After picking her up as though she weighed nothing, he settled her down in the water and joined her.

The night had cooled, and she sank into the blissful heat. Bubbles and hot water cascaded over them. For a while, the two of them just gazed at the moon. But there were many questions in August's mind. "When we were in the infinity pool before, you hummed fae magic. I heard you."

Jay ran a hand over his shaved head, then leaned back and sighed. "Having sex underwater doesn't work well for a woman. The chlorinated water might have got inside you with my fingers and hurt you."

"But you said the only magic you could do is culinary."

He rubbed his fingers back and forth across his forehead. "Yeah, I stretched the truth a little on that one."

She said nothing, waiting him out.

He gave another deep sigh. "I hate magic."

Sympathy rose within her, a shared bond. "I understand. I hate magic too. Because of who my mother was, I saw... Well, I experienced a lot. I saw a lot."

"Yeah, I get you, girl. My own mother, well, I don't think she was dark fae, but she's in a coma now because she tried to use magic to save my father's life. She's as good as dead."

"I'm sorry."

Jay shrugged. "That's what happens to half-fae who use more magic than they're capable of handling. I don't let Arlan know I have more power. I don't want to get his hopes up that I can help him. The call to light-fae magic isn't as strong in me anyway. I just want to be a cop, you know? I just want to be a regular guy." He gave a mirthless laugh. "Yeah, I'm pretty far from it, but that's what I want."

Their eyes met for an instant, his pupils huge and black. He bent at the waist, pressing his lips against her upturned mouth. He kissed her with tongue and teeth, desperate, gluttonous, aroused. August tasted the musky essence of herself on his tongue.

With some effort, Jay spun her around in the water. He pulled her against him, her back against his chest and his muscled arms around her. His shaft was brick-hard against her ass. She moved tentatively against him, enjoying the velvety smoothness that covered steel rubbing against her cheeks. She turned her head to give him a playful smile. "No sex under water? Are you sure?"

His smoky laugher exhilarated her, as ebullient as the fountains and bubbles of the spa itself. It occurred to her how much she genuinely liked him, beyond the fierce sexual chemistry between them; how much she wanted him to like her back, to want more from her than her potential for magic. Did he realize how rare the connection between them was? Did he care? And where did Arlan fit in? If there were problems between him and Arlan, would her involvement in their relationship make things better? Or worse?

Jay's big hands slid up the back of her spine, making it tingle. He caressed her thigh almost to her mound, trailed his fingers up her belly, between her breasts and to her jawline. "What I want now is your pleasure." His fingers trailed back over her nipple, and he whispered in her ear, "I think we can find something fun to distract you from worrying."

He positioned her so she knelt in front of a powerful jet, his big hand cupping her mound from behind in a possessive gesture. Then he splayed his fingers, spreading the folds of her lips, and gave her a small push so the strong jet of water shot directly onto her clit.

His mouth closed on the side of her neck, sucking the skin. His hands caressed her breasts, played with her nipples, while the powerful jet pounded her clit. He knew what he was doing. He pinched at her sensitized nipples.

The hard ridge of his cock pressed against her back, teasing her, caressing her. She struggled slightly to turn to him. But Jay was uncompromising. His strong hands held her firmly in place so the water jet continued to pummel her most sensitive spot. She leaned back against his solid form, giving in.

The rise of her orgasm came again, steady and strong in thick, growing waves, the sensations coursing through both nipples and clit, shaking her to the bone, She slumped against his chest, letting him hold her up in the water, worn out from yet another climax.

"Christ, you're beautiful when you come. I love you."

"What?" The words were so unexpected, they shocked her to the core. "I don't think we've known each other long enough to say that kind of thing."

"Consider it this way. Love is something I'm feeling. It's my emotion. It's what I'm feeling right now."

The only person who's ever said "I love you" to me was Dad.

And the one memory of Dad she could never get out of her head involved faded bloodstains on a pristine white bedspread. August headed up the steps of the spa and pulled a towel tight around her body.

"I love you." He said the words again with a strength and sincerity that brought tears to her eyes.

He stepped out of the Jacuzzi and put his hand on her shoulder, forcing her to face him. His mouth was on hers again, his lips confident and firm, his hands on her waist as he tasted her.

Her heart pounded a mile a minute from his kisses alone.

"Sweetness, why won't you listen?"

Her breath started to back up, her chest tight with emotion. "You could have anyone, Jay."

"Anyone, could I?"

She nodded.

"Well, that's great, sweetheart, because I want you."

Chapter Eleven

Professor Kruger returned from his work elsewhere in the country, and for the next five days, August immersed herself in scientific work. Kruger introduced her to other academics from the college and took her on fieldtrips to observe and record lion behavior.

Today she'd had had the pleasure of tracking the spore of a female lion Kruger had named Chido. He'd explained that Chido meant "wish" in the Shona language. Now their wish that Chido would breed had come true.

August and Kruger had observed the mother feeding with her cubs. As the cubs chewed on freshly killed warthog meat, Chido talked continuously to them in a series of low moans. Observing the mother-cub relationship had caused a hollow sensation in her stomach. She'd seen the warmth of love flow from mother to child, and she'd felt alone. But on an academic level, she enjoyed the chance to study them immensely.

Hours later, she'd returned to the lodge. The guest bedroom almost felt like her room now. She sat at the beautifully polished Zambezi teak desk that Jay told her had been his father's. Mambava leapt from the bed onto her chair, and then her desk. He lay on his back, showing his belly. He was a half-breed like her. Half Persian, half goodness knows what. Absentmindedly, she rubbed his belly, making him purr while she skimmed over her notes.

She took another sip of her coffee, typed some more. She was determined to get all her work typed up properly, but her mind kept drifting back to Arlan and Jay.

On a companionship level, she'd become a lot closer to Jay over the last five days. Jay would gaze at her with those deep eyes darkening and beckoning, and they seemed to hold a promise he would protect her forever. That if she was strong enough to accept his love, then he was strong enough to take on the world for her.

Being with Jay had finally come to be about more than his dark looks, fit body and powerful sex drive.

And yet she'd never been so...in lust with anyone, even in her dreams and fantasies. God, she'd been missing out. Just the thought of Jay made her womb contract, made liquid seep from her core.

She stopped trying to type. She put her head in her hands.

You're back to square one, kid, trying to numb anxiety and desire with work. When are you going to get a life?

But she couldn't make love to Jay when Arlan was missing.

Visions of flying bullets, dark dust and the headdress of the witch doctors she'd seen flashed through her mind, and her chest tightened. Five days and nights gone, and still no word from Arlan. What if they'd shot him? What if they had him trapped somewhere?

Tears stung her eyes. She couldn't concentrate. She couldn't even see her notes through her tears. August wiped them away angrily, pissed off with herself for being such a wimp, and for thinking of herself when Arlan might be lying somewhere with a bullet in his chest, for all she knew. Immortal or not, Arlan could be stranded and in terrible pain.

She jumped at the knock on her door. It was either the maid or Jay. Jay had been working long hours, and she'd seen little of him since rebuffing his declaration of love five days ago. It was kind of awkward. "Come in."

Jay entered, looking hot in his cop uniform. Uniforms had always done it for her. Brown eyes blazed in a face that might have been chiseled from stone. She knew he was frustrated by her rebuffing his advances. He couldn't understand why she'd turned away from him.

He nodded toward the cat. "Mambava's so greedy. The maids fed him twice, and I fed him. Don't you go giving him another feed." August laughed. Jay flopped into the chair beside her and grabbed a pen off her desk. He started fiddling around with it. "You working on that thesis thing again? Do you ever stop working?"

"Hey, Mr. Policeman, you're no slacker yourself. When did you get home from work?"

He spun on the desk chair a little, grinned and stretched his legs. "This was my last day at the city office filing papers. Just a bunch of boring admin work about how many poachers we've caught, et cetera. Anyway, you're looking at a free man. Three weeks paid vacation, baby." He tossed the pen back on her desk so that it shot off and fell onto the floor.

She reached down to pick it up. As she did, a thought about Chido's mate came to mind. "Hang on a minute." She sat back up, reached for her pad and paper, and started scribbling away furiously.

Jay gave an exasperated sigh. "You love your job, don't you, mate? You love studying those animals as much as Arlan does." He smiled at her. "Tell me about the joy you find in it."

She glanced up at him, startled. Never before had a man who'd shown sexual interest in her asked her these kinds of questions. Ryan had been a virtual stranger; she'd been a fool not to see his interest in her was only sexual, even aside from the bet.

"August?" He put a hand on her arm. She shook her head and bit her lip, feeling like a fool for being touched by his simple interest in her. He leaned in and inspected her more closely. "Oh hell, baby what's wrong? What's that frown for?"

She rubbed a hand on her forehead. "I can't stop thinking about Arlan, that's all."

"He's a Warrior of the Light. He may not have much magic, but we know he's an immortal half-fae. He lucked out in the genes department like you did. They shot him once, and he should have died. He'll return. He always does."

Her lips quirked up.

"What's so funny?"

"I just realized the goings-on of light fae are about as mysterious to me as fae power is to full-blooded mortals. I've only ever had dark magic in my life. I know zero about Warriors of the Light."

He slid his chair in closer so he sat right next to her. "Your mother was a piece of work, huh? She was seriously committed to the dark path despite only being a half-fae? That's what Arlan told me."

She nodded. "I don't know what Arlan would know about my mother. I guess maybe Kruger's told him some stuff. Mind you, Kruger *admires* her."

Jay made a "pffft" with his lips. "Everything I've heard about that guy makes him sound like a dick."

"Look, he's a bit of a pervert, but he hasn't laid a hand on me since I arrived here."

Jay's eyes narrowed dangerously. "*What?* Since you arrived here? You mean he laid a hand on you before?"

She shrugged. "Yeah, he made a pass at me once back in New York. I have to deal with him because there's no one else available in my department qualified to supervise my PhD. But it's okay. It's fine. I told him I seriously wasn't interested, and he backed right off. He's been nothing but professional since then."

A muscle twitched in Jay's jaw. "He ever so much as touches a hair on your head again, I'll scoop his eyeballs out with a rusty spoon and put them in his back pocket so he can watch me kick his ass."

She choked on her coffee, laughing.

He shook his head. "I'm serious, though. A woman like you should be treated like a precious jewel. You're the kind of woman that should be a man's reason for getting up in the morning and working a tiring day. You deserve to be protected at any cost. You deserve only the best from a man, from anyone."

August blinked back tears. No one took care of her. Not since her father had shot himself. He'd been unable to take the pain caused by his the illness, and unable to take the emotional pain when the doctors had said little May would probably die.

Jay laid a hand on her shoulder and gave it a squeeze.

He really cares.

He took the mug out of her hand and pulled her close. The musky, masculine scent of him almost made her swoon.

"Shhhh, sweetness, don't cry. I get that you're worried about Arlan. I get that you miss him." He ran a hand over her head. "Hell. I miss him too."

She waited for him to say more. The thought that the three of them might be fated mates filled her mind once again. Could he feel it too? Did he think it was possible? "I'm becoming obsessed. I can't stop worrying and thinking about him."

"I can't stop thinking about you."

Her cheeks prickled as blood rushed to them. The way he spoke with such conviction and emotion frightened her. She waited for him to reveal the truth about his relationship with Arlan, but instead, his mouth met hers. Her lips parted, allowing his tongue entrance. She responded with soft welcoming touches from her own tongue. The full-throttle punch of his kiss after five days of denial jolted her numbed system into overdrive.

She hadn't known before Jay and Arlan that being with a man could be like this.

His lips covered hers. The taste of him exploded inside her, the ripe, greedy heat of it. His mouth was hungry, ravenous, taking long, deep kisses that left her clinging to him. Fiery tingles of sensation coursed over her body, licked at her womb, making her slick and wet so fast.

Too fast.

She was almost drowning in the sheer ecstasy of being in his arms again. Yet it was somehow wrong. Arlan should be there. Arlan should be with them. She pushed on his shoulders, dragged her mouth from his.

What if they aren't your fated mates? What if that's all a myth, and they dump your ass later to be with each other? You won't be able to stand the pain.

"August?"

She opened her mouth to speak, then shut it again, trying to find words to express how she felt. Slowly, his face changed, developing a more primitive cast. "I've let you deny me for five days now while we both worked, sweetheart. No more. I'm not tolerating this another damn day."

She drew in a ragged breath. She'd had many glimpses into the different facets of Jay's personality since she'd been in Africa, but his dominant side gave her goose bumps. It called to the deepest, darkest part of herself and to all her secret fantasies. But she couldn't give in. "I'll be finished with my thesis in August. I'm supposed to go home then. I'm supposed to start teaching in September."

"I don't want you to leave when you finish your thesis. I don't want you to leave if we make the tower appear either. Whatever happens, I want you to live with us, permanently."

"You *really* imagine you're falling in love with me?"

"Imagine?" He laughed and pulled a face. "That's *really* not the word I'd use." He folded his arms and looked into her eyes. "Is that why? Is that why you've been holding back on me?" He leaned forward, cupped her chin in his hand, gently lifting her face. "Because I admitted how I felt about you? You didn't like that?"

"Well, no. Yes. Kind of... At least that's part of it."

"What is this? You don't think you deserve to be loved?"

She didn't answer him. Instead, she asked a question. "What does it feel like?"

"What does what feel like?"

"Love. Being in it."

"You've never been in love?"

She shook her head. "I don't think so. Infatuation, yes, for that guy I told you about at dinner. That's all." She brushed a lock of hair back from her face. "So how does it feel?"

"Terrifying. And good."

"For me, it feels like something's warming up inside me. Something that's been numb almost as long as I can remember. Really, it was dead even before the thing with Ryan."

"Because of your mother?"

She glanced up at him, moved to see the compassion on that strong, masculine face. It gave her the courage to keep sharing. "Yeah. I guess. Since my dad died and left me alone with my mother, I haven't really had the ability to feel much. I've just been going through the motions. Studying a lot."

He took her hand, stroked it casually with his thumb. "And you're *feeling* now? You have feelings for me?" His voice was so gentle, so hopeful.

She bit her lip and nodded.

And Arlan.

He had that look of adoration again. The touch of his thumb on her hand and his closeness made her pulse start to rise. His expression warned her there would be no going back now. "To be honest, I've realized you're the first person in a long time who's taken the numbness from around my heart. You and Arl..."

His lips brushed over hers, stopping her words. Every time he kissed her, there was a flutter in her heart and at the base of her throat. She pushed on his shoulders, determined to say more. "Are you trying to tell me that I'm the *only* person you're in love with?"

His eyebrows shot up. For a second, his face was marred by a scowl. Then it passed, and he smiled again, spreading his arms wide. "Do you see any other women in my life? Hwange Poaching Unit isn't exactly awash with sexy policewomen."

She narrowed her eyes.

"Well, okay, Arlan and I do know a lot of people, but, no, I don't have feelings for any other woman. Why would you even ask such a question? I don't need anyone else."

And this is where it all breaks down. Because you won't accept who you are. Because you're not being true to yourself.

Before she could think what to say next, Jay had his hands around her waist, pulling her down onto the lush rug on the floor.

He felt so good on top of her, his heat, the weight of his body, the smoothness of his skin. His warmth engulfed her. The soapy scent of his cologne, with its hint of citrus, and his own dark musk underneath made all her feelings for him come racing back. Desire burned hot to her core. It was more than his dark good looks, his fit body and intense lust. There was a connection there, a soul-mate connection.

But he wants Arlan and won't admit it. It's maddening.

He kissed her shoulder revealed by her wide scoop-neck dress. It was a pretty, thin, cream summer dress sprigged with flowers, one of only two dresses she'd brought. If she was honest with herself, she'd worn it in the hopes he'd come home and see her in it.

His lips skimmed the cleavage it revealed. August closed her eyes. He lifted her slightly so he could raise her dress up and over her shoulders. She opened her eyes to see him watching her with a fierce, heated expression that made her groan. She couldn't think; she needed to relax and let the burning gold of sensual pleasure wash over her as he slipped down her bra cups and took her nipple in his mouth. Her pussy pulsed so hard that it had become uncomfortable. Her wet nipple popped out of his mouth, and he attended to the other.

Once he'd given full attention to both, he pulled her dress back up a little, not pulling it back over her shoulders, but just covering her nipples with the material, and rocking back a little to make eye contact.

"I know you're going to want to go back to New York after you finish your work, your thesis, maybe after the tower appears, if it ever does, but I want you to know this all means a lot more than sex and the tower to me. I feel a connection to you I'm not willing to throw away, like we belong together." He bent his head and brushed her neck with his lips. Her heart beat so fast, she had to open her mouth to breathe. This wasn't how normal people fell in love, was it? It was too fast. And how could they square this up with Arlan? Something greedy in her wanted them both far too much and wouldn't accept just one.

"We haven't known each other long."

"I know enough. I know you're beautiful and sweet, and as intelligent and sexy as fuck."

She managed a laugh. The way he spoke was sometimes so hilariously adorable.

"And you're a submissive too. Which is the icing on the cake."

She swallowed hard, giving him a barely imperceptible nod. In response, he groaned and rained kisses up the slope of her neck, his hot breath in the shell of her ear. She ran her hands over his massive chest. The man was etched as if from marble, toned and divine.

"Did you like it when you were handcuffed to my wall? Answer honestly."

She sighed, no longer able to hold back or deny the truth. "I loved it, okay? You hit on one of my sexual fantasies. I'm not going to deny it."

Jay gave her waist a squeeze of approval. His smile said *tell me more.*

"I crave it, okay? I need it. I want more."

When he grinned down at her, the light of the devil glowed in his deep, dark eyes. He pinned both her wrists to the floor. "I think I can find a number of ways to distract you from worrying about Arlan until he comes home."

Chapter Twelve

Arlan clenched his teeth, a muscle twitching in his jaw. He couldn't believe they'd left the gate unlocked. What the hell was Jay thinking? How many times had they left themselves unprotected like this while he was gone? Had Jay forgotten the attack on August altogether?

Arlan fingered the wallet in his pocket. He had pictures of a new baby boy he'd saved and brought back to his parents to show both of them. His soul craved the opportunity to show this small success to the two people he loved more than anything on earth. In spite of the short time frame in which he'd known August, it was as though he'd known her forever, maybe in a past life. Deep in his bones, he knew she and Jay were his fated mates. His lion form knew their scent. They were *his*.

They just don't know it yet.

Arlan made his way past the pool and the spa, where coffee cups sat on the outdoor table. The back door was open too. He heard noise in the study and padded softly down the carpeted hallway toward the sound.

Moans. The horny bastard.

He should have known they'd be in the playroom. When he reached the room, he blinked, and blinked again, then ran a hand over his hair, unsure what to make of what he was seeing.

August knelt on the white satin sheets of the bed. Her hands were bound behind her back with the soft, bright pink bondage rope he and Jay used with female submissives. Rope that Jay had once even used on him.

For a moment, he wondered how she could enjoy being bound and tied after what had happened to her as a child. One day he would find the strength to ask her. But for now, his attention was dragged away by his cock. Hard as a diamond, it pressed against the zipper of his shorts.

She was trussed on her knees. Ass in the air. And, holy hell, she'd either shaved since he'd last seen her, or Jay had shaved her.

Jay had looped the rope in such a way that Arlan was left staring at her plump, bare pussy. It was open and ripe and...ready.

Lust crashed into him, a battering ram to his gut. Movement at the periphery of his vision caught his eye. Jay stood beside the bed, staring down at her, molten lust in his gaze. He held a paddle in his hand. A range of chosen toys lay on the table.

Fuck!

Arlan cleared his throat. Jay glanced up, and his expression changed. The relief on his face was for Arlan alone. And the liquid heat in his gaze wasn't just for August. Jay's dark eyes seemed to be trying to communicate a thousand things to Arlan. He closed them for a second, and when he reopened them, the angst and passion had gone, replaced by an arrogant grin.

"Ah, Arlan. You're just in time. Our little slave here has been naughty and needs punishing."

Slave? There was no way he'd be calling her slave unless she'd confirmed she liked it. Jay wasn't an asshole. August must really be into all this. Arlan walked around to the headboard so he could get a glimpse of her face. She turned her head a little at the sound of his footsteps, her head tilting at an awkward angle so she could see him. When she did, she broke into a brilliant smile.

Fuck!

He'd kill for that bright smile she gave him. It melted his heart. It calmed his beast. Soothed his soul that was aching after his last battle with evil. This was kind of fucked up, but she was smiling, she was happy. She was enjoying this.

And she's happy to see you. She's happy because you're safe.

A wave of joy swept through him at the realization.

As much as he trusted Jay, he still had to ask. "August, sweetie, are you okay with all this? Really okay?"

That breathtaking smile again. "Master Jay has been making some of my fantasies come true." She'd had to twist her head to see him, and now she dropped her gaze to the mattress again. The way she spoke, the soft, dreamy lilt of her voice, was as if she were in some kind of trance. And in her submissive pose, she was so graceful, so fucking beautiful.

Master Jay? Her sexual fantasies? His sexual fantasies? Okay. Fine. But what about...love? It wasn't jealousy he felt. Not jealousy of the relationship she'd built with Jay. No. No matter how often Jay pushed him away, he knew Jay was his. His fated mate. He could smell it. Jay would always come back to him.

He took another deep breath and looked into Jay's eyes. It was obvious he and August had established a world, a rhythm between them without him, but he had to be sure. "You've talked to her about safe words, about limits?"

Jay lifted an eyebrow, his only hint of sarcasm. "No fire play, no severe pain, no binding of the feet."

"What's she done to deserve punishment, then?"

"Working too hard. The first five days you were gone, her little nose was buried in zoology textbooks. She wouldn't let me near her. Since the sixth day, I literally had to drag her away from the books and haul her off to the bedroom every night."

After saying that, Jay gave her a whack on the ass with the paddle, making her gasp. This paddle was the one with the word *slave* engraved on it.

138

"August's told me she has a thing for being called slave. It's one of her fantasies. And she's a very interesting girl. She has a lot of lovely fantasies, don't you, slave?"

"Yes, sir." She winked at Arlan.

Arlan shook his head. "Does this slave have a safe word?"

"Zebra."

Arlan's lip quirked.

Jay smiled. "Watch this. She's a well-trained slave now." He walked around to face August. "Tell me what you want, slave."

"Please, sir, I want to suck your cock, sir." None too gently, Jay grasped August's hair, yanked her head back and shoved his cock between her gorgeous lips.

Arlan's own cock raged against his shorts, as hard as steel. He needed to touch her, needed to tease her. He looked into Jay's eyes.

"Punish our slave while she sucks me, Arlan."

Arlan glanced down at her. She was beautiful and so fucking sexy. Why was he even hesitating? He'd never had a problem sharing women with Jay. He'd never had a problem with casual sex either, and there was no doubt August was fully aroused and into this.

You know why.

Arlan swallowed a painful lump in his throat. He shoved the dark secret away. He had to compartmentalize this, not ruin the moment for August and Jay, and not ruin the chance to work sex magic. Today could be the day they made the tower appear. He couldn't afford to be a pussy about this. He needed to do the sex magic. It was as if he and Jay had changed positions. Jay, now confident in using August for the sex magic, Arlan having his doubts. So many thoughts and emotions flooded his brain, guilt warring with the desire to drop his pants and fuck her senseless.

Arlan took a deep breath. He grabbed the lightest flogger lying on the table and gave her a swat. "Ready for a set of ten, slave?" His voice didn't sound like his usual Dom voice with women. There was too much gentleness in it. Too much tenderness.

I feel far too much for this woman. She's my fated mate. Our fated mate.

"Yes, sir. I'm ready."

He steadied himself, brought himself back to reality, back to the *real* world, where neither of his lovers believed half-fae had fated mates, where neither of them was ready to fall in love with him. Hardening his resolve, he brought the light flogger down upon her creamy flesh. "One. Two."

August counted each stroke, obviously trained by Jay over the last several days to do so, her voice shaking with arousal as the count rose.

Arlan stared at the bright pink trails across her beautiful heart-shaped ass. His gut instinct was to fall on the bed and kiss each one. But he didn't. He was about to bust the zipper on his shorts. Jay had said she was being punished, so maybe now was not the time to give her his cock. He turned to Jay, the choreographer of this dance. "How did you plan to punish this delectable slave?"

Jay smiled casually. "Last Christmas, one of the toys from Nick and Kris's Toy Emporium was a butterfly vibe to use on a woman. Remember that? We strap the little vibe on her and let it stimulate her, let her think about her behavior for a while." August moaned, but Arlan noticed it was a *yes, please* type of moan.

He picked up the white butterfly vibe, a thin glass plug and a pink glass dildo almost as thick as his cock, and placed them on the floor. These were hand-blown glass, beautiful, functional erotic art that he had ordered from Kris and Nick's Toy Emporium. He smiled, sure his little mate appreciated the aesthetic beauty of their toys.

"Sir?"

Arlan bent and kissed the sweet curve of her back with reverence. His cock throbbed with the need to get inside her, and yet he couldn't, wouldn't let himself. He had to forcibly tamp down his lust.

He laid a hand on her hip. "You don't have to do this, honey. Not any of it. I want you to feel good about anything you do with us. If you want to try to do the sex magic with Jay alone, that's fine. If any of this is too much for you, please say the word."

August rolled her eyes. "Arlan, I wouldn't be doing this if I didn't want to. I want Jay, and I want you." Her voice caught on a sob. "I'm just so glad you're home."

He kissed her back again, nuzzled her hair. He picked up the little butterfly vibe and strapped it over her clit, then pressed the remote control.

"Please," August begged, her voice thick and desperate. "I don't want you to be soft or gentle. I'm not a piece of glass. I won't break."

Arlan dragged one finger between her lips. Her pussy leaked sweet honeyed cream. Inside him, the lion roared with need.

Chapter Thirteen

August was beside herself with delight and relief. Arlan was home safe. But she wouldn't allow herself to forget her new duties as a sub. Sweet agony swept her body, making it difficult to think. She had to force herself to concentrate in case Jay or Arlan gave her any orders. For the last five days, she'd had one Dom.

Now she had two.

Jay had attached silver clamps to each nipple, and the clips excited her, closing around her buds with pleasurable pain. Her ass was still nicely warm from Jay's thwacks with the paddle. But Arlan's strokes with the flogger had been too light, only teasing her with a hint of the bite she craved.

"Ready for fifteen more, baby?" Arlan drew the flogger gently across her skin as though to remind her of its power.

She nodded. But he didn't begin. Realizing he needed more encouragement, she finally whispered, "Yes, sir."

The first swish seemed ironically only to soothe her ass, still hot as it was from Jay's paddle. The second stung just a little.

But the third, the third actually hurt.

Oh God.

The room spun, and she almost lost her balance as Arlan finally got fully into it, raining down the strikes.

Swish, crack, swish, crack, swish, crack.

The pain and endorphins threatened to topple her. Arlan grabbed her hips, keeping her steady on her knees. When her breathing finally steadied, she felt the nudge of what had to be the glass dildo behind her. Arlan slid it slowly inside her, and she groaned.

As pleasurable as it was too be filled, she craved the thick heat of cock, the, rigid glass only half satisfying her.

Excitement rose as she heard the sound of Arlan removing his clothes. Without warning, Jay slid the head of his cock into her mouth again, and she sucked, leaning her head right back and pulling him deeper into her mouth until he touched the back of her throat. She managed to hollow her cheeks for extra pressure, let him out a little way, then sucked him back in, glorying in his moans.

Jay wanted his cock sucked, so she would suck. She groaned in frustration, because as much as she was enjoying pleasuring him, her pussy ached with need. And then her concentration on pleasuring Jay unraveled at the feel of Arlan's fingers lightly resting on her ass. The thought of the shameless picture she presented to him filled her mind. Little woman trussed up and shaved, everything on display. The thought made her moan around Jay's cock, and she had to force herself to continue licking as a myriad of emotions overwhelmed her.

Arlan pulled the glass dildo out, then gave it a thrust back in one, two, three more times deep inside. Then he removed it, making her quiver at the emptiness.

"Have you ever been screwed in here, August?" Arlan's fingers brushed over her back entrance, and she flinched.

The lust in his voice proved he'd got over whatever qualms had been holding him back before. "No, no. Never."

Arlan ran his large hand over her back as if he were soothing an animal. "Your ass is so pretty and red now. I'm going to plug it, and then I'm going to fuck you, angel."

She groaned at his words, then cringed at the feel of cold lube, and cried out when he sank a finger in her knuckle-deep. There was a burning, a flare of heat, making her buck back against her bindings and clench his finger.

"Shh, shh, baby. Ahh, you're so tight."

Despite her fear, she knew she could trust him, and while there was pain as he stretched her, there was a bite she craved more of.

Dark lust rolled over her, eclipsing fear, as she felt the press of the tapered pink glass against her ring. At first it didn't really hurt when the head slid in, but as it went deeper, the thickness became a fiery heat of invasion, a steadily increasing burn of pain/pleasure that made her strain at her ropes. She wanted to beg, plead, anything.

He teased her, tortured her, spreading her, dipping his fingers inside her empty aching pussy and swirling them around. He removed the torturous little butterfly vibe, applying his stronger, firmer fingers right where she needed it, working the hard little bud.

Pleasure mounted until she was ready to scream. Skin met skin. Arlan's body was on hers, the smoothness of his chest pressed against her back, his hot male flesh melting against her, the head of his cock finally where it should be, demanding entrance.

Arlan's shaft finally pressing against her slit until the ridged tip slid in.

Jay groaned, aroused, no doubt, by the sight of Arlan behind her. He was so gorgeous, so *hers*. His lips were slightly parted, and he tilted his head right back.

Jay pulled out on a cry, ropes of hot seed splashing across her neck.

Arlan gripped her hips tightly from behind and slid in, ramming his cock deep inside her pussy, touching her walls. He'd only been inside her a second, and she was about to come. She didn't know if she could move. His cock filled her pussy until she was out of control, chasing an orgasm so big and so deep, it felt like it was never going to come.

"Look at me," Jay commanded, and she stared into the black depths of his eyes. His expression commanded her to keep her own eyes open, to worship her Dom as her body exploded with pleasure.

Arlan continued to pump his hips, stroke her walls, work her clit and prolong her orgasm, until she cried out and shuddered from head to foot, until she thought she'd pass out from the strength of her climax.

Tears streaming down her cheeks, she collapsed onto the bed. Arlan snuggled into her, giving her a hug. She flopped on her side, almost ready to fall asleep.

And then she remembered just in time to focus all her energy on imagining the storm tower. Her brain seemed to vibrate as she concentrated, and she knew the two of them were doing the same. They concentrated for the full ten minutes that Kruger's last email told them it might take.

Arlan pulled up his underwear and shorts and took a deep breath. The intensity of his orgasm, of hers, of Jays... He didn't want to get his hopes up, and yet he believed in it. He believed it could be. Surely making the tower appear was possible. Excitement and adrenaline pumped through his veins as he raced to the window. In a minute Jay was beside him staring out the window too.

And....Arlan slammed both fists down on the window ledge. He scanned the horizon, then kicked the wall hard, leaving a dent in the plaster. "What the fuck?" Arlan swore again, and flopped backward down on the bed beside August. He managed to blurt the words out against the lump in his throat. "Sex magic's not going to work." He put his hands over his face and pinched his eyelids. "It's not the answer. Fuck! Fuck!" He punched his thigh. He glanced over at August and saw she'd fallen asleep.

"The dark dust is an evil thing. She's still recovering from it. Look, she hasn't woken up despite your tantrum."

Arlan rolled over carefully and studied her, but she was out cold, victim of another dark-dust sleeping attack. He brushed a lock of hair gently from her face. She lay there so sweet and perfect.

Mine!

Was she really? Was she really his?

A hand brushed his own. Jay reached for him, taking his hands and pulling him up from the bed and out into the hallway. Jay shut the door to the bedroom carefully and silently behind them. He leaned back on his heels against the wall, eyes narrowed and fierce as they raked over Arlan.

Staring the other man down was a battle of wills, and something new ramped up the electrical charge already in the air. The zap of it rushed across his every nerve ending. In the next moment, his breath whooshed from his lungs as Jay slammed him against the wall, an arm across his neck, his cock a bar of iron against Arlan's groin. "Goddamn you! Why the fuck didn't you call?"

He struggled, but Jay's massive arms and superior strength kept him pinned to the wall. "You... asshole... I was in my lion form the whole time."

Jay released the pressure slightly.

"I don't exactly have a fucking cell phone hanging from my tail, Jay. I didn't shift back until today."

The ache in his chest suffocated him—the ache for Jay coupled with years of simmering rage. "And *you*. Dumb ass! Why did you leave the gate open? Anyone could have snuck in while you were in the playroom."

Jay's superior strength now gave the bastard the luxury of being cool and in control. "I left it open in case you came home. Like you did."

"That was dumb."

Rough stubble brushed Arlan's upper lip as Jay's mouth came down hard. Arlan tried to move his head and break contact, but the kiss ignited into a melting, tongue-thrusting mouth fuck. Arlan couldn't help releasing a groan. Finally, his pride got the better of his lust, and he broke the kiss. "You stupid fuck."

Jay's mouth captured his again, and he sucked on Arlan's tongue. Arlan surrendered, but only for a second. He wasn't Jay's fucking submissive, and he was tired of all his bullshit. "You...you... When are you going to stop being such an asshole?"

"I missed you like hell, okay? Like part of my soul was ripped away. Can you understand that?"

Arlan raised an eyebrow. Couldn't Jay even see the irony of his own hypocrisy? "Um, yes, *I* understand it."

"Well, *good*."

Again the lips crushed down upon his mouth, punishing it, bruising it. Arlan's cock rose like a sword to war with Jay's. Warriors on a battlefield where no one knew the rules.

Jay's strong fingers kneaded his neck muscles. Arlan's hands went to Jay's shoulders reveling in the play of taut muscles, shifting his head to deepen the kiss. Drugged by the contact all the blood in his body traveled south straight to his cock.

A sound off to his left made Arlan turn his head and caught Jay's attention enough to break the kiss and turn.

Pure abject horror transformed Jay's face when he looked down at August.

The petite minx was still bound. She must have toppled out of bed and slithered across the floor like a snake. Now she peeked around the doorway.

Jay waved his arms. Everything on his face said *no, no, no*. He threw his hands up and then let them fall pointlessly.

August seemed struck dumb by Jay's horror. Jay mouthed the word *sorry*, then headed down the hall.

"Jay, wait!" August pushed the bedroom door all the way open with her elbow. Arlan hurried to her side, bent down and began to untie her.

"August." All he could do was whisper her name, although the thought of her slithering across the floor with her hands tied, just so she could catch them kissing almost made him laugh.

The front door slammed shut with an almighty bang, and Jay was gone.

Chapter Fourteen

Duvessa slapped the riding crop she was holding onto the desk in front of her, making Hendrik Kruger jump.

The woman was tall, strong and elegant, her cheekbones high and wide. He might have compared her to Grace Kelly, but Grace had never had that cruel twist to the mouth that excited and, yes, if he were honest, frightened him. He'd been very excited when she'd first invited him into the playroom of her holiday home, but now he was unsure.

Still her tight black dress revealed the delicious curves of her breasts. Looking at her tall athletic body, those ripe melons and lustrous chestnut hair made his cock hard enough to cut diamonds.

But when he gazed up from her cleavage to her face, the sneer she gave him dashed his hopes.

Kruger sighed and sank into a nearby chair. He imagined he'd had the same expression on his own face when young, unattractive students stammered or blushed in his presence. He knew he was an attractive guy. But Duvessa was way out of his league.

"Hendrik, when I was a baby, my fae mother abandoned me and left me with my human father. My father was an extremely handsome man, but he was *poor,* he was lowly. He made other humans coffee in some stupid coffee house, and he was religious. He beat me if he caught me trying to practice magic. I gritted my teeth, Hendrik, and I endured, and I swore I would never be poor as an adult."

Kruger nodded.

"I built up wealth and power over a long period of time." Duvessa went on tapping the crop on the desk as she spoke. "I had help from *no one*. And I don't intend to lose the nest egg I've built up. I intend to keep building it higher till the day I die." She put her hand to her forehead. "Things are not working out, I have...debts. Debts I should not have. I shouldn't have a mortgage on my casino like a common, imbecilic human. I was born the daughter of a fae princess."

Kruger smiled to himself. There was more than one way to interest a woman. "Once we find out where the witch doctors get their power from, we'll both be using it to build more wealth. We'll be rich."

Duvessa's lovely cerulean eyes narrowed.

Only the daughter of a fae princess could have such eyes. By the dark path, she's magnificent.

"If our parents hadn't interbred with humans, Hendrik, if you and I were full-blooded fae, we wouldn't have these mundane problems to worry about. We'd have an unlimited supply of money."

"Well, that may be so, but I don't find tales of the storm tower mundane. It's exciting to me, a mystery. How do the witch doctors tap all that power? All the research I've done indicates these people have very little fae blood of their own. Their magic comes from some other source. Once the tower is found, we'll solve that mystery."

Duvessa fixed him with an ice-dagger stare. "What progress *have* you made in ensuring the tower is found?"

Kruger squirmed. "It's under control. I have Arlan Leonard completely convinced that I just want to work this magic for the good of the children. He thinks I have no other motives. Jay and August are working with him. He told me your daughter's been *willingly* doing sex magic with them."

Duvessa frowned and tapped the handle of the crop on her desk. "I still don't like this Arlan being involved. He's rumored to be a Warrior of the Light. Why couldn't you just do all this yourself? Seduce my daughter?" She scrutinized him with a slight sneer on her face. "You're passably attractive."

The faint praise made Kruger clench his jaw, but he held himself in check.

"I have plenty of toys you could use on her here." She nodded at the riding crop in her hand, and then the toys on the wall of her playroom.

Kruger frowned, annoyed with himself that he'd thought she meant to play with him. His cock finally began to soften at her lack of her interest.

"Well? Answer me. Why don't *you* seduce her?"

He spread his arms wide, emphasizing his points with his hands as he spoke. "Duvessa, I'm forty-five years old. Arlan is young. Everything I've read on this indicates the magic works best if done by the young and so-called pure of heart. August is twenty-three, and Jay Nandoro is younger still. He's only twenty-one. It should be perfect."

"But it hasn't worked *yet*, has it?" Duvessa's snarl made his heart slam in his chest.

"I-If you have a problem with Arlan being involved, then I really don't understand why you wanted your own daughter involved. Maybe *she's* the problem. You've told me a dozen times you believe she's a Warrior of the Light herself."

Duvessa smiled. "No. What I said was that she was *born* a Warrior of the Light. And I believe that in all certainty. But I fixed it. August is no threat to any of our plans. Believe it."

"How does that work, exactly?"

"Low self-esteem in a half-fae kills their power. I'm her mother. I saw to it that she has none."

"None of what?"

"No self-esteem. She has none. Zip, zilch, nada."

"What?"

"The first man she ever fell for was the son of some friends of mine. They are the couple renting me their house here in

Zimbabwe, the house down near the Zambezi River. Ryan Garrison. Handsome young man. She never even knew I set her up. She was humiliated. I believe she gave her virginity to him."

Horror snaked down his spine. "You did that to your own daughter?"

Duvessa's eyes glittered. He swallowed so hard, they could both hear the sound of it. She raised a brow. "You seem surprised. You know I'm a daughter of the dark-fae princess Zenia, do you not?"

Kruger nodded. Terror gripped his belly. He'd admired the dark fae all his life. Or thought he had. But this? Abusing one's *own* child. Setting her up for some kind of humiliation with a man?

"You know I am dark fae."

He nodded again.

"Then *why* are you staring at me like that?"

Kruger shrugged and glanced down at the floor. "I don't know. She's your daughter, light-fae tendencies or not."

"Don't mutter and look at the floor, Hendrik. It's very unattractive."

"I'm sorry."

"Dark fae are above the common horde. We are too intelligent, too powerful to be tied to petty morality and the tedious path of virtue."

"Yes, but..."

"I have four daughters. I was more than happy to play mother to the two who obeyed me and respected my wishes. I had no use for the two who did not." She leaned forward, the coldness gone as the fire of rage sparked in her eyes. "I spent my childhood in a trailer, because my mother left me with a stupid human father who didn't know how to make money. Who *whipped* me with a belt for practicing magic."

"Yes, you said that."

Duvessa paused, and stared at him so hard his balls drew up. "*I* didn't let jealousy of others affect *my* self-esteem. I always knew I was above him. Above all of them."

Thwack! Duvessa smacked the crop against his leg. His cock went instantly stiff in his shorts, but he cried out from the pain.

Duvessa had no reaction to his scream. "You want to know why I knew I was better than my mortal father? Why he could never ever damage *my* self-esteem?"

He gasped, the zing of adrenaline racing through his blood. She referenced his fascination, his passion. "I know, I know, because of the diary. Your mother's diary. You own a real diary written by a full-blooded fae."

"That's right. Because my mother, Princess Zenia, left me her diary with its marks of magic. A diary explaining who and what I was."

He began to recover his composure. "I'd love to read it sometime, the diary. What an extraordinary thing. A diary written by a full-blooded fae containing information on the Fae Realm. To study such a document would be a dream."

"Silence!" She shook her head, her lustrous chestnut hair swaying as she poked him in the belly with her crop. "I am *frustrated*, Hendrik. I am exasperated. It's hideous to be trapped on this dull mortal plane with only a modicum of magic." She slid her hand back and forth along the smooth surface of the riding crop. Every muscle in his body clenched, waiting for her to strike him again.

But instead she dropped the thing on his desk and began to pace. "They are young, they are willing, they are all of them half-fae. They should have found the tower already." She stopped pacing. "Are you quite sure this Arlan isn't holding out on you? Maybe he's lying because he doesn't trust you. How can we really trust him when he's a Warrior of the Light?"

Kruger swallowed again, embarrassed by the creeping, unmanly fear that had almost made him dizzy. His chin rose. "I

153

am certain. Arlan trusts me completely. The fact that he's actually only a quarter fae to be precise, but he's a naïve Warrior of the Light just makes it even more likely the sex magic will work. He's a textbook example of the kind of people we need to make it work. They'll be doing the magic for good, to save the child prisoners, and then we swoop in and find the source of the witch doctors' power."

Duvessa shook her head. "I just find it difficult to believe these two men are as innocent as you say. Arlan may be naïve and scholarly, but I've seen their mansion while scrying. It's much larger than this house I'm renting here or even my mansion on Long Island. Where do they get their wealth?"

"It was inherited. Indeed, I believe Arlan's father chose the dark path. Not so his son." Kruger read aloud from the grimoire he had brought that now lay open on his desk. "Success at achieving sex magic requires two men of fae blood and a willing female of a superior nature forming what is known as a ménage. Elements of power exchange, submission and domination between the parties involved may also increase the chance of success. All participants engaged in sex magic must be pure of heart."

"What does that mean, pure of heart?" Duvessa's eyes flashed fire. "*Well?*"

"I...I've take it to mean that the participants must be somewhat naïve. Like the characters in a Disney movie. Innocent, lacking in greed, those who don't crave power, or ambition. That's my take on it, anyway."

"*Stupid*, you mean? Well, my daughter fits that."

"Your daughter is working on her PhD."

Duvessa waved her hand. "She's still stupid."

Kruger rubbed his temples with both hands. "She is naïve. She trusts me, for a start, even after I..." The image of August grabbing his hand before he could touch her breasts filled his mind. Perhaps it was still not a scenario to relay to a mother, even one who cared so little for her child.

A tightness in his chest, confused him. He wasn't a man used to feeling...guilt? August had been ridiculously forgiving and kind, more interested in focusing on her research than on questioning his motives.

Duvessa didn't seem to notice the unfinished sentence. She continued to silently read the grimoire. After a while, she shook her head and closed the book. With one finger, she traced the edges of the cover's elaborate embossing. "So you think all three of them are stupid, naïve, or whatever you want to call it?"

"Pure of heart?"

She tapped the cover of the book impatiently. "Yes."

"Arlan is, certainly. August, most probably. Jay Nandoro? I'm not so sure."

She sat in one of the leather chairs on the other side of his desk, crossing her long, perfect legs. "So it's possible he's the bad egg, and we simply have to replace him?"

"I...I don't see August and Arlan agreeing to *that* easily."

Duvessa gave him the most arrogant sneer he'd ever seen. "I guess I'll just have to do some scrying to see what the hell is going wrong. That's one kind of magic my worthless mortal blood hasn't robbed me of."

"Oh yes," Kruger said, exerting every bit of control he had to keep his voice even. "Scrying is something I've never seen, and I'd *love* to watch you do it."

I'd love it more if the three of them happened to be working the sex magic at the time.

Duvessa smiled as if she could read his mind. "Who knows what we might catch them doing, huh? And once we find out what the three of them are up to, we'll take matters into our own hands."

Kruger shifted in his chair again, his cheeks heating, when she glanced at his lap. "How?"

"I have *friends*. Other half-fae that admire me. They can help us capture them. We can experiment."

"What do you mean?"

Duvessa rose to pace again as she spoke. "Well, this threesome... It doesn't have to be those specific three, does it? We could try other half-fae with them. We could try different people."

"But it took me some time to persuade them to work together on this. And we don't want too many people knowing about what we're doing. We don't want to share the power source we find. Duvessa, the good thing about these three is their naiveté. August and Arlan, at least, have no clue. It's really only Jay Nandoro that I worry about. He's the possible risk factor in this."

"So we eliminate Jay Nandoro. Simple."

Thwack! Duvessa hit the desk again before she hung the crop neatly in its place on the wall.

Chapter Fifteen

Arlan's mouth was dry as though it were filled with sawdust. He wanted to roar and shift and scratch his claws down the wall.

But he needed to remain calm. For a start, he needed to untie her. His claws were itching beneath his nails to spring out. He inhaled deeply, drawing air into his lungs, one...two...three calming breaths. He looked down, saw his hands had become golden paws, his claws unsheathed. By force of will, he slowly made them contract.

He *would* stay in control. He would *not* shift now, for her sake. Arlan closed his eyes tight. When he glanced down, he had hands again. August swore as she nearly toppled over. He rushed to her side, bent down and untied what was left of her bindings.

"Hell. I am *so* sorry, little one. Jay and I... We're just a pair of screw-ups. Damn!" Arlan put his hands over his face, self-loathing like a choking fog around his throat. He dropped his hands. "Shit, I'm sorry about not untying you earlier. I was going to, but I got waylaid and distracted. That was a big fuck-up. I'm so sorry."

She laughed. "Yeah I noticed you got waylaid and distracted."

He searched her eyes, trying to gauge her emotions. "Exactly how pissed off are you about all this?"

The glint of humor floored him. "I'm not pissed at all."

Arlan shook his head, unable to comprehend her unexpected reaction. "Why the hell did you *do* that, anyway,

August? Topple out of bed and slither across the fucking floor like a snake? Oh my God."

She took hold of his hands and let him pull her into a standing position.

"*August.* Are you okay?"

Free of her bonds at last, she brushed dust from her knees. "I heard moans, and I wanted to *see* it, Arlan. I figured out pretty early that you and Jay had something going on. I'm not pissed off...because I'm turned *on.* It turns me on. As embarrassing as that is to admit."

Arlan's eyes opened as wide as they could go, while his dick stiffened in his shorts. "*Really!*"

"Really."

Arlan swore and laughed again. "You're really not upset?"

She shook her head.

"You're fucking incredible."

"I got that there was something going on between you and Jay almost from the first time I met the two of you. I've been waiting for you to just cut all the bullshit and tell me."

"Holy crap!" He shook his head, then and bit his lip to keep from smiling too broadly.

She shrugged. "I mean, like you, I've read about fae ménage and how it works."

Arlan nodded and then lost restraint. He pulled her close. She didn't fight or struggle when he embraced her, and her small body felt perfect in his arms, exactly right. A roar of contentment carried up to his throat, his lion eager for her touch again. He wanted to hold her forever. He still had the problem of telling her that he'd known her briefly as Gus, but that would have to wait.

When he looked down at her again, all his irritation with Jay, all his confusion melted away. All he wanted to do was kiss her, take her to bed, make love to her properly. "God, you're amazing, August."

"I'm thirsty is what I am."

He laughed, relief bubbling up in his chest. "Shit, I'm sorry. Let me get you some coffee or something."

"Coffee would be great."

They went into the kitchen, and she sat in the breakfast nook while he got the coffee ready.

"Where do you think Jay has gone?"

Arlan poured the coffee into round white mugs. "At the Mopane Tree, probably." Her brow furrowed. "It's a pub, a bar. In Harare."

"Ahhhh. So he's gone into the city."

Arlan opened the fridge, searching around for the milk. No sign of it. He slapped his hand against his forehead and swore. "Sorry, there's no milk. Damn." He slammed the fridge door shut again and turned to face her. "Do you mind, baby?"

She pulled a face. "Um, to be honest, I hate black coffee."

"Yeah, Jay usually just magics it up for us. We don't buy groceries much."

"It's all right, really. I'll drink the black coffee." She reached out and took the mug, had a sip, made another face.

Arlan laughed. "You hate it. Hey, I'll tell you what. You get dressed, and we'll go to the market. It'll be fun."

"Sure. There's just one problem."

"What?"

"I need some caffeine first."

Arlan laughed. He settled in the chair opposite her and put sugar in his mug, lifted an eyebrow to ask if she wanted any, and she nodded. She scrunched up her face as she took the first sip.

"Tastes terrible, huh?"

She grimaced again. They sat drinking in silence for a minute.

"I feel bad I haven't spent more time just the two of us," Arlan said. "I mean, as a zoologist. You must be enjoying yourself with Kruger. Doing all that research? I'd have loved to see those new cubs."

"It's fine. I kind of understand that you're a magic warrior and all as well as a zoologist. You're a genuine Warrior of the Light. It's something to be very proud of."

He shrugged. "It pretty much sucks when you have so little power you can't control anything."

She pushed hair back from her face and took another sip of coffee. "I get that. Maybe the three of us can fix it, eventually."

He wanted to turn the talk away from magic and talk about their shared love of science instead. "Have you and Kruger seen many big cats lately, besides lions?"

Her face lit up. "Yes, we saw a leopard in a tree. He was crouched on a branch, eating an impala."

"Leopards kill impalas by suffocation so the prey doesn't make noise and attract other predators. They need to climb the trees to eat so lions and hyenas won't steal their kill from them."

Her lip quirked slightly, and he silently cursed himself for telling her stuff she would already know. "Sorry, indulge me. I try to talk to Jay about this stuff, and he just looks bored."

August laughed, and he smiled. Her laugh always sounded like a bubbling brook and made him want to laugh with her and then kiss her senseless.

"I get that you're really in love with Jay." August covered her mouth with her hand as if she'd never meant the words to slip out.

"Would you be weirded out if I told you I'm in love with both of you?"

She blinked and set her cup down. He'd never seen a person so startled and surprised His brain chastised him. *Wrong time. Stupid...stupid...stupid.*

"I thought this was casual sex to make the sex magic work, to save the prisoners. You don't have to say stuff like that."

"I'm not saying it. I mean it. But I think you're in love with Jay."

"I do have strong feelings for him." She put her hands over her eyes.

A heavy weight settled in his chest. "I see."

"No, Arlan I don't think you do. All my life, I've listened to my mom bitch about how she hasn't met her two fated mates yet and blah, blah, blah. She had a girlfriend from the Half-Fae Network that she believed had found her fated mates, and for weeks she couldn't stop talking about it. She seemed consumed with jealousy, and she never talked to the woman again.

"All this business about the full fae living in ménage relationships, fated mates et cetera... I'd come to think of it as just more of her bullshit you know? But..." She shrugged.

"Now you've met us, and you're not so sure?"

She smiled at him, her soft blue-gray eyes conveying even more than her words. "Now...I'm not so sure."

It wasn't until he exhaled that he realized he'd been holding his breath for her answer.

"The thing is, I don't feel any...you know...telepathy with you guys, or anything."

"Well, from what I've read, that kind of thing only happens when one of your fated mates is in extreme danger. Possibly you need the help of the blue spirit stone as well."

"The blue spirit stone? What's that?"

"Pure turquoise. It's said to have magic properties among the fae."

"Even growing up with a dark-fae mother, I really don't think of myself as fae at all, you know, or maybe that's the main reason that the older I got, the more I avoided anything to do with magic, the more I studied my mortal subjects at school to try to get good enough grades to earn a living and move out. Not that I earn much of anything tutoring, but I make enough for the essentials."

You don't need to worry about money. We have more than enough, and it's yours, every penny.

She played with the spoon in her coffee cup, obviously too shy to look up at him. "The connection between the three of us is... It's intense. It's something I want to explore more. That is, if Jay can ever get over his hang-ups."

"I still can't believe you didn't get angry or upset over the two of us kissing. I'm sorry that happened. We're working on this project together, and I want you to be included in everything, and I want you to feel safe."

"Hey, I've had plenty of gay and bisexual men around me in my life. I'm a New Yorker. I've also heard plenty of talk about fae and ménage relationships, even if I never believed all of it."

"But still, August..."

"It's *so* not an issue with me. In fact, as I said"—her lips quirked a little, and she blushed—"it's positively a huge turn-on."

His balls tightened, and his cock turned to steel at her words and her smile. Breath bottled up in his chest, hope that he was afraid to hold on to. But he wouldn't ask her about her feelings for him. Not yet. "That makes some sense now that I think about it. That you're turned on, I mean. If full-blooded fae live in these relationships, the female would be turned on at the sight of the males making love."

"It does. That's part of why I think this is really possible."

"My reaction to you was so strong when I met you. I thought at first maybe you were using magic on me, like my ex Silvara did. Then it finally hit me that you were our third." He squeezed her hand, stroked his finger against her palm. "But unfortunately, Jay has issues."

"No kidding. But actually, dude, he has a point on one level."

"What's that?"

She touched his arm. "Well, it *is* illegal in this country, Arlan."

162

Arlan blinked. "You mean gay and bisexual sex? Yeah, Jay told me he wove protection spells around us to protect us. But he's only a half fae. To be honest, I thought he was fooling himself about how powerful his magic is." Arlan shrugged. "Other times he'd say he could only do culinary magic, so he contradicted himself."

August shook her head. "Jay told me you were tough but naive. Too involved with your animals and your own research and worries about the kidnapped children to notice the rest of what goes on in the world."

"Jay said *that*?"

"Goodness, Arlan, how do you think you guys have managed to avoid detection and trouble? Don't you read the paper? Haven't you read what Mugabe has to say about homosexuality? That it's unnatural and degrades human dignity?"

"Of course, I read the paper. I just thought that... I guess I thought my being a Warrior of the Light protected me in some way, because we've never had any problems."

.August took another small sip of her coffee, then set the cup back in its saucer. "Well I suspect it's Jay that's been protecting you. I think he may be more powerful than you realize. My guess is he's been using magic to protect you all this time, and it's been a strain on him."

Guilt twisted in his gut, and she seemed to notice his distress. She shook her head. "I'm sorry, Arlan. Maybe I shouldn't have said anything. I'm only guessing. It's an issue between you and Jay."

"No. You could be right, and if that's true, it's something I need to talk to him about. There have been far too many secrets, in this house already. I don't want to keep secrets from my fated mates."

As soon as he said it, a vision of eleven-year-old Gus flashed before him in his mind, and he winced at his own hypocrisy. His stomach clenched, and he let go of her hand.

She frowned "What's wrong?"

"I was just thinking how fast scorching sex can turn into searing-hot guilt."

She shook her head. "You're still feeling guilty about kissing Jay? Seriously? I told you... Or is it about Jay? You feel guilty about what you feel for me because of Jay?"

Tell her the truth now, asshole. But his mouth still couldn't form the words. He couldn't bear the thought of seeing more pain and hate in those beautiful blue-gray eyes.

Chapter Sixteen

Tendrils of hair clung to the sweat on the back of August's neck. The memory of the back view of Arlan, the muscles of his golden ass clenched as he passionately kissed his gorgeous, dark lover, would never leave her mind. Jay's hand had been wrapped in Arlan's hair, pulling him demandingly close...

Arlan brought her attention back to the present when he stopped, put his hand on her shoulder and pointed to a handsome white rhino grazing, his powerful molars cropping the brittle yellow grass. His dull gray hide blended perfectly with the dusty vegetation he fed on. Arlan clapped his hands to let the creature know he was passing, not wanting to surprise the beast. She admired the effect of perspiration shimmering on Arlan's muscular shoulders, bared by his sleeveless T-shirt.

Farther along, Arlan stopped to take a few pictures of a purple heron with his phone.

Lavender jacaranda petals lay in cascades across their path as they walked through the market hand in hand. His fingers were so wide, there was a hint of pain as they stretched hers, but the strength of his big hand felt comforting. Made her feel safe.

Unfortunately, as they finally got near the market, the heady honey smell of the jacaranda trees didn't smother the stench. Fresh kills, the carcasses still oozing, made her nose wrinkle. August thought it might be elephant flesh; it didn't smell like any meat she knew of.

Lisa Whitefern

A woman wearing a traditional headdress and beads and a worn denim skirt seemed to be following them. She finally held out a hand. "Please, lady."

Arlan reached in the pocket of his shorts and pulled out a handful of Zimbabwe dollars. "*Maita zvenyu.*"

"*Unotendei? Zvakanaka.*" The woman walked away, her flip-flops slapping in the red dust.

"I thought you weren't supposed to give money to beggars. I mean, it says in the guidebooks they can mob you."

His green eyes held a hint of arrogance. "Do I look worried?"

No. No, she supposed he wouldn't be worried. He was all alpha, a Warrior of the Light and a were-lion. He had little to fear.

"So you two go to this market a lot, you and Jay?"

"Not usually for food and drink, 'cause Jay magics it up, but we like to support people here by buying this and that. I know a guy here that sells milk. I'll get some other stuff from him, make him happy." He winked, and that slow smile she'd come to love lit the green and gold in his eyes. Her own lips curved in response, and a sweet peace filled her mind.

He took her hand and they walked on. August stopped to peek at a stall filled with colorful flat shoes decorated with traditional Zimbabwean patterns. When the man started pushing her to buy, Arlan held up a hand, and she smiled at the man apologetically. Arlan bought a small dyed rucksack the man was also selling.

"Lady, best shoes in the area, you buy now," the man tried again, blocking her exit from his stall. Arlan made a low growling sound in his throat, and the man backed off, wide eyed. August grinned at the unexpected hint of his were-lion showing through.

With one hand on her shoulder, Arlan steered her through the crowds. They passed stalls selling thick black twist tobacco, baskets, carvings and Shona sculpture. A woman was selling

166

painted wooden masks. She had only rough wooden crates to display them on. A little boy about five was rolling a tiny metal car along the top of the crate. August frowned. They both seemed familiar.

"Nhamo." The woman dropped the mask she had been holding and swore. Arlan bent and picked it up. "Nice work."

The woman stared at him, her expression filled with awe. "I-I..."

"Hello, Mukuru."

The child stopped playing and stared at him. "How'd you know my name?"

Arlan just smiled and ruffled the boy's hair, then picked up about ten masks. "I'll take these."

Nhamo's mouth dropped open. Arlan lifted his shirt and took some money out of the pouch around his waist.

Nhamo gulped. "Thanks, boss," she managed.

Mukuru suddenly ran up to August, his toy car clutched in his fist. "Look, it's a car. It's blue."

Nhamo smiled. "Been teaching him English."

August crouched down. "It's a pretty cool car."

Mukuru threw his arms around her legs. "I like you. You're pretty."

August laughed, heat rising to her cheeks. "Thanks."

Nhamo suddenly made eye contact with Arlan. "I'm expecting another baby. I've heard rumors good people are trying to find the tower. The were-lion and his friends. I pray they can find it before I have my baby." She grabbed his hand. "Please, if you know anything about these things, if you're the... If you know anything, please don't let them take the baby."

Arlan blanched. "The rumors you heard are true. There are good half-fae trying, Nhamo. That's all I can tell you. They're trying."

August's heart went out to the woman. She gulped a lump forming in her throat, and all she could think to do was smile and nod. Arlan put the masks into the rucksack, put it on his back, and they continued on.

When they came to a jewelry stall, August slowed to a halt. Arlan hugged her from behind, his arms safe and warm around her, as she looked over the items. Her gaze was immediately drawn to a stunning turquoise pendant on a silver chain. Arlan drew in a sharp breath.

"What?" She wriggled around in his arms to face him.

"I have to buy this for you."

"What? No you *don't.*"

"Don't you like it?"

"It's gorgeous, but really, I was just window shopping." She set the pendant back down. "I'm saving money to rent a bigger apartment when I get home. I'm not buying jewelry and stuff right now."

"August," Arlan said through gritted teeth, "are you going to take a gift from me, or do I have to spank you when I get home?"

His words sent lust curving deep in her belly. Blood rushed to her cheeks.

"Boss, you buy for the lady. Very good quality. The best!"

Any white man here was called "boss". It made August cringe a bit, but it was standard. "You don't need to buy me anything." Even as she said it, a wave of pleasure swept through her at the thought that he wanted to.

Arlan tilted his head. "When reading about the fae, have you ever read about the blue spirit stone?"

"The what?"

"A turquoise stone of this exact color, this pretty robin's-egg blue, is considered a spirit stone. It is said that if the stone is worn by the fae, it can help them bond with their true fated mates. Fae call it the blue spirit stone."

"I... Like I said, you don't need to buy me anything."

Arlan pulled her close. "Listen to me." He captured her chin in his hand and tilted it up so she had to look at him. "In the short time I've known you, you've become the most important person in the world to me other than Jay. I believe you're our third, our woman, our fated mate. I want you to be with us."

Her heart beat so fast, she was sure everyone in the market could hear it. He gently traced her lower lip with his thumb. His sensual touch and his intensity made her positively melt. He truly wanted her. Her heart was lost. It simply slid out and dropped at his feet. Her tongue was too thick for speech.

"Boss, boss?"

Arlan broke away and paid the man. He took the necklace, then, putting his hands on her hips, he turned her body a little and draped the chain around her neck, lifting her braid and fastening the clasp at the back. She breathed in his scent of cedarwood and musk.

He pressed his mouth to the side of her neck, warm against her flushed skin. His tongue flicked over her earlobe. His hands on her waist, he spun her round and kissed her face, slow and sweet, cheekbones, eyelids, the corners of her eyes. She heard the low whistles around her and didn't care about the public display.

Finally, he brushed his lips over hers. The drugging taste of him flooded her body, made her knees week. He tilted his head, deepened the kiss. The longer the sweet torment went on, the wetter she became.

Slam! A bolt of pain exploded on her shin, forcing her to push back and break the kiss.

"Fucking hell!" Her hand went down to her bruised leg. "What *was* that?"

Arlan pulled her back into the jewelry stall and pointed. Just up ahead, she saw what he was gesturing to, a young boy pushing the hand cart that had grazed her.

"You okay?"

"I guess we we're blocking the path. Yeah, I'm okay, just a little bruised." She gazed up into Arlan's beloved face. He reminded her of her father in a way. He had Donald Peak's fine qualities—warmth, integrity and kindness. The one thing he had that her father had not was bravery. Arlan tucked a lock of hair behind her ear, his expression full of concern. "Poor baby. That was my fault for being a dumb ass and kissing you in the middle of moving traffic."

"So this blue spirit stone, it's supposed to help connect fated mates? Do you think it can help us with our problem with Jay?"

Arlan shrugged. "Magic is unpredictable. And it might just be a silly superstition. But I wanted to buy it for you. Will you accept it?"

She couldn't find words to answer him.

"It's supposed to strengthen the psychic intuition between mates. Help warn one when another is in danger, that kind of thing. I want you to take it, August. I want you to accept it willingly."

She swallowed. "Thanks again. It's beautiful." A simple lift of his brow was his *you're welcome.* She glanced down at the pendant, rubbing her finger over the stone. "Are you worrying about Jay right now as much as I am?"

"I'm trying not to, trying to just enjoy the time alone with you. He's such a damn closet case."

Depression crashed down on her without warning. She should be happy just to be with Arlan now. How greedy of her to want them both, how foolish to remain unhappy without Jay when her day with Arlan was so beautiful.

"Boss, you buy the lady, matching earrings? Ring?"

"Yes."

"No!"

But he already had his money out. She could feel her cheeks brighten, embarrassed by the extravagance. *When was the last time anyone bought you a gift?*

She took the pale green peridot studs—her birthstone—from her ears. Arlan took the elegant turquoise stones in their silver setting from the little box, and she placed the studs in it. Then he brushed back the tendrils of hair that had escaped from her braid as she put the new earrings in. The wave of bliss that swept through her toppled down years of walls built around her heart.

Arlan leaned forward and lowered his head. She closed her eyes, anticipating another kiss, but they flew open again when his tongue flicked against her earlobe. He took the soft lobe between his teeth and sucked it into his mouth, earring and all, making her groan as wetness seeped from her pussy. Arlan, let go, slipped the ring on, then, laughing, pulled her back into the stream of foot traffic. She noted a mobile van among the more rudimentary stalls. An old man with a wrinkled face, pooched and puffy, waved to them through the window.

"That's my friend, Zivai," Arlan said.

The mobile van sold sadza, the staple food of Zimbabwe, made of cornmeal, other food and various drinks.

"Want sadza, boss? Goat meat sandwich? Coca-Cola? Lemonade?"

"Some milk please, Zivai."

Zivai gestured around the back. "You come to the back door, easier for me. Fridge back there."

Arlan shrugged and took August's hand again. They made their way around the back of the van into a secluded area and round to the back door. Arlan paid for the milk. "You want lemonade or anything?" She nodded and reached for her purse. He held up a hand and paid the old man. The sweet, cold taste of the drink was divine in the heat. She stood still for a moment, enjoying it.

Zivai swore as he dropped something inside the van. Arlan told him good-bye and led her off a few yards to some shade beside a wall.

A random sense of foreboding suddenly gripped her, and the bliss of the sunny day, of the cool lemonade, the jacaranda trees, the gift of the necklace and earrings, the joy of being with Arlan, all suddenly drained away into some crack in the universe, until there was nothing left but anxiety.

Shocked by her own change of mood, she wasn't entirely surprised when Arlan's mood also changed. She could sense it, strong in her mind, like a psychic connection.

"I have to tell you something. I can't lie to you anymore." His expression had gone from playful to deadly serious. "I love you. I have to stop being a... I have to tell you the truth right now."

"What?"

"You may hate me. You may rip that necklace off and throw it at me."

"I didn't hate you when I caught you with Jay."

"No, you didn't. You were amazing." Arlan took a deep breath and leaned back against a stone wall. "I was one of the kids. I was one of the teens, one of the half-fae kids your mother babysat so other half-fae could go see tourist attractions in New York. I saw the games your mother played."

Tears sprang to her eyes. "Wait? *What? What?*"

He looked up at the sky. "I told my father about what your mother was doing to you the day I was there. He wouldn't listen. No one listened."

Humiliation burned her face like fire, making her body shake. "What did you see? Why didn't you tell me this before?"

"I didn't want you to hate me."

He heard the names your mother called you. He witnessed your shame. He did nothing. Like everyone else, he did nothing.

She shook her head and backed away from him, her hands out in front of her. "How old were you? No. I don't even want to know." She turned, ready to run.

"August, *no*. For God's sake."

She kicked him in the kneecap. As he swore, she bolted. She could hear him behind her. He caught her easily and grabbed her arm.

Angrily, she turned to face him. "Go away! I'll walk home alone."

"No. Give us a chance. Talk to me."

She struggled to think, to find a way to express herself. "I don't even remember you. I don't remember your face."

"A lot of kids passed in and out of your house, right? Your mother did a lot of babysitting?"

He watched her expression go dark at the memories. When she turned and looked about to run again, he pulled her into his arms. Though she shoved and strained against him, he held her firm against his chest. Her heart kicked against his as she struggled. "I'm so sorry, I'm so sorry, Gus."

"Don't you *dare* call me that. Let me *go*."

"No. I won't. You've been let go too often, and by too many people who should have been there for you."

A sound somewhere between a sob and a laugh burst from her throat. "I had my father's love and my grandmother's. I wasn't alone. I don't need your pity, you asshole."

"Why didn't they stop Duvessa? Your grandma? You father? Someone in the neighborhood?" She didn't answer him. But he saw it on her face. He understood. They were weak. They were afraid. Everyone had been weak and afraid of the terrifying, wealthy dark-fae princess. Everyone was weak, and everyone sucked ass, including him.

August shook her head. "I don't remember you at all. How old were you when you saw...it?"

"I was twelve."

She stopped. Some of the bitterness left her expression, and his heart lurched back to life. "Twelve? That's a baby. You would have been in middle school then. I thought you were older."

"I'm just a year older than you, August. You were eleven at the time, and I was twelve.

Her voice was a soft whisper. "What could you have done? You couldn't have done anything." Tears shone in her eyes, and he pulled her closer. She whispered into his chest, "I have nothing to be mad at you for. You were a baby."

"Yeah, you do. I'm an asshole. I should have told you sooner."

She shrugged, and he brushed the hair back from her face. "Can you forgive me? Can I make this right between us?"

"Arlan, I'm not going to hold something against you that happened when you were so young. I'm horribly embarrassed that you saw that, though."

"Your mother is the one who should be ashamed. In fact, the bitch should be in jail. You realize that, don't you?"

"I doubt a mortal prison could hold her anyway."

"You're too good for me *or* Jay.

Again, she simply shrugged and shook her head.

"August, I have to ask you... What I saw... I saw your mother had you tied up. So it bothered me when I first saw that Jay had tied you up."

She patted his arm. "It's okay. Really." She gazed up at the sky, then looked him in the eyes again. "I've talked to my counselor about it back home. I don't think it's unhealthy. Maybe it's a way of redefining that experience and the abuse, but, whatever, it turns me on, so I really don't care."

She smiled at him again. Joy warmed him. She really did enjoy it. She really wanted both him and Jay, and she didn't care that they were Doms, or that they loved each other. Arlan pressed his lips to her neck. "Are you okay, now? Are you ready to start home? We can talk more about it all when we get there."

174

She nodded. He took her hand, and they started on the long walk back toward his house. The sun was a big red ball low in the sky, guiding their way. But when she spotted a bench under a Musasa tree, all she wanted to do was sit down on it. Her legs shook and she realized how weary and numb she was from such an emotion-filled day.

"Let's sit down for a while here."

"Sure, sweetie. Hey, I'll tell you what. I can get you a coffee, one with milk this time. There's another mobile shop we passed a little way back that has good coffee."

"Thanks, I could use some caffeine. I didn't realize how exhausted I was."

She sat on the bench, and he kissed her forehead and smiled. "I'll be right back."

August leaned back and gazed up into the branches of the tree. Cicadas chirped and somewhere nearby she heard a bullfrog croak.

She shuddered as she remembered his confession. Arlan had been there and witnessed her humiliation. Witnessed her being treated like nothing, like less than nothing by her own mother. But he still respected her. He cared for her regardless.

She touched her new earrings, then the pendant. The gifts were beautiful, and she loved what they represented to Arlan, even if he was mistaken that the two or three of them had any kind of preordained connection. But what she loved most was getting to know him more. What an amazing personality he had, so kind, so strong. She'd met him when she was a child although she didn't remember it. A tear slid down her cheek, and she brushed it away. She'd been so friendless, perhaps if things had been different, if her mother had been different, she and Arlan might have been friends.

"Well, well, if it isn't little August." A menacing voice cut into her thoughts.

Ice-cold horror lanced through her. The man before her was huge, well over a foot taller than her, with a chest that spanned a wide breadth. He had unusual eyes. Glittering, jewel-colored eyes. Fae eyes.

The hands on her shoulders from behind the bench were enough of a shock. But the voice sent tremors down her spine.

"You bad girl. You *never* do what you are *told*."

A rough cloth covered her mouth, a taste and smell she well remembered, so chemical, yet so sweet. Panic shot through her. She thrashed more, tried to turn her head, knowing it was hopeless.

Spots formed before her eyes, her vision dimmed, graying, edging toward black.

Chapter Seventeen

August hadn't really expected to wake up, so when she did, it was a great shock.

Heart racing, she opened her eyes and wiped the grit from them. She was lying under a blanket on a thin mattress with a hard floor beneath. A dull throb pounded at her temples and the base of her skull, making it difficult to concentrate and get any real idea of where she was. The effects of the dark dust were worse this time. Kneading pains poked between her shoulder blades and deep inside her hip, knee and elbow joints.

Pinpricks of light seeped through sheer curtains from a window very high above her. That was the first place she looked. Up and toward the light. When she glanced down again, a scream tore through her mind. The thick metal bars of her cage stood at two-inch intervals. A large water bottle hung on the side with a metal straw hanging down. There was a toilet. A prison toilet. No seat.

They intend for me to be here for a long time. Or someone's been kept here before.

Panic swelled again with the need to...do something. Then the sense of hopelessness returned. Why was Duvessa doing this? Why now?

A soft whimpering came from somewhere in the room. August's blood froze. She willed herself to calm down and slow her breathing. As she adjusted to the dimly lit room, she noticed there were two other cages rigged up like hers with water bottles on the side. Arlan was asleep inside one of them.

Was he also knocked out by dark dust? Or had they used some other drug?

Oddly, the other cage contained a man who looked no older than maybe...seventeen. The boy pressed his fist to his mouth as though trying to stifle a scream. Tears ran down his cheeks.

Other than the three cages, the room was like your typical basement, filled with old junk. It was a huge mess, with a couple of old tables also stacked with more junk, and many things she might have used as weapons if she could have reached them. She scanned the glass bottle, the umbrella, the lamp, then crawled off the mattress and searched the interior of the cage again for something, anything she could use...

Among the mess and the junk, she saw them. A huge bulk multipack of her mother's favorite brand of cigarettes lay on the table. The brand name caused her memories to flash back. August's stomach clenched. Every muscle in her body went painfully rigid.

Mother will punish you.

Her mother would punish her with them as she had when she was a child The glowing tip would sting, the pungent smell of burning flesh would combine with the stale cigarette smoke and...screaming.

The sharp click of heels tapped against the floor outside the room, and a key scraped in the lock. August choked down rising bile. Her gaze automatically dropped to the floor. The shoes were black patent leather, six-inch heels making her imposingly tall mother even taller. August steeled herself and forced her eyes upward to gaze at her mother's face.

Her mother's beautiful, Grace Kelly face wore that ridiculous TV newsreader smile. The one she put on when she really wanted something. That smile that had charmed so many of her half-fae acquaintances into doing whatever she wanted. As if that could possibly work now on her daughter, whom she put in a cage. Duvessa was crazy.

A flood of memories transformed August's fear into a haze of rage. "Mother, why did you do this?"

If she focused on the rage she could forget the memories of violence. She could forget what it felt like to have her arms burned by cigarettes, or the humiliation of her mother slapping her face, in a room full of other children. She bit her lips so she wouldn't cry.

Duvessa said not a word, just scanned her up and down, and after a couple of minutes of silence, the rage faded. August reverted to the age of ten, trembling, panicking, her mother's frosty silence weighing on her like a stone.

A whimper came from behind her, and she jerked her head around to stare at the teen boy, now awake. Arlan was still out cold. "What's wrong with Arlan?"

Duvessa glanced over at him. "I had to knock him out with chloroform like I did you.

"*Why?*"

"Well, look at him. His shoulders are as wide and broad as a doorway. Must be nice for you, holding on to all that muscle while he sticks it in. Hmm?"

"You're disgusting."

Duvessa smirked and stepped closer, then stuck a finger through the bars, touching August's chin. The change in her mother's expression was almost tropical, the cool newsreader gone, the evil seeping through. Duvessa started to hum. A tightening sensation under August's forehead, then between her temples made her wince. *Mother's trying to use magic to break into your thoughts.* August jerked backward, slamming a mental door between them.

Duvessa gripped one of the bars of the cage, pointing at August with her other hand. "There, ha. Ha! You see? You *slammed* me out of your mind just now. You couldn't do that if you were really as mundane and human as you pretend to be. Even after all I did to try to drain you of magic, you *still* have a little power." She shook the bars, frustration on her face. "You must have had so much to begin with. Why didn't you choose to cultivate it and join the dark path with your *mother*? I could have made you great. It didn't have to be like *this*."

August blinked in surprise. Duvessa gestured around the room. "You could have simply worked with me. Been a proper daughter. Your father and grandmother ruined you."

"They *nurtured* me."

The two women stared into each other's eyes.

"You're not even *mortal*." Duvessa whispered.

August raised her chin, her voice shaking. "No, I guess I'm probably not mortal. But how do you even know that? You tried to kill me, didn't you? That illness that May and Dad and I had... You?"

Duvessa went silent again, still, her face cold and blank like the dark side of the moon. "Caused that? Yes. I caused that. I put it in your food. Yes. I was curious."

"You put *what* in our food? You were curious about *what*?"

"Dark dust. I was curious which of you had inherited the immortal gene. If any of you. Of course, I know I have it. I'm the daughter of Princess Zenia. But with your father's genes in the mix, well, I didn't know."

Dark grief mixed with bright rage. "You killed him? You made May sick when she was only four years old. And you *killed* him!"

"Your father didn't love me. He made me sign a prenup."

"With good *reason*. You knew you could get around it by...killing him and making it seem like an illness."

She pushed back from the bars of the cage. "Your father killed himself. The fool shot himself in the head. That was not my fault."

August leaned forward, her head against the cool metal of the bars, remembering the bloodstains on the plush white carpet in what had been her sister's perfect bedroom. "He was in unbearable pain, and the doctors told him his baby girl was going to die."

Duvessa's lips quirked in a sardonic smile. "And they were *wrong*. She was *immortal*. She survived. But the idiot shoots himself in the head. And now your *immortal* sister May is off in some ridiculous place pretending to be a cowgirl or something."

"Montana"

"Alive and well in the state of Montana, so your father was a huge fool."

"You would have killed him anyway?"

"Maybe."

August's mind raced, trying to comprehend what she was hearing. Trying to comprehend the incomprehensible. "But you never did any of it to June or April. You never tried to poison them?"

Her mother pressed up against the cage again so she was face-to-face with August. Her eyes became yellow, the pupils turning to slits—the eyes of a salamander, a fire fae. Fear bubbled up to the surface again. "Your older sisters always gave me the respect I deserved. They worked on their magic every day. I knew they were both superior. I knew they'd be dark fae. So I never doubted they'd be immortal too, any more than I doubt I have the gene myself. Besides, I had no reasons to want to get rid of them. They never gave me a moment's grief, either of them."

Her stomach dropped, hollowed. It still hurt to be rejected. It hurt that her two older sisters knew how to tiptoe around her mother, how to please her. June had chosen the dark path herself. April didn't really have any ambition to be dark fae. She was just clever. At least she and April were friends. "Why did you even marry my father? You despised him."

Letting go of the bars of the cage, Duvessa drew herself up to her full height. "I needed heirs. I wanted to breed."

"To *breed*?"

"It's an idiotic question, August. Naturally, if I'd known any full-blooded fae, that was where my interest would have gone. You know I didn't know how to get to the fae realm. I knew only half-fae."

"So?"

"So your father was eager, he pursued me, he had more money than most men I knew. I figured he'd used magic to acquire it, that he must be more of a dark fae than he let on. How wrong I was. Only after we were wed did I realize that he was truly weak. That he worked in drudgery like a mortal to acquire wealth."

August's lip curled. "The ways you acquire wealth are weak and disgusting. I've been inside that casino of yours."

Duvessa smiled. "Glamorous, isn't it?"

"Attraction spells to draw people to the slot machines, to the roulette table. I could smell the manipulative magic you use. Nothing about that place is natural. You *enslave* people in there. You ruin their *lives*."

"Most human beings and dark fae use what gifts they've been given in life to their own benefit, August. But not the light fae." Duvessa's lips thinned. "You are a bunch of fools. Did I need a fool for a daughter? This is exactly why I had to kill your fae power. By the time you were eight or nine, I realized you had chosen the light path, that in time you would be called to be a Warrior of the Light and want to help stupid mortals, and just fuck everything up. You would have ruined my life. We would have been *poor*."

"We could have lived off the money Dad made and been more than comfortable. He earned a *good* living."

"Ugh. Your father spent all those hours selling real estate, stupid mortal drudgery. He had no time to be my lover or to do anything fun with me. Seriously, he was better off dead. I was so bored."

August bit her lip. There was no use rising to this bait. At times, her mother could be as immature and as callous as an

Internet troll. She was enjoying her daughter's outrage, provoking it, poking at it. So August kept her voice deliberately calm for her next question. "You still haven't answered my first question, Mother. Why did you kidnap us?"

"And you still haven't answered *my* question, daughter. Why did you suppress your magic all these years?"

"I didn't. You..."

Duvessa smirked, and August mentally kicked herself.

...damaged my self-esteem so I wouldn't be able to perform magic.

She didn't need to say it. It stood in the air between them.

"I made the right choices for our family, August. We're close to being wealthy enough to have whatever we want, but we could be wealthier and more powerful still. You just need to work with me. If you would consider..."

The whimpering in the opposite cage grew a little louder. She realized how much the conversation must be scaring the teenager. She swallowed. Guilt at her thoughtlessness for scaring the kid even further washed over her. She pointed to the cage. "Who is that young man?"

Duvessa glanced over at the cage. "Oh, him. I believe his name is Johan." Johan's sobs now seemed to have doubled him over like punches, and he collapsed in a heap.

"Mother, what the hell are you doing? He looks maybe seventeen? Why are you kidnapping people?"

Duvessa glanced over at the boy. "Oh no. Johan is twenty-one. He just has a youthful face. Must be one of the advantages of being pure of heart."

"What?"

"Pure of heart. Apparently that's what you are, and your zoologist were-lion friend, and Johan. It's supposed to help with the sex magic."

"I don't know Johan. Who is he? Where did he come from? I don't understand any of this." She squeezed the bridge of her nose, trying to keep calm.

Duvessa's heels clicked on the floor again as she walked over to peer into Johan's cage. "Johan is your new sexual partner."

"What? You are *crazy*." A knot formed in her belly.

"For the sex magic"

"That's about saving children locked in a tower. What do you care about any of that?"

Duvessa leaned back against Johan's cage. "That Jay Nandoro is a dead loss. I've scryed on him. This is his replacement."

August gripped the bars of the cage. "Jay. What have you done with Jay?" She scanned the room as if there might be another cage, though she knew there wasn't.

"My darling daughter. *I* haven't done anything to him. But your *friend* Jay Nandoro is one drunken mess."

She stared at her mother for a moment, remembering that Arlan had said Jay had gone to some bar, or pub, or whatever they called it here. "What do you mean?"

"I scryed on Jay Nandoro today. He looks like an alcoholic slob, from what I saw. He's very handsome, but ultimately he's inferior. You will be performing the sex magic with Johan instead. And with Arlan too. Lucky girl, Arlan Leonard is one attractive son of a bitch, all those golden muscles."

"You're *gross*. Why do you even care about the sex magic? Why are you getting involved?"

Duvessa raised one eyebrow. "Why do I ever get involved? Why do I ever do anything? For money. For *power.*"

As powerless as she felt, August tried to make her voice firm. "Well, whatever your plan is, it's not going to work. You need to let us go. Maybe if you let me out of here, we could talk more. Keeping us in cages is... It's criminal."

Duvessa smiled. "What do I care if it's a criminal offense? No jail cell could hold me. If you'd let me teach you dark magic when you were a little girl, you could have freed yourself from any cell. Yet another reason for you to regret your foolishness in choosing the light path."

Chapter Eighteen

Jay woke on a bare concrete floor, his hangover thudding against his temples, drill bits trying to work their way out and leave circles in the top of his skull. Wherever he was, the scent of yeasty beer and cigarettes was strong, with a faint smell of urine and vomit underneath. He touched his head and felt a sticky patch of blood. He struggled into a sitting position and glanced down at his shirt and shorts. Both were stained with grime. He was grubby, humiliated, emotionally drained.

As his memories of the day returned, a swamping wave of black depression rolled over him. He touched the small bloody patch on the top of his head and scanned the room. People were drinking and laughing and playing pool.

August!

Her image flashed in his mind's eye.

Since he'd met her, she was at the forefront of his mind much of the time. His gut knotted just remembering her surprised face. He wanted the impossible from her. He wanted her to stay with him forever. He wanted to be at the center of her heart, as she would be at the center of his. He wanted a woman who didn't care that he also desired Arlan, that he couldn't, try as he might, break free from that relationship. And that was impossible. That was madness. Maybe that was how things were in the Fae Realm, according to Arlan's research, but the three of them lived here on earth.

Jay touched the blood on his forehead again, grimacing at his stupidity and the pain.

"You all right, boss?"

Jay jumped at the intrusion into his thoughts. A man with skin that shone almost blue-black reached out to give Jay a hand. A Shona man. Jay ignored the hand and hauled himself to his feet. "Don't call me boss. I'm Shona too." Not for the first time, Jay felt irritated that his skin was pale enough that Africans here never took him for one of their own, and yet he knew most Europeans saw him as black.

"Jay Nandoro? Well, I'll be! It's Jay Nandoro."

Jay did a double-take. "Dr. Tongai?"

The older man grinned at him. He was a lot slimmer than he'd once been. He hadn't seen the psychiatrist in years.

"Shit, Dr. Tongai. Let me buy you a beer." Swearing, he patted his shorts and gave a huge sigh of relief. His wallet was still there. Opening it, he sucked in a breath. All his ID and credit cards were still in place, even his eighty dollars. Amazing. At least his height and muscle still counted for something in this world. Even when he was passed out. Even if he was a...

He rubbed his forehead, not wanting to think about what August must think of him now. Her poor heart was probably broken. And someone else had long ago put the haunted look in those beautiful blue-gray eyes. Now he'd added to her pain. Self-loathing and guilt tightened his chest.

The two men walked over to the bar. Jay pulled out some money and handed it to the guy behind the bar. Once they had their beer, they took their drinks back to the rough wooden bench and table.

He slapped the man on the back. "What are you doing here, man?"

"Why wouldn't I be here? Can't a shrink have a drink?" He grinned, and Jay felt his own lips tilt up at the edges in response. As embarrassed as he was to see the man, he was still taken in by his charm.

"You had one drink too many before I arrived, I see. You're bleeding, you know."

Jay pulled a face. "I know. This place is a dump, though. I thought a man like you'd be drinking somewhere classier than the Mopane Tree." Jay gestured at the blackboard sign that advertised only scuds, the slang for big plastic containers of local beer that smelled of raw yeast and tasted like earth. Made with maize, it was a drink and a food in one.

The doctor shrugged. "My nephew works here. And sometimes you just want a scud." He took a sip of beer. Then stopped, frowned and reached a hand up to almost touch the spot on Jay's head. Instinctively, Jay shrank back. "Listen, Jay, you better put something on that fast in case it gets infected. I'll see if they have a first aid kit."

His former psychiatrist headed around the back of the bar and started talking to a young man. He gestured at Jay and returned with the kit. Jay had to slouch so the shorter man could put disinfectant on his head wound while he swore at the burning.

The doctor covered the graze with a thick square plaster. "I might have thought a man with your wealth could find a classier place to drink, Mr. Nandoro?"

Jay shrugged. "Sometimes my mood is seedy. This place fits."

He walked back around the table, sat down and took another sip of his scud. Jay studied the man as he drank some of his own strong yeasty beer. Scud always had a surprising lemon aftertaste. "So what's it been, two, maybe three years? And you don't wear glasses anymore."

Tongai gestured to his eyes. "Contacts."

"Thought so."

"You ditched me all those years ago. Ran out on me, Nandoro."

Jay rubbed his fingers against his temple, trying to relieve a bit of his headache. "I don't really want to talk about that, man."

"Your uncle prepaid for an additional month's counseling you didn't even show up for." Jay shrugged. The doctor leaned forward and whispered, "A suicide attempt is a serious thing, Jay."

His insides went tense. He pointed at the doctor, cutting off his speech. "That was years ago."

"But..."

Jay gave Tongai the look. The look that always shut Arlan up. He motioned to the plastic container. "I bought you a drink, old man, and that's *all* I paid for. Drink your scud."

Dr. Tongai shook his head and took another mouthful. "You can come visit me anytime."

"It's not necessary." Jay peered more closely at Tongai. He was thin. He appeared healthy, but...the horror of the thought made him nauseated. "You've lost a lot of weight since I last saw you, Doctor. You don't..."

"No, Jay, I don't have the disease. I don't have HIV. I'm thin, but I'm not *that* thin. It's just stress, you know?" He shrugged. "Life is stressful here."

Jay's whole body relaxed, and he raised his plastic container in a mock toast. "Life is hell in Africa."

Dr. Tongai lifted his own drink, then the old man's gaze went to the doorway, and his mouth dropped open. "Oh God, no."

Jay turned his head to focus on what he was staring at. Three men had entered the pub. One glance at them told Jay they were bad news. Early thirties, black wraparound sunglasses, black Levis, gold chains; one of the men was short, but the other two were huge, hulking men. One of them appeared European possibly South African, the other two might be Shona. Jay's eyes met those of the largest man, and a muscle twitched in his jaw.

The shorter man nodded toward their table. The two heavies approached them. "Hello, *Doctor*." The man's lip curled. He practically spat the word doctor.

One of the larger men stepped forward. "Where's your *boyfriend*, Doctor?"

The way the man said boyfriend made the hairs stand up on the back of Jay's neck. The doctor blinked rapidly. "I don't know what you mean."

The other large man drummed his fingers on the wooden table. "Steven Zinyoro. Stop playing dumb."

"My *friend* Steven's visiting his mother."

"My *friend* Steven's visiting his mother." The thug's high-pitched falsetto imitation of Dr. Tongai made Jay's nostrils flare as his body tensed.

The short man grabbed the back of Tongai's shirt. "Own your filthy deeds, Doctor." The man's Afrikaners accent was thick with contempt. "Answer me this, Tongai, are you *gay*?"

"Well, I'm not very happy right now. But I might be if you let go of my shirt."

Before Jay had time to think, one of the other thugs grabbed Tongai's arm. "My buddies and I should turn you over to the cops, fudge packer. But you never know. Play your cards right, you might get lucky."

"Yeah." The man wearing the most gold chains poked Tongai in the chest. "You might get lucky. Where's your wallet at?"

Jay grabbed the Afrikaners man's wrist and twisted it backward, making him let go of the psychiatrist. "We were just leaving." Jay's teeth ached from gritting them. His vision was dark with rage. He wanted to kill all three men, but his headache still jackhammered in his skull, and he didn't need the grief or trouble.

The largest man blocked their path. "Well, mate," the man said in a poor imitation of Jay's boarding school accent, "we have business with the fag, so you'll be the one leaving. *He* stays."

Jay's right eye throbbed like a heart. He wished he had his phone. He wished he had his gun. The doctor sucked in a sharp breath and whirled around. The other heavy had Dr. Tongai's hand pressed down on the wooden bench, trapped in a viselike grip.

"Motherfucker," Tongai swore in pain.

"Wallet."

"You're...not...blackmailing me." Tongai's words came out between gasps. The man squeezed harder, and pop of cartilage echoed over Dr. Tongai's screams. Getting it together at last, Jay landed a sharp right hook on the man's jaw. The man's head snapped back, and he careened into the table. Jay grabbed the beefy wrist of the other large man, whose fist came flying at him, stopping the punch, then shoving the man against the wall with enough force that the guy's head gave an audible crack as it hit the concrete bricks.

From behind him, Jay heard the snap of a blade. His blood pumping so fast it deafened his hearing, he jumped aside, missing the man's first lunge. The other two men grabbed him, knocking him into the pool table. Trapped on both sides, both men holding his arms, pinning him against the table, Jay felt his pulse race.

The brute sneered at him. "You're dead, *mengzi*."

Jay thought the Shona word meant stranger, or maybe asshole. It hardly mattered when he felt the sting in his flesh.

Chapter Nineteen

The basement door creaked on its hinges, and Kruger entered the room. August was frozen in time, staring at him, while Duvessa looked on, amused.

"*You!*" Indignation overwhelmed her terror. "*You!* I gave *you* a second chance. I trusted you."

Did she see guilt momentarily flash in his eyes?

"Ah," Duvessa said, "you're here at last, Hendrik. How are we going to do this whole thing? This sex magic?"

"I don't fucking know."

Duvessa whirled to face him. "This was *your* idea, to replace Jay Nandoro with someone younger, more naïve."

August turned her head as Johan let out a gasp of protest or pain. Her hand through the bars, Duvessa had a fistful of the young man's hair. She was clearly enjoying his palpable terror and pain.

My God! My mother. This is a woman I loved. I loved you once. In spite of everything, I loved you because you're my mother.

"Stupid." She heard herself voice it out loud. Her mother merely raised an eyebrow at her words. "What's stupid?"

"Trusting him."

Kruger actually had the grace to flush. "This was *not* my idea, Duvessa."

"Of course it was."

"No." He waved his hand at the three cages. "This was never the plan. You kidnapped these people? I can't believe this."

"Well, what else are the cages down here for?" Duvessa tucked a lock of hair behind her ear. "For keeping people in, I would imagine. What has gotten into you today? We discussed all this."

"We *discussed* it, but I told you I didn't think August and Arlan would be keen to find a new third." Kruger sighed. "I had things under control. They were doing the sex magic. If you just had some patience... You never said you would *kidnap* them."

"They were not performing. It needed to be done." Duvessa glared. Her eyes flickered like guttering candles, turning August's blood to ice.

"*Look* at that kid." Kruger gestured at Johan. "He's scared out of his mind. He's probably wet himself. How well is he going to perform?" The professor raised his chin. "Sex magic is supposed to be done by consenting, happy participants." His voice quivered with what August could only guess was frustration, though his speech was impassioned. He was...forgetting himself. "I had the key to all that power in the palm of my hand. I had it all planned out, under control. You messed everything up, Duvessa."

August watched with a mixture of horror and resignation as the change began. The beautiful cerulean blue in her mother's eyes began fading, transforming to amber. The pupils became slits as the glamourie dissolved, and the salamander traits of the fire fae appeared. "You *dare* ssspeak to me like *thisss*? In front of *her*?" She jabbed her thumb at August. Johan screamed as her grip on his hair tightened and she banged him against the bars of his cage. Released, the young man slumped to the thin mattress on the floor.

Duvessa began to hum. And August was not surprised when Kruger fell forward onto the table with an "Ooof." A variety of objects tipped over. Some rolled off the table and clattered onto the concrete floor.

She was more surprised when Kruger's belt undid itself and his pants and boxer shorts fell down to reveal a gym-toned butt.

A whip that lay among the clutter jumped from the table into Duvessa's hand. As Kruger bent to pull his trousers back up, Duvessa struck him hard across his still-bare ass. The blow must have stung—he cried out. A thin pink line appeared.

"Duvessa!" Kruger called out her name in agony.

August couldn't tell if Kruger was chastising her mother or if he was aroused. She feared the latter.

Duvessa lifted her arm, and August hid her face behind her hands so she could only hear the thwack of the whip.

Twenty thwacks, twenty screams.

"Duvessa, Duvessa." He was pleading now, begging, crying. Were the tears from pain? Or from loss of dignity? Duvessa wore her TV-presenter smile again. The whip clattered to the floor.

"So. Tell me your plan, Hendrik. Tell me how we work this sex magic."

Kruger breathed heavily. "I...I'm sorry. I'm sorry."

"Forget that. Tell me the plan."

"Well... We'll prepare the three of them. Get them ready for the sex magic."

"How?"

Kruger leaned back against the desk, sweat beading on his brow.

August averted her gaze quickly at the sight of his erection.

"We want to do this properly so that the magic really *works* this time. So we can tap into the mysterious power these people have. You know there are certain objects that can be placed around the participants so that..."

"Yes. Yes. We saw Arlan line up all those little trinkets." Duvessa sneered. "It didn't work."

"We've figured out at least part of the issue is that Jay Nandoro isn't pure of heart. He's a cynical type with some kind of chip on his shoulder, so that was some of the problem. Another problem might be that—"

"Why not just get on with it? Have them mate in the cages right here."

August gasped, bile rising in her throat. This would be rape, and her mother involved. It was grotesque.

"Um, no. No, that wouldn't work at all." Kruger sounded hesitant, but his words gained in strength. "I think they must be properly groomed first, oiled, their fingernails cleaned and trimmed, that kind of thing. I'm sure that would help."

Silence.

August didn't want to see her mother's face, and when she did, she wished she hadn't. Glimpsing the serpent's face beneath the glamourie had always scared the hell out of her, always made the black dog of depression return. It sat heavy on her chest. The sensation felt like all hope had left the world.

Chapter Twenty

Anger and adrenaline soared. Jay touched his chest. Blood seeped from the gash the thug had managed to make even as he jumped aside. It was only a slash, but it still stung like a motherfucker.

The fae humming began in his throat before he'd even made a conscious choice to try magic. Tendrils of silver and blue appeared at his feet, coming out of his toes. Wow, he'd never had magic seep from his toes before.

His hand was behind his back, bent painfully by one thug, but as he concentrated, light poured out from his fingertips He focused on a pool ball behind him that he could no longer see. Jay fought to concentrate. With his mental powers and his magic, he hurled the ball at the third man, the short one, as hard as he possibly could. The orange ball with the number five on it went sailing over his head, careening through the air.

SMACK.

The pool ball hit the man straight between the eyes. Blood streamed from the round wound, making him look like some three-eyed monster from a horror film. One of the thugs let go of his arm in shock, and Jay drove his elbow backward into the guy's gut. The other creep grappled with him, not about to let go.

Jay took a deep breath, shaken by the use of a kind of magic he'd not tried since childhood. It still fucking scared him to use it for anything. Images of his mother flashed through his mind—playing with her, drawing with her, singing with her, doing culinary magic with her. Her lying blank-faced in a hospital ward. The memories randomly flashed in his mind while he grappled with the swearing, grunting jerk.

Jay blinked, and clenched his fists, humming louder than before.

Indigo light flashed in diagonal streaks. A pool cue slid across the table and smacked its edge, then rose through the air to press across the man's neck. The man fell silent, his face a mask of shock and terror. He let go of Jay to use both hands to try to pull the stubborn cue from across his neck. Crowds had formed around the bleeding man. Few had noticed the pool cue's animation.

One man had, though.

"Witch! Monster!" The accusation was one of whispered horror. It was the fat bartender, his face purple. "Get out of my pub. Fiend! Witch! Monster!"

Jay glanced around at the dozens of witnesses, but it was a pub. He could claim they were all drunk. Most of them stared at the slumped and bleeding men, not at him, anyway.

The pub owner raised his voice and shook his fist. "Get out, get *out*."

Jay pushed the doctor ahead of him, past several gawkers and out the front door. Footsteps pounded behind them. As they ran down the street, Jay still heard someone behind him. He didn't want any more trouble. His brain split with headache pain. Already nauseated, he didn't want to use any more magic and he didn't want to fight.

He whispered, "Run," in the doctor's ear, and he and the doctor started pounding the pavement. Jay sent up a prayer of thanks that he'd worn his Nikes. After several blocks, the doctor was panting and whimpering in pain.

His hand!

Jay rounded the corner and swore. He stopped and leaned back against a brick wall, looking left and right. Whoever had been following them wasn't there now. Dr. Tongai moaned again, and Jay cringed at the memory of the sound of cartilage popping in the doctor's hand. He'd momentarily forgotten how much pain he must be in.

Jay touched the pocket of his shirt, which was still sticky with blood from where the thug had cut him, and sighed. "I don't even have my phone. How bad is your hand?"

"I'm in pain, Jay. A lot."

The older man's complexion had a green tinge. He looked like he might vomit from the pain.

"Do you have a cell phone on you? We could call a taxi or a doctor."

Tongai shook his head. "Battery is dead."

Jay swore again. The last thing in the world he wanted to do was healing magic. The magic that had put his mother in a coma. But she had been trying to heal his father's vital organs. This was just a crushed hand.

Dr. Tongai held the first aid kit out to him. "Good job grabbing that thing before we left, but I think you know as well as I do that nothing in there is going to fix this."

"Bloody fuck!" Tongai nodded and moaned again.

"Give me your hand."

Tongai dropped the case. "Why?"

"Just do it."

Dr. Tongai held out his arm. Jay grasped the doctor's hand and began to hum and then sing in fae, remembering his mother, remembering how she'd done it when he'd twisted his ankle as a kid. He held the old man's hand up to his mouth, breathing warmth on it, the threads of healing spiraling in his mind. Beneath his fingers, the magic swirled, the cartilage healed, the damaged hand became strong.

Tongai panted hard and fast. "What the fuck? What did you do?" He flexed his healing hand. "More magic. All that shit that went on in the pub? Holy crap, I always thought all that half-fae nonsense was just a bunch of kooky people running around being weird. Just some delusional fringe group."

"Did you think you imagined what happened in the pub?"

"I thought I was maybe losing my mind from a combination of alcohol and pain. I thought I was hallucinating.

Jay leaned against the wall. He closed his eyes to fight dizziness and nausea. Maybe it was finally time to break it off with Arlan once and for all. Their love was far too dangerous in this country. He couldn't live with himself if some dudes like that attacked Arlan, or August somehow got hurt.

Chapter Twenty-One

When August awoke, she glanced down at her palm, where she still clutched some strands of hair. Rather than give in to the depression, she'd decided to try to braid some strands of her hair into a thread. If she had a few threads, she could make a cord, perhaps use it as a weapon against Kruger or whoever might open the door of her cage. It was better than just lying there being depressed.

But she had drunk from the bottle attached to the side of her cage. And the damn thing must have had a sleeping draught in it, or, more likely, more fucking dark dust. Her mouth felt like it had been stuffed with cotton. She remembered feeling so dizzy that her arms and legs had stopped working, and she hadn't even been able to get her eyes to focus. Now they felt gritty.

She fought against the remaining stranglehold of the drug, struggling to wake properly. Gradually, she became aware that she wasn't where she'd expected to be. She was lying on a towel. Her fingers splayed on...smooth wood. Not the thin mattress. Wherever she was, it wasn't her cage.

It was very hot in here, and the scent of steam and soap and lavender filled her nose. She opened her eyes fully. Steam floated all around her. Music came from another room, but no other sounds indicated people nearby. She ran her hands down her slick body. She was oiled—and completely naked. Her pulse took a sharp upswing as adrenaline surged.

She swung herself into a sitting position and brought her wrist to her nose. Someone had slicked up her naked body with a lavender-scented body oil. Her heart pumped with a ragged fierceness that scared her. Her turquoise pendant still hung between her breasts. She clutched it, felt its smooth surface and took deep calming breaths.

Someone pushed through the plastic strips that hung down as a curtain blocking off this steam room. August gasped.

Kruger.

Frantically, she stood up, grabbing the towel to cover herself.

"Hey, hey, hey," Kruger whispered as though to a frightened animal. "I'm not here to hurt you, August." Even as he said it, he glanced down to her breasts.

August tightened her grip on the towel wrapped around her. Anger helped her brain to awaken and become more alert. "Where am I?"

"Your mother is renting this place from some very wealthy half-fae. You're in their private gym and exercise area. This is the steam room."

A sense of excitement flooded her, even with the dreaded Kruger here. She wasn't in the cage anymore. She glanced around the steam room, but there was no way to dash past Kruger. He would catch her. "But why? Why am I here?"

"Listen, August, I told your mother all that garbage about how we had to get you looking beautiful, oiled, scented and perfect for the sex magic. It did that for precisely this purpose." He seemed pleased with himself.

August wasn't sure she understood his change of heart, but then she remembered Duvessa beating his ass with the crop. *She humiliated him. That's why he's changed his mind. Her aggressive dominance with him backfired. He no longer admires her.*

"Two half-fae women trimmed your nails and everything in preparation. They've gone out to for a bite to eat now.

"What are you saying?"

"This is your chance to escape, August."

"Oh my God!" She clutched the towel to her chest. "Thank you. Thank you. Won't she..."

"Kill me? For helping you escape? Your mother is a demon from hell, but I think I can outsmart the dark-fae witch." Kruger's eyes were cold stones in the steam. "She'll never know I had a hand in it, as long as you don't do anything stupid now. So don't waste time. Get moving."

August stared at him. "Um... I'm *naked.*"

Kruger threw up his hands. "Hold on." He pushed through the plastic strips and left again. Her heart continued to thump painfully. In a few minutes, he returned with shoes and a tote bag and a red velvet dress that was way too big.

She held it against her body. "This is my mother's dress. And those aren't my shoes either. I don't know whose shoes those are."

"They took your clothes away for cleaning. I have no idea where they are. This is what I could find."

She realized she was being ungrateful. Kruger was putting himself at considerable risk. "Thank you." She pulled the dress on over her towel, ignoring his obvious disappointment, as his gaze still lingered on her chest.

"And take this. It's going to get dark soon." He handed her a flashlight, which she put in her tote.

"Thank you again."

"I'm out of here. There's no way I'm getting caught by your mother. You'll have to fend for yourself now."

"Well... Wait... What about Arlan, where is he?" She bent to put the shoes on. They had a slight heel but they actually fit. Perhaps they belonged to a maid or something.

When she stood up again, he was gone. She yanked the towel out from underneath her dress and sighed inwardly.

Pushing through the plastic strip curtain, she found herself in an impressive, well-equipped gym area. An enormous flat-screen TV was set to some rock video channel. She scanned the room frantically. Some of her gratitude to Kruger evaporated as she realized the coward had scampered away and wasn't going to give her one more iota of help. Her gaze alighted on some small handheld weights. Just the metal bar without the weight could make a decent weapon.

She'd never been one for small handbags. The tote bag was just big enough that it would hold the little metal bar. She slipped it inside. Spying a drinking fountain, she went and drank. Even if it slowed her down, she needed water. It felt like heaven to her dry throat and mouth. Even as she drank, she turned her head to the side to survey the room, her ears on alert, vigilant for any sound, sick with the fear they'd come back too soon.

She wiped her mouth and scanned the area. There were three doors, and she had no clue which way Kruger had gone or what the safest way out was. Taking a gamble, she grabbed the handle of the first door and headed down the corridor. Glancing up at the wall, she saw a portrait. She did a double-take. Her jaw fell open as cold settled in her belly. The portrait was of a handsome young couple. The older man looked so much like Ryan Garrison, it could have been his father.

She shook her head. *Impossible.*

She couldn't be wasting time on nonsense like this. She gazed down the end of the long hallway to the door. *Just run, you fool.* She hoped her pounding footsteps wouldn't alert some unknown someone in this colossal mansion.

She reached a big door, a back door. She pushed, but it wouldn't budge. *Breathe in. Breathe out. In. Out.* August pushed harder. The door swung open. In the dimming light, she could make out jacaranda trees, and, in the distance, euphorbia trees. The smell of jasmine hung on the air.

She really had no idea where she was. Leaning against the door, she covered her face. She'd just have to wing it. In the distance, a hippo snorted.

She noticed Kruger's Land Cruiser parked in a car port.

She ran down a paved pathway through the immaculately tended garden, dodging a spitting water sprinkler. And then she heard it: a car coming up the driveway. A silver Lexus, with her mother at the wheel.

Fear slashed to her heart. She swiveled around and stood staring as Duvessa stopped and climbed out of the car.

Chapter Twenty-Two

The Flame Lily All-Night Café was located on Crassula Road in the center of Harare. The interior was decorated with many paintings of the stunning Zimbabwe flower. Jay took another sip of his coffee. "I never had any idea you were..."

Dr. Tongai smirked. "What? A little bit lavender?"

Jay laughed and ran a hand over his shaved head. "Shit, man, a little bit lavender."

Dr. Tongai put a finger to his lips as the waitress approached. Jay glanced down as the waitress poured more coffee into his cup and placed a warm croissant in front of him. They waited until she walked away, unwilling to risk her hearing their discussion.

"You still live in that big old mansion with your friend?" Dr. Tongai asked.

Jay glared at the doctor, daring him to say more. Daring him to make the comparison.

Hell, he didn't have to make the comparison. *You told him. You told him about Arlan all those years ago, dumbass.* "Yeah, I do."

The doctor glanced after the waitress. "We need to leave this country, Jay. Zimbabwe is not a safe place for us to be. It's not worth it."

"Who is we? Who is us?"

"Steven and I, you and I? This is not a safe country for our kind."

"What do you mean, our kind?"

"You know what I mean, Jay."

In his mind's eye, he saw Arlan in his lion form, running across the savannah, his coat a blaze of glorious gold. "It's just not that simple for us, for me."

"Arlan doesn't want to leave?"

Jay bit his lip. "Something like that."

"Steven and I are leaving. He got a job in New York. You and Arlan could..."

"Shh, for fuck's sake!" Jay began humming a protection spell very low. It was the easiest, most invisible magic he knew.

This kind of spell couldn't protect you once people had noticed and locked their attention on you. It was only good at hiding what people hadn't noticed yet. It would misdirect people's attention, distracting them.

Jay smiled at Dr. Tongai's open-mouthed expression. He was obviously still adjusting to the whole concept of half-fae and magic being real.

When Jay finished, the doctor regained his composure. "More magic?"

"Protection. So we can talk." Jay pulled a face. "God knows I know you want to talk."

"And you don't?"

"No." Jay bit into his chocolate croissant, still warm, sweet and delicious. The coffee here was rich and flavorful too. I had no idea there was such a great all-night coffee house in this part of Harare."

"I come here a lot."

Jay continued to eat in silence.

"Jay." The doctor tapped on his cup to get his attention. "Why throw up one of your...what do you call them...half-fae protection spells, if you're not going to talk to me?"

Jay rolled his eyes. "Because I know you're going to talk about being 'a little bit lavender' and all that shit, and you could get us attacked. No wonder you were so interested in

trying to drag details out of me about Arlan all those years ago."
He frowned and took another bite of the warm pastry.

"No wonder? Because I'm gay, you mean?" Dr. Tongai took
a sip of his black coffee, very calm, very cultured.

Jay envied the man that he could be so unruffled now after
being called all those vile names and being attacked. It hadn't
fazed the doctor half as much as it should have. He was still a
man who was secure in himself, secure in who he was. The
doctor said, "You're suggesting I might be more interested in a
client if he were a gay man?"

Jay shrugged. It was exactly what he'd been implying,
although it seemed a terribly rude accusation when the doctor
put it in words.

Tongai gave a little half smile. "It's only natural for human
beings to be interested in those who have similarities to
themselves. I suppose I do take a special interest, have a special
fondness for those clients of mine who are gay or bisexual. I'll
make no apologies. Of course, it's even more rare for clients to
expressly come out to me in this country, the laws being what
they are."

"It was the laws that were the last straw for me. The laws
that made me do it."

"Do it? You mean the suicide attempt?"

Jay raised his brows in a yes gesture. "My boarding school
days were over. My dad was dead, my mother in hospital, and I
was expected to go back to a country where the stuff I did with
Arlan could get me killed. I was still a kid. I was barely
eighteen."

"And now you're twenty-one?"

Jay shrugged and nodded.

"If I remember correctly, your family expected you to come
here when your high schooling was over. You didn't want to.
Your uncle prepaid for sessions with me, but you didn't show
up for the final month of them."

"Yeah, well, he didn't have to be doing that, for a start. Kind of crazy when Arlan and I inherited so much money I could have paid for my own damn counseling. *If* I'd wanted any."

"He's a good man, Chitavati, and a fine lawyer."

"Uncle Chit. Yeah." He took another bite of his croissant. The doctor simply waited. Jay finished his mouthful and sighed. "I was actually going to keep visiting you. I liked you. But once I mentioned Arlan, you kept pushing me. I mean, I knew you wanted me to talk about that some more. I didn't want to then. And I don't want to now. Drink your coffee."

Dr. Tongai took his glasses off and polished them on his shirt. His patience was as irritating as a sore tooth. But the warm chocolate and pastry in Jay's mouth and the great coffee was starting to put him in a better mood. His headache was receding. He sighed again. "You *really* want to have a session here, Doc?"

"I didn't say that. You said it. Are you sure it's me who wants to talk?"

Jay shook his head in frustration. August's face flashed in his imagination. He set his croissant down and put his head in his hands. He could use someone to talk to about *her.*

Dr. Tongai began to sip his coffee. Moonlight shone through the window onto his blue-black skin.

"Fine. It was a long time ago." Jay shrugged. "I can talk about it. Funny thing is, if I hadn't admitted to Uncle Chit that it was a suicide attempt, no one ever would have even known that's what it was."

"Hypothermia. You stayed out in the snow outside your boarding school, if I recall correctly? No jacket. You were hospitalized."

"I hated that school in Christchurch. I hated being different. I hated having to leave school and not knowing what the hell to do with myself. Arlan and I had planned to return to Zimbabwe. Same-sex relationships used to be considered okay here, even fortunate, especially among the Shona. But once those new laws came in..."

"Those laws Mugabe passed about homosexuality?"

"Kissing, handholding, even hugging someone of the same sex are all illegal under Mugabe's new laws. I couldn't handle reading about it. It made it all worse."

"Made all what worse?"

Jay felt his face flush. "Everything. Dad's death, Mum's coma, the fact that I was..."

"Gay?"

"I'm *not* gay."

Dr. Tongai raised his brows. Jay made himself say the other hated word. "I'm bi."

The doctor waited. Jay knew it was a shrink's way, to leave him to do the talking, that he wasn't necessarily judging. But he felt defensive anyway. "*I am.*"

He thought of August. Her sweet smile, the light flush to her cheeks when she was aroused or embarrassed. Her passion for the animals she studied. He admired her. For the first time ever, he'd thought about having a woman as his wife, not because it would make him normal, but because he wanted *her*. "There's a woman."

The doctor remained silent.

"There *is* a woman. This is not a phase. This is not a stage of pretending to be bi before I 'come out'. I *like* women. I want *this* woman."

"I see." Dr. Tongai took another sip of coffee.

Even thinking about August's smile did crazy things to his pulse. If he'd ever had any doubt that he was bi, August had changed that completely and forever. Embarrassed, Jay shifted to adjust the front of his pants. One thought of August made his cock rigid.

"So does Arlan know? Have you told him about this woman?"

"Yeah, he knows. He's okay with it. The problem is, she knows about me and Arlan. She caught us...together."

"I see."

"It's a mess, Doc. I've fallen in love with her. She has these soft gray eyes, and she's super intelligent like you, a PhD. She's..." He put his face in his hands and mumbled between his fingers. "I get the freakin' wedding march playing in my head thinking about her. It's fucking insane."

"Are you sure that's not..."

"No. I know what you're thinking. I know what your type thinks. It's not about wanting to be straight."

Tongai's lips quirked. "You're making some assumptions about me. Why do you think you're doing that?"

Jay shrugged.

"So what have you said to Arlan about this? You said you were still living with him?"

"He's in love with her too."

"Oh."

Jay lifted his face from his hands and laughed. He knew the doctor was being a doctor, trying not to make any judgmental or leading comments, but Tongai was shocked. Jay could see it in his eyes.

"So that's another problem?"

Jay ran a hand over his head. "That bit's actually okay. Arlan isn't mad at me. We're still friends. It's just this woman, August. She didn't know I was involved with Arlan. I kept it from her. She caught us together. It was horrible."

"So now she's angry?"

"Yeah, probably...shocked. Disgusted, I guess. I left the house when she caught us. Went to the Mopane Tree."

"So what are you going to do?"

Jay shrugged. His stomach felt awful, greasy. "I'll hang out here with you for a while. Maybe I'll..." Jay stroked his bristly jaw. It had been way too long since he'd had a shave. "Could I stay with you? Stay at your house for a while?"

"Why would you need to stay with me?"

"I just need time to think. If I wasn't using protection spells, Arlan and I would be in jail by now, living together like we do. I worry, Doc, you know, I don't think my magic is so good I couldn't fuck up, leave a gap in the protection spell. And even if it wasn't illegal, everyone at work would hate me if they knew. You get that? Even August hates me now. I'm sure she does."

Tongai smiled sympathetically. "I just don't see that prolonging your confrontation with the two people you have feelings for is going to help you any."

"I love this woman." He remembered their last kiss and how it had gone from sweet to sensual to mind blowing.

"So you break it off with Arlan. Simple."

"No. No. It's not... I can't do that." Jay put his hands to his head. "You said you never believed the half-fae were anything but kooks. So you don't know about the kind of relationships they...we have."

"What do you mean?"

"Never mind." Jay finished his coffee. "Fae have a different idea of love and relationships from mortals. It's just different."

"Is your friend Arlan a half-fae as well?"

"Actually, only quarter-fae. One grandparent."

"Does he have magic like you?"

"Yeah. No. Not like me. He has magic, but he can't control it at all, so he can't do much with it. It just kind of comes upon him. He's involved in this stuff... He's a Warrior of the Light. He has a calling to do good to help people. He's been fighting some of the witch doctors in his city."

"The wealthy ones? I always considered them scam artists."

"We think they have some magic. They're getting it from somewhere. Unfortunately, the wealthy ones aren't helping people with their powers."

"I see. Well, you have some big issues to work on here."

"That's why I asking to stay with you. Just until I get my head sorted." He wiped his mouth with a napkin from the table. "But forget it." He threw the napkin down. "I'll go to a hotel."

The doctor raised a finger. "One week, Jay. One week you stay with me. Then you go home and face your friends."

He smiled. He had his debit card in his wallet. Staying away from the mess at home for a week would suit him just fine.

Adrenaline pumped through August's body, her lungs stung, and her ribs ached from pushing air violently in and out, but she wouldn't stop running.

With your tiny legs, you better run as fast you can, because she'll easily catch you. She always catches you.

She'd not had the nerve to check behind her. But that didn't mean Duvessa hadn't found some silent way to chase after her. Visions from the past flashed in her mind. A tiny Gus, age six, seven, eight, nine, running, running from her mother, heart slamming in her chest, until she ran into a corner of the mansion and was beaten or lassoed by magic before she could get to the front door.

This time, she'll kill you. This time, she'll actually do it.

Panic gripped her belly at the sound of a rustling bush behind her. She *had* to keep running. She would aim for the river, where her scent might mix with the scents of other creatures.

Yellow grass rippled like waves ahead of her down to the Zambezi. The scent of the river was strong, and the spoor of various animals—hoof prints and paw prints—lay in the mud before her.

Don't breathe too loud, run, run.

She swore as the low heel of her shoe broke off. Kicking her feet free of them, she kept running. Now prickles stung, making every step like fire.

Ahead, dozens of birds of prey feasted on the carcass of a rhino. August veered sharply to the right, avoiding, the gorging birds that barely reacted to her small form running past them, so intent were they on their meal.

Unlike in New York, the dark of night here fell with the suddenness of a closing curtain.

August grappled in her bag for the small flashlight Kruger had given her. She switched it on as she ran, swiveling the flashlight left and right in search of night creatures whose eyes would glow like reflectors in the bright beam. As scared as she was of her mother, there was no point in ending up being attacked by a wild animal.

Her sight blurred as sweat dripped into her eyes. She lifted her hands to wipe it away and pitched forward into the grass, letting out a scream. Someone had grabbed her ankle.

She tugged again. Her hands went to the turquoise pendant around her neck, clutching its smooth surface.

A force compelled her to hold it as tightly as she could.

Chapter Twenty-Three

Jay awoke with a flicker of fear in his gut. Moonlight shone against closed eyelids. With a groan, he blinked and stared up at the open window. Finally, he swore and swung himself out of bed, grappling with the floor-to-ceiling mosquito netting. The hairs on his neck began to prickle. His sense of foreboding made him wish he had his nine-millimeter Glock 17, or at least his extendable baton. Why had he brought nothing with him when he left?

Because you were making love before you slammed out of the house, dumbass.

He pulled the shorts he'd left on the floor of Tongai's spare room back on. The horrible feeling of fear increased. Must be an intruder. He froze and stopped to listen. Crickets and cicadas; the grunt of a hippo mocked him with its deep belly laugh. He pushed the bedroom door open and crept down the thickly carpeted hall.

The door of the doctor's bedroom was open, and the man was peacefully snoring. Jay peered in on him and smiled. He really was a likable guy, and wise. Jay sighed.

He stood for a while just listening to Tongai's snores and the other night noises. The irrational, illogical lancet of fear, of foreboding, slid further into his stomach. A sudden sense of claustrophobia came over him, making him desperate to just get outside and into the night.

He flung the front door open and inhaled the sweet, dry night air. He could hear small night creatures skittering across the grass, and the eerie whoop of a hyena. Blood roared in his ears, and sweat beaded on his brow. His body became so hot that he pulled his shirt off and threw it on the ground.

Searing pain sliced across Jay's back. He doubled over, falling onto the grass, gasping. Shock at what was happening had him shivering. The tearing pain came again, and he could barely breathe. The sensation was like a gang of trolls hammering spikes into his joints. His body convulsed again. He let go, slowly allowing his wings to unfurl. He hadn't done this since he was a child flying with his mother at her urgings. He'd had no need for it. Flying might be fun for full-blooded fae, but the pain of wings coming out was something most half-fae tried to avoid.

He knew he needed to do this now, though. Some psychic sense had him sure his mates were in trouble.

At first his wings were crinkled and flat. Clenching his teeth against the pain, he bent backward in an acrobatic position to pump blood into them and help them flesh out.

His wings had not come out since childhood. Since before his mother's coma. He'd flown with her a few times, a rare activity because of the extreme pain it caused half-fae.

Looking around, he laughed to see how he'd startled a poor family of baboons.

Fear firing his blood, he began pumping his wings hard, so hard that he powered up into the air, up, up, up, until he was higher than the trees. He remembered being a tiny child beating his little wings against the wind, but now it was the dry season in Zimbabwe, and his flight path was easy.

He followed the faint trail. The trail left by the scent of evil, of dark fae and sinister magic. Instinct told him something or someone had ensnared his mates, and he could smell their magic now. He moved his wings at a faster speed now to fly higher and higher. It was important he get high enough that no pure mortal would see him and get a shock or call the media. They didn't need that crap. Rather than go through the potential pain of trying to shrink his form as well, he hummed his invisibility spell.

Thank God for the full moon. Cold and silver, it soothed the fire in his back and the ache in his wings.

Stronger than the pain in his wings and the fear in his gut was the agony in his soul.

Whatever danger his mates were in now was his fault. The image of August's shocked face when she caught them kissing flashed in his mind again. He'd been such a *goddamned* pussy. If he hadn't run out on them, she'd be safe now from whatever was after her, or had her, safe from whatever it was that every instinct in his body screamed out he had to save her from.

He continued flying until he had a panoramic view of the Zambezi below him, silvered in moonlight.

He'd give anything to hold August again, to inhale her sweet, feminine scent. Whenever he was alone, he could think of nothing but her moans when he and Arlan made love to her, the sweet taste of her passion, the memory of ecstasy on her face. His dick ached, and he swore at the stupidity of getting turned on in this situation.

And now both of his mates were in danger. All his senses howled that they were. But it was August he flew to rescue now. He focused on thoughts of her with all his strength in his quest to find her... He could almost taste her sweet essence on the tip of his tongue. How could he have ever doubted that she was his true mate? And if he had one fated mate, then... They both had to be. It hit him like a blinding flash that he was truly in love with both of them.

Within his mind, he saw another strange light shimmering like fireflies and irresistibly beautiful. This was more than a stray daydream vision. Somewhere on the earth, this strange light was real, and he had to find it.

August tugged and scratched once again at the wire noose that had pulled around her ankle. Her eyes watered with pain and frustration, blurring her vision. Wire cut into the flesh of her ankle, hurting her terribly so she couldn't think.

Once she was able to see clearly against she noticed a pearly luminescence shining on the grass and on the little stones around her.

Confused, she glanced down at her necklace and saw that it was glowing. Then she realized she was glowing too. Gasping, she clutched at the necklace.

My fae magic.

She had never known, never believed she had *this* kind of power.

August turned to face the car and toppled over into the grass, screaming as her flesh tore on the poacher's wire noose.

They drove the Land Cruiser right up near the Zambezi. Moonlight danced on the surface of the river. Rather than the Lexus, her mother sat at the wheel of Kruger's vehicle, bathed in the glow of August's own magic. She had the door open now. In the backseat sat a large man, someone a lot larger than Kruger.

Duvessa climbed out of the car, went to the back and opened the trunk to take out a backpack. August struggled to right herself, her heart slamming like an imprisoned bird. She turned her head, determined to face her mother, determined not to cower, and set her lips in a grim line. The man stepped out of the car, and *yes*, it *was* him, Willem, a vicious brute of a half-fae. He'd often been around her childhood home, laughing when her mother "punished" her. The man acted as a bodyguard of sorts to Duvessa.

Dread formed a knot in her belly, but she clenched her jaw and blinked back tears, determined not to give Duvessa any more satisfaction.

Her mother looked as flawless as ever in the moonlight, her hair lustrous, her bone structure perfect. August knew it was the fae glamourie her mother used that made her so tall and stunning, yet still she felt a twinge of envy. She muttered a curse as her mother came to stand beside her.

"You should have known I'd be watching you in my scrying bowl, and I'd catch you sooner or later. I had to change cars for the rough terrain out here."

"I hate you."

Duvessa rolled her eyes. Then she knelt to examine August's ankle. She opened the backpack, and to August's surprise, she took out what looked like a first aid kit. Duvessa opened the kit and took out some bandages. "This isn't a good time for you to be hating on me, considering you're caught and bleeding, and I'm the only one here to help you. Ironic that you were caught by a poacher's snare."

"What do you mean ironic?"

"I mean with all your crazy animal do-gooding and what not." Duvessa examined the wire noose.

"I'm a zoologist, Mother, an academic and wildlife conservationist, working to protect endangered species. You still don't even understand what I do for a living, do you?"

"I get what you do." Her mother grappled around in the large backpack and finally just picked it up and shook it upside down. Some sandwiches wrapped in plastic and a water bottle fell out onto the ground, along with what looked like a makeup case, a wallet and a pair of wire cutters. "Ah there they are." She picked up the wire cutters. "I came prepared to help free you from this, so don't do anything silly like start running in the dark again. You're glowing, for one thing, and Willem has long legs. You won't stand a chance running from him with your stumpy little legs. He'll catch you quick."

Against her will, tears slid silently down her cheeks.

Duvessa shook her head. "Why the fuck are you crying and acting like I'm going to kill you?"

"You tried to kill me once before."

"Oh, I did not. Not really. I always knew you had the immortal gene. It was simply a test to make sure, and to kill your pathetic father."

"You're a psychopath."

Duvessa stopped cutting and glanced up at August. "That's a very rude thing to say. And very silly considering it's a term that relates to mortals."

It was on the tip of August's tongue to apologize, and then she shook herself. Her mother could always twist things and make her feel in the wrong.

"I am not a psychopath. I'm dark fae. I'm self-interested. It's the realism necessary to live successfully as a half-fae in the mortal world." Duvessa went back to cutting the wire. "A trait you lack and would benefit from cultivating."

"Just let me go, Mother. I'm not going to fake pretending we have a relationship anymore. Just let me go."

Duvessa finished cutting the wire off and put the tool back in her bag, then began to spread cream on August's wound.

"Why are you doing that? Tending my wounds so I'll be pretty for the sex magic? It's not going to happen. I will not have sex with Johan."

Duvessa sighed. "Listen to me. Stop and think a bit. I mean yes, I treated you badly as a child, but it was all for a good reason. Just look at you." She gestured to the glow. "You have plenty of power and not the sense to use it properly. By damaging your self-esteem, I did my best to keep you from getting involved in all the Warrior of the Light garbage and ruining all my plans for wealth, for this family, for *your* family... You never approved, yet you had a *luxurious* childhood."

"You provided a luxurious home, when you weren't torturing me, yes."

"You had *everything*. You had a beautiful bedroom, a spa pool, a tennis court, a swimming pool, a huge entertainment center. I can't understand why you even left. I didn't kick you out. You left. And went to live in some shoebox you could afford with your 'job'. Anyway, I stopped punishing you years ago, so I don't know why you're acting so scared of me." Duvessa wrapped the bandage around August's ankle and began humming a healing spell.

The skin under her ankle bandage began to knit itself back together. "Stopped punishing me for what? All I did was study and get good grades. What the hell did I ever *deserve* to be punished for?"

"For choosing the light path."

"Mother..."

"*No.* You listen to me. I was so proud of you when you were tiny. You had so much magic potential, and then you chose to squander it, so I cut it off. You would have ruined me and our family financially, and I would not allow it."

The light radiating from August danced on the metal body of the Land Cruiser. She rubbed her temples. As much as she hated to ask Duvessa for help, she needed her mother's knowledge.

Duvessa picked up the water bottle and took off the lid, which she dropped in the bag, then took a sip of water. August looked at the package of sandwiches lying on the ground, and her stomach growled. She wondered what kind they were. Her mother put the makeup case, the wallet and sandwiches back in the backpack.

"Mother, why am I glowing?"

Her mother pursed her lips and rested her chin on her fist. At last, she shook her head. "I don't know."

"*You* don't know?"

"It's some kind of strong magic, obviously. Magic you've always possessed but that I suppressed by damaging your self-esteem. But you shouldn't just be glowing with power like that." Duvessa's brow wrinkled. "I've seen a glow like that with newborn babies." She stepped back and observed August critically. "It relates to new things. Something new is occurring.

New power is collecting itself." She shook her head. "Well, hopefully all that power will be useful for the sex magic."

August glanced at Willem. If she ran, they'd catch her, tie her up and throw her in the Land Cruiser. All she could do was try to reason with Duvessa. She swallowed hard against the lump in her throat, trying to find the right words. "Let us go now. Let Arlan go, and let me go." It was all she could think of to say.

Duvessa folded her arms and pouted. "I don't understand why you suddenly have a problem with the sex magic. You were *happily* doing it before you found out it was something your *mother* wanted you to do. You were more than happy. I saw you in my scrying bowl. You were consumed with lust."

Heat crawled up her neck, and she swore under her breath in exasperation. "Mother, forcing Arlan and me to sleep with Johan would be rape."

Duvessa's mouth suddenly dropped open, and August turned to see what she was staring at. A huge male lion stood glaring, his golden eyes glowing like laser beams in the night. He must have padded his way over to them on velvet-soft paws.

August knew lions. She had studied them for enough years to know the worst thing you could do when faced with one was run. The best thing to do was freeze, to stay completely still and wait for the giant beast to decide you weren't a threat.

But Duvessa screamed and ran for the car. She leapt into the open boot of the Land Cruiser. The lion crossed the distance to the car in an instant.

She wondered why her mother wasn't using magic and realized with relief that terror had frozen her abilities.

"Back! Get back from me. I'll use magic on you," Duvessa threatened.

Her mother's legs stuck out of the trunk of the car. August winced as hooked yellow claws ripped into flesh. Duvessa screamed. The lion pulled at her so she fell back out of the car and slammed onto the ground, moaning with pain.

Then August noticed Willem crawling along the ground. Something shone in his hand. He didn't have a hunting rifle, but he had a pistol. Shock galvanized her and filled her with a diamond-hard hatred.

Oh no, you fucking don't.

She loved Jay. She loved Arlan. This lion was either one of the beasts she loved or her lover Arlan himself. August carefully slid the metal bar she'd stolen from the gym out of her bag. Duvessa's scream's sounded like shrieks from a horror film, but she couldn't feel sympathy. When her mother struggled to sit up, the lion placed his giant dinner-plate-size paw on her belly.

Though her mother had for the most part healed her ankle, residual pain made her wince a little with each cautious step, as she crept up behind Willem, who was gaining on the unsuspecting lion.

That lion could be Arlan if he's escaped somehow, and Willem's going to shoot him.

Willem crawled on his belly like a snake. August was right behind him. Fury had risen within her in a momentous wave, all the years of being at the mercy of Duvessa and this man, her bodyguard. Years of denied love.

She brought the metal bar down on Willem's head. *Crack.* She felt the jarring impact all the way up her arms, heard the brute's curse through the rush of blood to her head, and brought the bar down again. *Crack.* All the years of hating her mother's minions from the half-fae network filled her with rage. "No, you will not shoot one of the men I love." *Crack.* "You creatures will not ruin my life anymore." She could barely hear the man's moans over the sound of her own rapid breathing. *Crack!* "You will not harm me. You will not harm my lover." *Crack.*

All the years, she'd suffered abuse, and no one had helped her, no one had protected her from her mother.

Willem had ceased moaning and struggling to right himself.

"For God's sakes, August, you'll kill him! Hit the damn *lion* with that thing. Get him *off* me," Duvessa screamed.

A wave of nausea rolled through August at what she'd done. She shook from head to toe, but she had saved Arlan.

"Willem's still breathing. You haven't killed him. Stop standing there like a little idiot and get this beast *off* me."

The lion cuffed Duvessa's head and stepped away. He stared into August's eyes. Duvessa sat in the grass, her back against a tree, tears streaming down her face as she grasped her mauled knee.. She muttered, "I'll get you, you bastard."

The dark fae wiped at her tears angrily with her fist. She set her jaw and began humming. Fire rippled across the ground, her mother's fire-fae power. Her dark magic.

No, no, no.

Fire snaked across the ground. Some of the flames looked like blue tongues tasting the grass, until the lion was surrounded by a circular wall of flame on all sides.

August screamed, but gold sparks flew from Arlan's coat. His own magic.

Arlan's magic fought back, repelling the flames so they only formed a ring around him and didn't scorch his fur. But the ring of fire seemed enough to trap him where he stood. Duvessa's humming had changed pitch, and August understood Duvessa was now healing her leg wounds.

August strode across the grass to get closer to Arlan. But when she got close, the heat became unspeakable, intolerable. "Arlan!" she cried out to him in fear, wondering what she could do to set him free from the circle. She didn't notice the hands on her until it was too late. She struggled wildly, kicking and screaming. Duvessa, so much taller and stronger, took the thrashing in stride.

Her mother yanked her hands roughly behind her back and bound them with what felt like cord. August thrashed and kicked, cursing herself. Arlan roared with rage every time he tried to approach the heat, but he couldn't breach the flames.

Her mother lifted August, easily carrying her toward the trunk of the car. August looked up. High above her in the distance, a winged figure appeared silhouetted against the moon. She gasped in surprise as the figure began to glow. Instinct made her glance around at Arlan behind her. Yes, he too was surrounded by a haze of gold. All three of them glowed with power, like the pendant around her neck. The pain of craning her neck to look at Arlan made her look back up at Jay. His wings were beautiful. As he powered toward earth, they sparkled with every color of the rainbow. Jay had true-fae wings? That was something her mother had never managed. Duvessa had always been furious that she didn't possess the power of flight.

Her mother shrieked as Jay came flying toward her, and August fell upon the grass. Duvessa backed into the Land Cruiser, her hands in front of her. She closed her eyes and began an intense humming.

Jay dropped to the ground beside August and began to untie her. Seeing the horror on Jay's face, she turned to glance at what he was looking at. Her gut pitched as her mind struggled to process the sight.

Behind them stood an enormous salamander, perhaps seven feet tall. The reptilian skin of the beast glowed red like hot coals, its malevolent eyes a shimmering jet black. A peppery musk emanated from the reptile, surrounding them until they all began to splutter and cough. The monster breathed out a torrent of dark dust until their throats burned with pain. And August remembered something just in time.

"It might be illusionary, false fire magic, Jay. That thing isn't *real*. Don't believe in it, and it won't kill you."

She said it just in time as fire poured out of the creature's lungs, replacing the illusionary dust. Her mother had enough fire magic to create small fires. She'd burned August in the past. But huge fires like that, and huge salamanders and snakes... No way. Duvessa was only half-fae; it just wasn't possible. This was an illusion.

Despite the knowledge, the pain of the heat all but swallowed her whole. She rolled, rolled and rolled to get away, to try to kill the illusionary flames that seared her body.

Not real, not real, not real.

When she stopped rolling, glowing red snakes surrounded her.

Not real, not real, just her mother's stupid nasty, illusionary magic.

"You're both going to die." Duvessa laughed.

"Who's got the gun, asshole?"

August whipped around to see Jay had Willem's pistol. But he had it trained on the snake closest to her and not on her mother. "No, Jay. Focus on her. On *her.*"

But Jay seemed frozen with shock at the sight of the reptiles. Gradually the creatures transformed and coalesced into one enormous cobra with a huge wedged-shaped head and a tongue that flickered in and out. The snake's eyes glowed with the fire power of its fire magic. It reared toward them, breathing more dark dust.

August's fingernails made half-moon shapes in the sides of her arms. Every nerve in her body thrilled with elemental fear, even as her mind knew this was not real. Her mother wasn't powerful enough for it to be real.

The dust burned her throat, but it didn't knock her out.

It's not real. The monster's not real, so his dark dust isn't real.

Jay's gun tracked it. He was going to waste a bullet.

"No. Point it at her, at *her,*" August shouted.

The snake reared up on its coils and spread its neck in a threatening display. A red glow outlined each of its scales. The eye-shape pattern on the back of its hood was mesmerizing.

Through the smoke and sulfur, Jay finally pointed Willem's pistol at her mother.

Her mother's lip gave a nearly imperceptible quiver. The dark fae's jaw twitched. She'd *never* seen that expression on her mother's face before. She'd seen her angry, she'd seen her excited, but she'd never seen this. This was Duvessa Peak, scared.

The sun punched a little gold through a gap in the clouds. At last, the long night was ending. Jay thumbed back the hammer on the little pistol and aimed at the fire fae, while his body screamed with pain from the flames. The ring of fire remained around Arlan's lion form. The dark fae struggled to maintain it. She seemed to him to be losing her energy.

Duvessa backed toward the Zambezi, getting closer and closer to the water. "You won't shoot me."

Arlan roared from behind the flames. Incredulous, Jay lifted an eyebrow. "Give me one reason why not?" But he knew why he wasn't pulling the trigger.

"I'm *her* mother." She aimed a finger at August. "You love *her*, don't you? So you can't go shooting her mother."

"You were kidnapping her, you *crazy witch*. She doesn't need you for a mother."

You've never hurt a woman in your life. But she's a monster. Just shoot her.

Conflicting voices raged in his head.

Duvessa sighed and rolled her eyes. "My plan was simply to take her home and make her *behave*. I know what's best for her. I'm her mother."

He raised the pistol and pointed it at her head. "*Not* good enough. From what I heard, you were about as crap a mother as a person could be."

Duvessa sniffed. "I'm sure I inherited the immortal gene anyway. You won't kill me."

"Then it doesn't matter if I shoot you."

The dark fae spluttered even as she backed toward the water, her knee still bleeding from the damage Arlan had done with his claws. *Silly woman used her magic up on threatening us with fake serpents, and fire, and forgot to heal her own knee.*

Duvessa glared at Jay. "You're not the type to shoot a woman."

She had him. Even if she was dark fae.

And a child abuser.

He cocked the pistol. "*Wrong.*"

Duvessa held up her hands. "I have magic that can help *him*. Arlan."

"Pffft. That fire you got around him is gonna die out. You can't maintain it much longer. You're losing energy."

"Not that. I don't mean *that*." Desperation turned her voice to a whine. "I can help him control his shifting, dammit! *Listen* to me." Seeing the surprise on Jay's face, Duvessa grew more confident. "I've been watching you for some time, scrying on the three of you."

"Why?"

"I have a right to keep track of my own daughter's whereabouts."

"So what does any of that have to do with Arlan's shifting?"

"I can take the bulk of the curse off him."

Keeping the gun on her, Jay glanced at Arlan behind the flames.

The curse removed. Arlan no longer at the mercy of random shifting. Arlan's heart's desire fulfilled?

He glanced over at August.

"She spent years studying everything about magic. She could lay her hands on him." August shook her head. "She's pretty clever with magic. Hell, some people say she's a genius."

Jay didn't miss the touch of irony and bitterness in her voice. He ached thinking of all the pain she'd suffered. The envelope of light around August's turquoise pendant brightened. "Arlan needs this, Jay, doesn't he? He needs control over his shifting."

"Right, what is that magic pouring from her necklace? And why is she glowing? Can you answer me that?"

Duvessa froze. "Fuck," she whispered. "That's the blue spirit stone."

"What does that mean?"

Duvessa's jaw clenched. "It means the little do-gooder has found her fated mates. *That's* what it means. I've spent my whole life looking for mine, or hoping one of my *obedient* daughters would find theirs, and *she* finds them. God dammit! Anyway, I can take part of the curse off Arlan, okay? So don't shoot." She sounded desperate. "You can stop pointing that goddamn *thing* at me." She began to hum.

Jay still didn't trust her, and as great as the temptation was, he didn't turn to check out Arlan when she started to hum. He kept the gun trained on her, and maybe that was what made her humming so frantic.

The louder Duvessa hummed, the brighter the red light pouring from her hands became. When Jay dared a glance out of the corner of his eye, a rooster-red halo of light surrounded Arlan's head.

Arlan spluttered and coughed. He was in his human form at last, and the wall of flames that had surrounded him flickered and died in an instant. Duvessa had stopped exerting power over the illusion.

"*Jay*. Fuck! Look up."

Jay turned. August stared up at the sky. He followed her gaze to see pale blue and orange streaks stretching across the horizon.

Morning.

Then a hunting rifle flew through the air toward Duvessa.

Jay stepped back. "What the fuck?"

"She must have magicked it from the trunk of her car," August shouted.

The hunting rifle did a nice swirl in a circle before it landed in Duvessa's hand.

Chapter Twenty-Four

Clever. The little swirl the gun did through the air was a nice touch. A little flourish to show off her power before sealing his doom. In the distance, Jay could see a large troop of about thirty baboons loping along on their hands and feet. He fought not to give in to the primal fear crawling in his gut.

Duvessa slapped at a mosquito on the back of her neck with her free hand. "Oh, August, August." She shook her head in mock sadness. "You should have known better. Really, you should have." Her mouth formed a satisfied smirk as she aimed the rifle at Jay.

"So you were faking. You couldn't take the curse off Arlan," August shouted. "You aren't really powerful enough to remove a curse like that?"

Her daughter's desperate attempt to distract her from Jay only made Duvessa smirk. "No. I took the curse off your sainted Arlan. He won't be transforming into a lion anytime soon unless he chooses to. I know my kind's magic. Silvara's more powerful than I am, I must admit it. I wish to God I could pull off a curse like that. But, yeah, I know how to undo that kind of thing."

"You can't shoot Jay. I get that you're furious with him, but you can see now, the three of us are fated mates." August clutched the glowing pendant in her hand for emphasis.

There was a tightening under Duvessa's eyes. August spoke quickly "You want the sex magic to work, right? Well, trying to fix Arlan and me up with Johan would *ruin* everything. You *have* to see that now. The three of us have far more power together. Come on, Mom. You know I'm right."

Jay could read the combination of avarice and envy in the dark fae's expression. She wanted their power, and their money and their...their love connection. She craved that for herself.

Duvessa was furious. And she was also trapped. Because surely August was right.

Duvessa didn't lower the rifle.

"Mother if you want the sex magic to work, if you want to find the witch doctors' tower, then you'll let us go and let us do this by ourselves, *our way.* You'll know when it's done via your scrying, and you can do..." August waved her hand, "...whatever dark magic you have to do in relation to it. Killing Jay is the last thing you want to do, if you ever want to see that tower."

Her mother was going to kill them all. She would never feel Arlan's arms around her again, or Jay's. She would never know their love. It struck her that the two of them made her feel whole, made her feel real, in a way she never had before. Even the universe was trying to tell the three of them that they were fated, that they were meant to be together. But her mother would snuff the life out of their union before it even began.

In the distance, an elephant and the mopane trees were black silhouettes against the red-gold dawn of the morning sky. Her mother's beautiful Grace Kelly face didn't change, but her lips grew white.

Jealousy.

Duvessa blew her bangs off her face. "I haven't found even one of my fated mates."

"I know, Mother. I'm sorry."

"My father never let me have pretty things. You know that, August? He never let me have anything cool. I would have worn shabby clothes to school. I would have been an outcast if I hadn't been able to magic up a few things." She slapped a mosquito off her cheek. "I'm never going back to being poor." Duvessa's lip quivered, something August had never seen before. "You think you're so clever, don't you. Your fated mates are billionaires." She gestured at Arlan, then at Jay with the gun. "You think you're superior to me."

"Are you in some kind of financial trouble?"

Duvessa's eyes suddenly shone with unshed tears. "I should have known better than to trust an idiot human. But he was supposed to have this great reputation for financial planning. My investments have tanked. We could lose everything."

Her mother gazed at her with such vulnerability, all her usual bravado stripped away like leaves in an autumn gale. "I'm your mother. I gave you the breath of life. You owe me."

No, I don't. But Duvessa held the hunting rifle directly at Jay.

Bile rose in August's throat. She gave herself a little leeway because her mother was terrifying to nearly everyone. But she was so tired of kowtowing to Duvessa's crazy demands, to backing down and submitting. "I do owe you, Mother. We will do what you want. Johan just wasn't the right person. Jay is the right person."

"Jay *threatened* me with a pistol. Why would I trust him now?"

From the grass, Willem gave a whimper.

"And look at what you did to poor Willem. You could go to jail for that. I never thought you had that in you."

"There are two witnesses here who will say it was self-defense." Jay's voice was surprisingly languid.

"It wasn't self-defense. Willem was trying to kill a man-eating lion with that pistol."

Jay glanced over at Arlan. "I saw Willem about to kill a man."

"You lying piece of filth."

"*Duvessa.*" Arlan wiped the soot from his forehead with his shirt. "Willem is still alive. Put the gun down and call an ambulance on your cell phone, and he might be saved. In fact..." Jay bent and pulled a cell phone out of the man's shorts. "I'll call them myself."

"Drop that fucking thing!" Duvessa pointed the gun at Jay again.

Chapter Twenty-Five

A brown-headed kingfisher flew over the river. Its shrill whistle echoed across the plains. "I said drop it." Duvessa's whisper was almost drowned out by the barks of the large troop of baboons coming their way.

Jay dropped the cell on the ground and raised his hands. "Guess you don't care about your friend after all, Duvessa."

"Never mind that for now. I need you to promise you'll help me." She waved the gun around. "I need money, dammit."

She'd seen her mother almost like this before, and this was when she got the most crazy and unpredictable. *She's cracking up. She's losing it.*

"Mother," August choked out, "we will. We want to. We want to help you. Any way we can." She consciously tried to make her voice as soft and undemanding as possible. "Please, put the gun down."

Duvessa's eyes shimmered with tears of sadness or rage, but she didn't lower the gun.

August had to think of something to distract her mother from shooting Jay. "Look at all those baboons back there, mother. Their scientific name is *Papio cynocephalus cynocephalus.* Look, they're foraging for bulbs and grass roots. They're probably drinking at the river."

"What? What are you even babbling about? You know I'm not interested in your stupid animal obsession." Duvessa didn't even turn her head. She focused on Jay. "She was always so nerdy, unappealing and short. Practically a dwarf. I didn't think any man would be interested in her. It's not right, you know. In fact, it's ridiculous, that while I'm facing bankruptcy, *she* finds her fated mates. And you two are rich as Midas." Some of her normal cunning returned to her face. "But maybe I don't even need the sex magic. Maybe I don't need to call up that stupid tower to get power and money."

August's gut clenched. Duvessa had played with identity theft in the past to illegally get her hands on extra cash, but that had been with the death certificates of already dead people. "You're talking about murdering Jay and stealing his identity? That won't work, Mother. You won't be able to kill me, for a start. You're the one who said I was immortal. You failed to kill me with that dark dust in my food as a child. You'll fail again."

A muscle twitched in her mother's jaw. "I won't fail."

August tried to make her voice soft and placating. "We can use this power to help you. Don't be jealous of us. Just let us help you."

"*Jealous.*" Duvessa whirled around and pointed the hunting rifle straight at August. "God *damn*, you ungrateful *brat.*"

The gun made a slick mechanical sound as Duvessa chambered a round. Fumbling with the safety catch, she fired.

At the last millisecond, August swerved to the side. Her shoulder stung and a screeching noise rose up behind her. The sinking in her gut hurt more than the small nick of the bullet. That her own mother would actually, really *shoot* her filled her with indescribable sadness.

August clamped a hand on her shoulder to stop the blood, and tried to ignore the pain.

Arlan raced to her side. The combination of rage at seeing her hurt and concern about the swarm of baboons fogged his mind. Only yesterday he'd read in the news about a couple of tourists attacked by baboons looking for food. He shook his head, needing to concentrate on August first. He pulled his shirt over his head and pressed it to her shoulder to stem the trickle of blood, it wasn't serious.

Lisa Whitefern

"It's just a nick. I'm okay."

Arlan nodded but kept the shirt in place. He gestured at the baboons with his other hand. "Probably river guides and tourists have made them used to humans. They know they leave food around. There are an awful lot of them but if we all leave them alone they'll leave us alone. Just let them do their thing.

Yellow baboons swarmed the Land Cruiser, climbing and jumping on the roof. Others tugged at the doors. About five others, led by a large male, were heading straight for them.

Duvessa still held the gun on them but seemed shell-shocked at the sight and sound of so many baboons. One of them, a smaller one, probably a female, grabbed the backpack lying on the ground.

"Oh, the sandwiches." August laughed.

"My wallet's in there!" Duvessa screamed, grabbing at the straps.

"Don't fight with her! She'll hurt you," August shouted over the barking.

The stupid woman continued playing tug-of-war with the baboon. "There's two hundred dollars in there."

In a blur of yellowish grey fur and fangs, the biggest male rushed at Duvessa to protect his female. Leaping and baring his fangs, he slammed her head sideways with the back of his hand, then slapped her again and again, dragging her down until he was able to bite her neck. Her low scream of pain tore through the air. Duvessa stepped backward a few times, then slipped on a small rock, shrieking and falling into the Zambezi with a splash.

It all happened so fast, Arlan could barely believe it. A hint of glistening gray-green scales rose from the water before a snout appeared. Then a crocodile grasped Duvessa's thigh in its jaws and pulled her under.

A dozen or more green-gray crocs appeared, but the dark fae was no longer in sight. She'd been dragged clear under the shimmering surface of the Zambezi.

Chapter Twenty-Six

"Are you all right?" Arlan whispered in her ear. August shuddered. Her whole body was still trembling. He'd insisted on doing everything for her since Jay had gone to work—made her a light dinner, run her a hot bath. Now she was sleepy. She loved sitting curled up like this in his lap. She stared out her bedroom's large window at the azure blue of the African sky and the panoramic view of the savannah beneath.

"Look at me."

She turned her head and met his gaze.

"Are you sore anywhere but your shoulder?" He lightly touched the edge of the bandage.

"I have some mild tinnitus from the sound of the gun going off, but that's all."

"Yeah, I've had that too, but it's not bad. Better leave off the caffeine for a while. I heard it makes it worse."

"Why can't I stop shaking? It's been hours."

Concern crossed his face. "It's hardly surprising after all you've been through, baby girl. Listen, maybe this is still the wrong time, but I need to ask you something important. Something we've talked about before."

"You can ask me anything."

"Good. Okay. Do you fully believe we're fated mates? The three of us. Or were you putting some of that on for your mother?" His voice was so sincere and full of love, it brought tears to her eyes. "Because we both just have to work on Jay now." His eyes shone with love. "We could even make the bond stronger, maybe with a wedding."

"I can't think about all that."

"I see. Okay."

But he didn't seem okay. Anxiety churned in her belly, fear that he'd misunderstood. "I don't think you *do* see. Arlan, excuse me for being a little messed up after everything that's happened. It's really not about you."

His gaze softened, and he threaded his fingers gently through her hair. "I see how much she hurt you. Every time I tell you that you're beautiful, every time Jay or I compliment you, I see in your sad smile that you don't believe us. You and Jay both keep putting off what the three of us could have together. There's no reason to put it off anymore. And I think if all three of us could commit, we could make the magic work. and save those kids." He was silent for a moment. "Do you believe I love you, August?"

She drummed her fingers on the bedside table and stared out at the darkening blue of the sky. She was in love, but she couldn't cope with his questions. "I do believe that you love me. But I have no idea where that leaves the three of us, considering Jay's issues. And it's just really difficult not to think about my mother right now. Do you understand?"

"Not really." His tone was as blunt as his words. "She's worthless."

"If it turns out she's alive, I still have to deal with her."

He gave a slight, disappointed nod. She laid her hand on his. "I do love you. When I thought for sure she was going to kill us, I..." She gulped and pushed her shoulders back. "I thought about how you'd never touch me again. How I'd never have either of you touch me again." She shook her head. "I swear I was more bothered about that than I was scared of dying."

"You're immortal."

"We don't know that for sure. My mother said she couldn't kill me with dark dust, but I don't know for sure that I'm immortal. But, anyway, I do love both of you. I do want to help you make the magic work. But until I know what's happened to my mother and whether Willem is still alive, I'm not going to be able to concentrate on anything else."

He pulled her into his arms, pressed a kiss to her cheek and shuddered out a breath of his own. "Let us love you, hon."

She couldn't find words. A tight knot twisted in her stomach, wanting release. It wasn't easy for her to find words to respond to his compliments or his protestations of love.

She heard Jay's footsteps. "Jay's home." Arlan nodded. "Arlan, whatever happens, I don't want to come between you and Jay. I couldn't stomach that, okay?"

"That's not..." He trailed off when Jay entered the room.

The foolish dread that had been waiting launched itself into her throat. "You're home. What did the police say? Did they manage to track anything down? Did you ring the hospital about Willem?"

A muscle in Jay's jaw twitched. He sat beside her, touched her arm. "Yeah, we did. Sorry, baby, it's as we thought."

"They're both dead?"

He nodded. "Willem died before the ambulance even arrived at the hospital. He's well known to the police as a thug. They seemed to believe me that Willem was struck on the head in self-defense. They just want to take your statement and Arlan's later."

"Did they find her body?"

"Yes. Apparently, it floated to the surface. At least...what was left of it. That bleeding knee of hers, I guess it attracted all the crocs to feed on her."

She brushed away her welling tears with angry fists. Arlan's arms wrapped around her from behind. He kissed the top of her head. The hot, dark scent of his body infused her senses. In her stomach, confusing emotions swirled. "I'm stupid, right? Why the fuck would I cry for her?"

Jay looked stricken. "Because she's your mother?"

August gave a hard swallow. Jay got it. She stroked the rough pattern of the bedspread with her fingertips. "I would never have stopped wanting her to love me, you know that? I'm so stupid."

"Hey." Jay grabbed her chin. "You are not stupid. She was your mother." He brushed his lips against hers, claiming her, and she melted back against Arlan, who held her in a firm, comforting embrace. Their warmth and unconditional affection for her thawed bitterness, anger, humiliation.

August leaned back, gazing up at Arlan. She bit her lip. "Obviously, this is a good thing. I won't be upset about it for long. It's just kind of a shock."

Jay nodded. "Don't blame yourself for being a loving person." A muscle in his jaw twitched. "She made her choices."

Arlan kissed the top of her head. "Dry your tears, baby. She's so not worth it."

"That's a bit insensitive, mate." Jay stood up.

Arlan let go of August and leaned back against the headboard, his eyes hooded. "You'd know."

"You're still angry with me?"

"Why did you run away last week? Why did you tear out of here and go to the pub?"

Jay gestured at August. "Are you kidding, mate? You really don't get it? She *saw* us kissing. I never meant for that to happen." Jay reached out to touch Arlan. "But things are different now."

Arlan flung Jay's hand away. "Why? I'm so sick of your bullshit."

"I thought she'd be disgusted. I thought she'd be hurt. Don't make this about what happened afterward, because how the *fuck* could I know all that was going to happen?"

Arlan's lip curled. "It's you who're disgusted. Disgusted by who you are and disgusted by *me*. Was it because my claws came out? Was that part of the reason?"

241

Jay slammed a hand on the wall above Arlan's head. "I've never been disgusted by *you*. Ever. I don't even know why you have these issues about being a were-lion. You're beautiful when you transform. And now you have control over it. Just accept who you are, man."

Arlan laughed in his face. "Really funny coming from you."

Jay's lips thinned. "Maybe, but regardless, I've never felt disgusted by you."

"Yeah, mate, you have. And maybe it's not about my being a were. Maybe it's only about wanting to fuck a man. I don't even fucking know with you, but you have all these excuses. You wanted to make this about August being disgusted. But guess what? She already *knew*. Despite everything you've done to hide it, it was *that* obvious to her that we were lovers." Arlan massaged the back of his neck, trying to relieve some of the tension in his body. "How long have we been doing this, Jay? You sleeping in my bed, and then backing off and sleeping in the spare room? You coming to me for sex and then backing off again, trying to hide what's always been between us? How long have I been letting you do this?"

Jay shrugged. "Since high school." Arlan shook his head. A world of sadness welled up in Jay's eyes. "How can I get you to forgive me?"

Arlan put his fingers to his temples. "Jay, I've always known you were my fated mate. And maybe I've been a goddam pussy letting you walk all over me, but my gut kept telling me to stick it out with you."

"But August—"

Arlan gestured at August. "Look at her necklace. Just look at it glow. You know what it means."

"That's the blue spirit stone?" Jay asked.

August fingered the glowing pendant.

"Yeah, Jay. A turquoise pendant doesn't normally have a pulsating light circling it." Arlan's voice was very sarcastic.

"That's the stone you've been talking about all these years? The one you wanted to give me."

"The one you told me you didn't want."

Jay pulled a face. "I'm a *guy*. Guys don't wear jewelry, unless they're hippies or something, I wasn't going to wear some stupid pendant."

"I know, Mr. Macho, you're so straight acting. Like I said, you're ashamed of what we do, ashamed of who you are, and ashamed of me."

August swallowed the lump in her throat. It hurt to see Arlan's pain. They both looked so fierce, so gorgeous. If they rejected her in the end, it would all be worth it just to have been with them for a while, to have had this adventure. However much her heart would break when she went back home alone, it was still *worth it.*

Jay's hand shot out to capture Arlan's face. His voice a harsh whisper, he said, "I've never been ashamed of anything about you. Of being gay or bi, yes. Of myself, yes. Nothing about you. I'm proud of everything you've become."

"Then accept what we are, Jay. Accept that we're fated mates, and we can *do* this thing."

Jay turned to August. She wanted to speak, but her voice was choked by the slam of her heart. His expression was so intense, so dark. "You really weren't upset, August?"

"Jay, I lived among half-fae a fair part of my life. A bisexual lifestyle is no shock to me." She played with her pendant. "I think Arlan's right that the three of us really are fated. And he's right that the thought of the two of you together does turn me on." She swallowed and knew her cheeks were flame red. "It turns me on a lot."

Jay brushed his lips on her forehead. Then her lovers' eyes met, and August's arousal spiked, sudden and delicious. She placed her hands on the backs of each of their heads, guiding their mouths together.

In an instant, it became a very open-mouthed, tongue-thrusting kiss. Jay grabbed Arlan's golden-brown ponytail. Arlan rocked his hips forward, his white-knuckled hands gripping Jay's shoulders. Jay, the muscles in his arms bunching, braced himself on the headboard and thrust forward.

They pulled off their shirts so she could see their flat abs. Arlan's golden skin shone in the light that streamed through the window. Jay glanced over at August. "Nearly losing you both made me realize how wrong I've been."

Arlan shrugged. "You needed time to sort yourself out. I get that it's pretty macho down at the station."

"Yeah, they wouldn't approve of this." He slipped his hand beneath Arlan's butt cheek on the bed, and August guessed he gave it a squeeze.

"Now you—" Jay gestured at August.

"What?"

"Get your fucking clothes off!"

August gasped at the savagery in his tone but didn't hesitate to obey. When he got that intimidating tone in his voice, there was no way she could resist.

August unbuttoned her blouse so that it hung at her sides, completely open. Jay's dark eyes gleamed with heat. She laughed, breaking the tension. "Have you ever seen a bra before?"

"I thought I might never see you in one again." He reached around her to pull her shirt off her arms, tossing it on the floor, unfastening her bra. He looked over at Arlan. "Get those pants off."

Arlan undid the belt of his shorts, and slid them and his underwear down his legs, and tossed them off the bed, then lay back down completely naked. Jay gazed at Arlan with lust in his eyes to match her own. This was what she'd been dreaming of. This was what she wanted. The intensity of them staring at each other made her nipples pebble.

Jay walked around to her side of the bed and sat beside her. She jumped when he suddenly lowered his head and his lips touched her breast. The sound of her blood whooshing in her ears drowned out the mild tinnitus. Her pussy throbbed, yet they'd each only looked at her and each other with desire, only touched her breast, nothing more.

"Have you ever seen such gorgeous full breasts on such a petite babe?" Jay murmured.

"No, I've never seen any tits that pretty ever before." Arlan's voice dripped with an eroticism that had her quivering. His touch caused tremors that speared straight between her legs.

Jay dipped his head and laved the taut nipple. Arlan sucked the other nipple into his mouth. She cried out, arching her back, pressing her nipples deeper into their mouths. The sensation shot straight down to her pussy, causing her to cream and her clit to throb with need.

She reached to put her hand on Jay's head and push him farther down on her breasts, but he restrained her wrist. Her heels dug into the mattress, and she rocked her pelvis against Jay's hip. She throbbed; she ached; she wanted them both.

Arlan released her breast and began licking her torso, setting every area he touched on fire. He grasped her free hand and held it to his shaft, rubbing it up and down.

Jay let go of her wrist and opened the bedside drawer, pulling out the lube and a couple of toys.

A dildo? Or a vibrator? And is that a glass plug?

"You really want to watch two men, August?"

She looked at the lube, the toy and then at Arlan.

Arlan raised an eyebrow. "Who's the toy for, mate? Not me."

Jay put them on the bed and said nothing.

"And the lube? That's for her?"

Jay shrugged, making an ultra-innocent face.

Arlan's eyes widened.

Was that fear in his eyes, or lust?

Chapter Twenty-Seven

"We've only ever—" Arlan spluttered.

"Just shut up."

"Seriously? Since when do we do anything that involves lube? Don't try to prove something, Jay."

Jay put a hand over Arlan's mouth "Shhh." He kept his voice low and dangerous. "I told you to shut up."

They'd only ever sucked each other off. Arlan had always just accepted that he wouldn't go *there*. Jay smiled. Things were going to change. After a moment, he slowly removed his hand from Arlan's mouth. Soft lips left an electric tingle of moist heat on his callused palm.

One side of Arlan's mouth quirked in a disarming way. Jay thought of how often he'd seen that smile, a thousand times or more. He knew Arlan in almost every way it was possible to know a man, mortal or fae. He knew secrets about him that Arlan didn't even know about himself. "Are you going to shut up, now?"

"Yes."

"Yes what?"

Arlan looked at him, a hint of defiance in his green-gold eyes. Jay threatened to cover his mouth again. "Yes, sir?"

Jay laughed and grabbed Arlan's ponytail. "I *knew* it. You little whore. A Dom with women, and a sub for men. Or at least, a sub for *me*." He ran his finger over Arlan's jaw. "That's what you were born to be."

Arlan swore quietly under his breath, then groaned.

Jay glanced over at August, saw the lust and need on her face. She was so *hot*, so ready for anything. He'd never met a woman he was so compatible with. He handed August the vibrator. "Here, you might need this."

He could practically feel the heat coming off August as she blushed. Laughing, he gave her thigh a squeeze and got down on his knees. He pressed his face into Arlan's flat golden abs, inhaling the hint of the savannah he suspected would never quite wash away from his lover's skin. Sunlight shone through the window, glossing the tip of Arlan's cock. Pre-come left a pearly sheen on its surface. Jay ran a finger along the marbled veins. It struck him that Arlan's cock was as pretty as any pussy. Arlan gripped Jay's shoulder, his tense muscles quivering in anticipation.

"Don't you worry about that lube for now, pet. Let's relax you first." He focused on the man he loved, running his hands up to Arlan's chest, stopping to tweak his nipples, making that beautiful shaft rear up. "You want this, mate?"

"Yes." It was a whispered growl, as though Arlan didn't really want to admit it but had to against his will.

Jay smirked. Arlan thought he wanted to be dominant and toppy, and the were-lion certainly could be with women, but when Jay wanted him, he caved every single time.

"So where do you want me? Where should I start? Here?" He began licking a trail downward, tasting sweat and salt, kissing his way down to the beautiful shaft he'd ignored for far too long. "Here maybe?" Jay grazed his fingers over Arlan's sac and winked at August. Her fists were gripping the bedspread, her eyes wide, her breathing uneven.

Arlan's head fell back on a gasp, his chest heaving with excitement. Jay flicked his finger across the pearly drop of pre-cum. "Or would you prefer here?"

Arlan managed only a grunt in response.

Jay sucked the thick hot tip into his mouth. The salty taste hit his tongue with potency. He ducked his head to suck on Arlan's balls with deep tugs.

Arlan groaned "Please," and Jay grinned, knowing that Arlan would regret begging later. Finally, he placed another open-mouthed kiss on the head. He filled his mouth with Arlan, sighed at the sheer pleasure of tasting him, sucking him. He rolled his tongue along the underside and groaned, knowing he was sending delicious vibrating sensations up and down Arlan's dick. The shaft was so smooth, hard and broad. He sucked strongly, taking as much in as he could. He'd rarely done this for Arlan, and he owed him. His eyes watered, but he continued, massaging the prominent vein on the front of Jay's cock that he knew so well.

August was a sight to see. All bouncing, oversize tits and wet, gleaming pussy, she hadn't turned the vibrator on, but she was stroking it softly between her lips, sliding it over her clit.

Jay slid his finger up her thigh until he could rub her soft, damp folds and really see her nub. He stroked her wet pleasure button, delighting in her moans and her deeper groan when he thrust his finger in. He breached her deeper, and deeper while she clamped down on him.

He started up a fast, thrusting tempo, sucking on Arlan and finger-fucking his girl, giving pleasure to both his lovers, getting painfully stiff himself but focusing only on their pleasure.

Jay concaved his cheeks, pulling Arlan farther in, creating a tight vacuum, just listening to his moans.

He stroked her thigh and pulled off Arlan to say, "Sweetie, can you help with the lube now?"

Arlan's body tensed up all over.

Jay stroked Arlan's hair. "Shh, shh, relax, mate." In a decisive move, he spread August's legs farther than they'd been, holding her thighs wide apart. He pushed the vibrator away that she'd been too shy to turn on. It fell on the bed by her side.

"What are you doing, Jay?"

"Shh." He rested his fingers on her pulsing, puffy sex lips, enjoying how ripe and needy she was. "Just getting things ready." He picked up the fat glass anal plug and stroked it over her clit, making her jerk, then plunged it into her hole, sliding it in and out. "This should get it nice and wet. Now sit up, August. You need to help me."

Seeming to recall herself, perhaps realizing how lewd she must look, August sat up, blushing. He squirted a generous amount of lube on the butt plug for good measure and handed it to August.

"Roll over, boy." Trembling, Arlan did as he was told.

Jay handed her the butt plug. Shock registered on her face as he indicated with just a lift of his brow and glance at Arlan's ass what he wanted her to do. But obediently, she pressed the tip of the glass plug to Arlan's tight star. Arlan yelped and jumped, but August placed a hand on the small of his back.

Jay watched her teasing the area in soothing circles. When she breached the rim, inserting it, Arlan's sharp intake of breath alarmed him.

"Are you okay, mate?"

"Hurts some," Arlan choked out. "Feels weird."

"Trust us, mate, it'll be all right." Jay began massaging Arlan's scalp. August glanced at him for permission to go on, and he nodded. August pressed the plug all the way in, eliciting another gasp from Arlan.

Jay's mouth watered as he took in the full picture, the broad, golden shoulders and the muscles in his back, tight bubble cheeks you could bounce a coin off of. And pretty, shy August, penetrating Arlan with the glass bulb. She picked the vibrator back up and slipped it between her closed legs again, so he could just see it peeking out.

The sounds the two of them made went right to his cock, which seemed to get even harder. He allowed himself one rub against the bed.

Lisa Whitefern

"Roll on your side, now, pet," he commanded.

Arlan shook but did as he was told, rolling over so that Jay could get a look at the long thick cock that had haunted his dreams and nightmares for so long. It seemed to stand out thicker and longer than it ever had before, if that were possible.

What a fool he'd been, afraid of what was only natural for his kind. He gave the awesome mast three lazy, teasing tugs. The sounds coming from Arlan's throat now sounded distinctly feline. Whatever Duvessa had done or not done, his golden-skinned lover was still a were to his core. Jay put his other hand on August's vibrator. When she didn't release her grip, he slapped at her hand. A high-pitched, feminine whine tore from her throat as he confiscated the toy.

Jay forced her legs wider apart, brushing his finger across her sopping clit, thrusting a finger in her tight, delicious channel, testing it, probing it, curving his finger up to brush her G-spot, rubbing her clit with his thumb, making her plead.

"Please, please, Jay,"

He shifted her hips a little, angling carefully, and in one hard shove, he pushed her snug pussy on to Arlan's shaft. His lover groaned long and loud as he sank into her wet heat.

Instinctively, the were-lion rolled on top of her without Jay having to order it. Jay moaned at the sight of the plug still clenched between the cheeks of his perfect muscular ass.

Greedy August tilted her hips and gripped Arlan's ass, trying to take in as much as she could. Jay slapped her thigh. "Be *still.*"

She whimpered. Arlan ignored him, as though his command had been only for August. He raised himself on his forearms and began to pound into her without mercy, as though trying to claim her as his own.

"I said, be still." Jay gave Arlan's bare ass several smacks until he froze in place. Again Jay smiled at Arlan's final submission to his will.

"Oh God, Jay, she's so fucking tight and hot."

250

"You'll be tighter." Jay's lips quirked as Arlan's butt muscles automatically clenched in defense. He couldn't wait any longer. He'd waited far too long. Jay tugged a little at the glass plug. "Relax, mate." He gave Arlan's ass another hard slap. Arlan stiffened, and then after a second relaxed, and Jay pulled the plug out.

"Don't pretend you don't want this," he whispered in Arlan's ear. "You've always wanted this, you little whore." He palmed the left cheek of his lover's ass. Arlan shivered, groaning and shaking with obvious need.

"But I'm gonna be polite and ask if you want it."

Arlan swore. "You're an arrogant prick, Nandoro," he hissed.

Jay continued to palm the cheek, rubbing his thumb against Arlan's hole. "Yeah, baby, you want this?"

August whimpered with frustration beneath Arlan, arching her back to try to get more of his cock.

Jay smacked him again. "You're keeping the lady waiting."

Arlan let go of a held breath. "Yes, goddamn you. I want it."

Arlan rocked, arched, and pushed his ass higher in the air, pulling away from August so she groaned.

"Spread your legs, mate."

The were-lion obeyed, spreading his legs farther apart. August moaned again, and Jay realized Arlan was stroking her clit. It made his cock jump and get even harder. He was done holding himself back. He was joining them. He would always be joining them from now on. Today was the day he would fully and completely be with those he loved.

Arlan's biceps and triceps bunched as he pushed up and back. Jay slowly parted his lover's ass cheeks for the first time. He heard Arlan moan and imagined his lover feeling warm air whisper across his pucker.

He let one hand cup the muscled left cheek and poured on more lube, then selected a packet from the bedside table. He tore open the wrapper of the fae condom with his teeth.

Arlan swore again. "I can't take it anymore. Please, Jay, fuck me. Let me fuck her."

Jaw tight from lust, Jay positioned himself at the were-lion's hole. The tip breeched Arlan's defenses, and Jay thought he might come right there and then. Never had he imagined it would be so warm, so tight. He surged forward slowly, taking care to watch for any sign of discomfort from Arlan. When he finally sank his cock in as far as it would go, Arlan sighed out long and loud.

"Mine!" Jay said savagely, and he meant August beneath as much as Arlan.

"Yours," August whispered in response.

Jay slapped Arlan's thigh.

"Yours," Arlan choked out.

Jay gasped with emotion. Arlan pressed his ass back as though trying to get Jay to go deeper.

"Yes, yes, baby, do that again, please."

Arlan did as Jay commanded. Then he heard August's moan as he slammed forward again, pushing Arlan deeper into her.

The pleasure was becoming too much for Jay to bear. He steadied himself, concentrating on not coming. Arlan flattened his back and pushed out, tight, so tight. Jay allowed another moment to get control of himself again and get used to the sensation. Then, grabbing Arlan's hips, he set up a brutal pace.

Oh my God, I fucking love this.

He dragged his cock in and out, the heat and pressure nearly blowing his mind. Arlan's tight ass sucked at his cock like nothing he'd ever felt before. Even as Arlan moaned his own pleasure, Jay could feel Arlan's hand moving beneath him, frigging away at August until she cried out her orgasm on a sob.

Jay kept the pace hard and steady.

Then Arlan slumped, and he was the one shouting as he came inside their precious gift of a woman. His body tightening around Jay's cock was almost enough to make Jay see stars. August groaned and then giggled. Arlan shifted his hips, sinking into her again, and August cried out, another orgasm obviously rippling through her.

Arlan had never been one of those guys whose cock instantly went soft once he came. He always stayed stiff awhile. Jay rammed in deep again, and his balls tingled as a shiver ran down his spine. His orgasm crashed over him with all the subtlety of a runaway steam engine, leaving him panting and dizzy.

They landed in a tower of limbs.

He lay against Arlan's back, aware of every rippling muscle, every glorious dip and ridge of his gorgeous lover. Jay dragged air into his lungs, unwilling to leave the tight clasp of Arlan's body.

"*Focus*, both of you, *focus*." Jay could barely hear Arlan's whispered plea.

He swore under his breath. He'd almost forgotten about the tower, but he took the time to envision for half a minute. Much good that shit ever did. All it did was spoil post-orgasmic bliss.

In the complete silence, Jay kissed Arlan's shoulder. He spread his arms around both of them, hugging them, protecting them. "God, that was *hot*. I love both of you. I don't want to take another step in this world without you both. Not ever."

Heat blazed across his cheeks at the deafening silence that was their response.

August swallowed the enormous lump of emotion back into her throat. Jay's sweet words were like a hand reaching out that she could see but not quite grab on to. The wild, romantic declaration of love seemed somehow so unlike Jay that she hadn't been able to find her tongue. She noticed Arlan hadn't responded to Jay's words of love either, even though she felt him shaking.

Jay sighed and rolled off them. Arlan did the same, drawing August into his arms.

"I guess you two just got overwhelmed with how hot the chemistry was between the three of us. Huh? That's all." Jay's tone of voice and expression were cynical as hell. "Neither of you forgives me?" He looked at the ceiling. "Well, fuck. I guess you have every right to tell me to go to hell after I've screwed you around all these years. So fucking forget it." He sat up. "Jesus Christ, I just... Can't you fucking understand? I didn't want to love so much that I'd feel sick to my stomach at the thought of never seeing someone again. I had those feelings for my mother. She might as well be dead. I thought I could ignore those feelings for you, and then having intense feelings for August too... And, yes, I didn't want people to call me a fag, but I'm over that shit. I don't care about that now." Jay's face was beet red. He swung his legs angrily over the side of the bed, yanked on the red silk robe that hung from the bedpost and belted it. "Fuck it. I'll go take a shower."

Arlan held up a hand. "Um, guys, I'm more worried about what's happened to this condom. I'm not sure it held up—"

August couldn't help laughing. "Jay, you haven't even given either of us a chance to even speak."

"So speak."

"Jay, I love you. Arlan and I both do. I know what you risked to try to save us from my mother. You've changed me. Your love has changed my very core, changed the roots of who I am." The pendant she wore glowed stronger, brighter than it had before, and she knew why. A wave of bliss and happiness washed over her. "Look at this, Jay. Look isn't it obvious what it means?"

Arlan slapped a hand against the headboard "For fuck's sake, will you guys pay attention for a second? This thing *burst.*" He held up the condom. "Baby girl, I think we might have to take you to a doctor. I mean, if you want to take the morning-after pill. And, Jay, I think we're all just feeling volatile after what happened. We do forgive you, both of us."

August put her hand on Arlan's shoulder and gestured at Jay. His eyes were wide, his mouth agape as he stared out the window. She struggled to sit up and peer out the window herself, at whatever he was staring at.

In the distance, on the yellow grass of the savannah, stood a massive gray stone tower, stretching up to the clouds.

Chapter Twenty-Eight

"Does he know what he's doing?" August asked breathlessly as she called out to Arlan. Jay had run ahead of them and was nearing the tower. Memories of crying mothers and their precious stolen babies filled Arlan's mind. The dizziness of relief at finally making the tower appear almost overwhelmed him. And while he'd lain, shaken, on the bed, Jay had dressed and gone.

"I don't know. Let's just try to catch up."

They reached the bottom of the lodge's stone steps and started crossing the wide space of dry yellow to get to the tower.

"Jay, wait!" they both called to him, and finally he stopped and turned to glance at them.

Holding August's hand as they ran to catch up to Jay, Arlan slowed his pace for her. Sweat beaded on her brow as she ran, and he wanted to wipe it off for her. Finally, they reached the spot where Jay stood.

An unseasonable wind blew the red dust of the savannah around them.

A circle glowed around the huge circumference of the gray stone tower, pulsing and shimmering with a white-hot light. Lightning zigzagged around and above the storm tower.

"Why is the tower like that?" August bit her lip. Arlan wanted to reach out and hold her.

"It's a ward."

"You mean a magic ward?"

"It's the witch doctors' spell of protection."

"So, what, we're going to be struck by lightning and die if we try to save the children?"

Arlan shook his head. "Remember, I've dealt with these bastards before. It's why I told you to take your necklace and earrings off before you left the bedroom. No metal. I don't know where the witch doctors are getting their power from. But I think at most these people are only half-fae. I've noticed gaps in their magic many times. I think there'll be a gap. We just have to wait."

Jay put his hand on August's shoulder. "If there's a gap, I'll run in. You two stay out here. I have more power than either of you to fight whatever's in there."

August shook her head. "We're fated mates, three into one. We're not leaving you behind."

"I have more magic to fight them, though. I could—"

"Now!" August shouted. Sure enough, the lightning had stopped, but it could start again at any moment.

Jay ran toward the huge wooden doors at the bottom of the tower and flung them open to reveal more stone steps lit by a single bulb. Jay didn't hesitate to run up them, and Arlan and August followed close behind.

A wave of heat hit Arlan, giving him a fright. He braced himself against the shock of it and entered the stairwell. They kept running until they were both panting, and his throat and stomach muscles ached. The stench of sulfur, matches and eggs gone bad made him gag. Poor August gagged too. He grabbed her waist and pulled her to him on the top step. Sweat trickled down the back of his neck. The heat wasn't completely unbearable, but it was as if someone had left central heating on too long at too high a level.

"Oh my God, how can the children bear this heat and the stench? We have to find them." The anguish in her voice hurt him, and made him admire her sweetness at the same time.

"The heat helps with dark magic somehow."

August nodded. "I remember this smell from my childhood. The smell of my mother's dark magic and that of her friends. Arlan, I don't think these are really witch doctors at all. I think they might be dark fae. Maybe even from the Half-Fae Network. But they've found some way to make their power stronger."

Jay nodded. "Maybe, but don't let the smell get to you. We can't hesitate."

Arlan set about flinging open the doors of rooms on any floor they came to. Many were piled high with coins and jewels. The witch doctors seemed to favor rubies. Some of the rooms were lavish bedrooms, plush with red velvet.

But there were no children.

The three lovers continued running up stairs. Arlan pushed open one of a set of huge wooden doors. It opened only partially so they couldn't see anything. Needing to know what was inside, he squeezed through. August and Jay squeezed through after him. The doors slammed shut again behind them, plunging them into almost complete darkness.

Arlan noticed an odd wheel spinning up high. Pinpricks of light whirled along the walls and ceiling. A brush of air passed over them. They could hear babies crying from other rooms, the sounds of little footsteps running.

It seemed to be coming from above and beneath and somewhere on this very level all at once. Somewhere in this tower, there were many, many children, but none in here.

He started to find his way out again to go search for the children. But as his eyes adjusted to the darkness, he thought he saw men. The flickers of light from the spinning wheel gave him a vague impression that at least three of them were massive and muscular.

Security guards.

The big, grim men walked toward them. One finally spoke. "Arlan Leonard?" The huge bastard had a thick Afrikaners accent.

"What's that up there?" Arlan shouted to distract the men, and because he really wanted to know.

The big man just swore and lunged at him, pushing Arlan up against the rough stone wall. He pressed his hand across Arlan's throat. Another man grabbed his arms, forcing his hands in front of him. Humming, the huge man managed to make a rope from somewhere fly through the air. It bound Arlan's hands tight before he even had time to think. They had to be half-fae security guards, the biggest and the best. Probably giants in their family tree, deliberately bred for this purpose. And powerful. That magic was quick.

August shouted as the other men grabbed her and Jay, restraining them. The big man held his hand over Arlan's throat and used the other to trace a blade over his hip. In the dark, another shorter man suddenly grabbed his arms.

"Tell me what those lights are," Arlan gasped.

"It's a fire wheel. The rhythmic blasts of light drain their magic."

"Whose magic?"

"Them. The rhythmic blasts of light drain their magic when they sleep, drains it from their dreams. The wheel of fire spins and retains the magic. Magic for us to enjoy. As we deserve."

"You mean you're stealing from the children."

The man only smirked at him. "Are you ready to die, were-lion?" The evil tone of the man's voice frightened him almost more than the blade in his hand. The knife traveled up and down his body, tracing the vulnerable organs on the right side: kidney, heart, lungs. The half-fae played with him like a cat playing with a mouse. "Because you *are* going to die, idiot. Your constant interference has made a trial of what should have been simple."

Arlan struggled and twisted but couldn't break free of the men. He'd have to try to stall. "Who are you, anyway? I get that you're half-fae. You're security. But what are you doing here? What is all this?"

"For fuck's sake, let him go, Gert! Don't kill him."

All of them turned toward the voice. Kruger stood in the now open doorway, holding a very large, old-fashioned book with an embossed cover of some sort.

"Professor?" August cried. "How did you get here?"

Kruger tapped a finger against the cover of the book. "Your Grandma Zenia's journal. It taught me how to scry."

"How the hell did you find that?"

"That was my car your mother drove down to the Zambezi River. She left her journal in it."

"Wow. She never let me near that journal. Not ever." August shook her head. "Do you know these men, Professor?"

"Yes. That's my cousin. He's a half-fae, prides himself on following the dark path."

Gert grinned. "Don't you also pride yourself on being dark-fae, Hendrik?"

"Not anymore. I don't pride myself on ever having been involved with any of you."

Gert gaped in seeming astonishment. "What? What's gotten up your ass, Hendrik? Upset you weren't invited to the party?"

"I stopped being a greedy loser, that's what. I realized I have a good job, and that's all I needed. I realized I don't need more money and power. Not if it means hanging out with you creeps."

"Pffft. You're mad because you weren't invited to be part of this. And now you can get lost, old man. The Half-Fae Network never was impressed by you. You were always low on the totem pole."

"These children, these villagers are *people*, half-fae just like us. And you've been stealing their kids because they're poor?"

Gert laughed. "Piss off. Go back to studying your animals. Silvara and I aren't sharing anything with you."

"Silvara?" Arlan stared at him.

Kruger's eyes grew wide. "What?'

Gert laughed. "Yeah, your were-lion lady friend, the one you were once so close to. She's mine now." He smiled smugly. "And, yeah, the two of us have been running this scam, taking any half-fae babies from the villagers around here, draining their power and making it our own. Soon, the two of us will be as powerful as any full-blood fae, and rich beyond our wildest dreams."

Kruger's mouth dropped open.

Gert clucked his tongue. "Regret not being as smart and handsome as your cousin? My heart bleeds for you."

"The two of you? What about all these other people involved? The witch doctors?"

Gert shook his head. "They aren't witch doctors. That's part of the scam. They're from the Half-Fae Network. Some are Zimbabweans. They've been fooling people that they're witch doctors for a while now." He shrugged. "Why not, if it works? It makes them more malleable. They do have a little magic power, so why not call themselves witch doctors if that's what makes the villagers compliant?"

"You are such a piece of—"

"There are a lot of babies with half-fae blood in this area, Hendrik. And their parents are poor as fuck. They live in mud huts. They believe their magic. Kids are evil anyway. Why not just take them?"

Rage at the injustice rose to mix with disgust in Arlan's heart and mind. "That's *not* true. Only some villagers believe that. The mothers don't want their *babies* stolen."

Gert sneered at Arlan. "Listen, loser. The kids are better off *here*, where they get toys and shit. They have nice rooms. We don't treat them bad."

"Apart from ripping them from their mothers' arms and draining them of their magical power. That power is their birthright, asshole."

Gert guffawed. "Their parents can't even pay to house them properly. They have no rights."

August said, "Yes, they do. You're stealing from *children*."

"Ever heard of survival of the fittest, dumbass?" Gert retorted. "Those of us in the Half-Fae Network didn't ask to be stranded in the mortal world. It's our *birthright* to get to the Fae Realm, but we're doing something about it and getting it *back*. Personal responsibility. We're helping ourselves. If these kids' parents are lazy and can't make money to save them, that's their problem."

A red veil covered Arlan's vision, and the rage inside him boiled over. He twisted a fraction more in his bonds until he was at the angle he needed to be. He aimed true and winced as his lucky kick hit precisely where he'd intended it to. Gert's tortured groan almost made him feel pain in his own balls.

"Oh, you'll pay for that," Gert growled.

Arlan ignored the angry security guard and looked at his fingernails. "Holy crap, why haven't I changed?" He'd been so sure all the stress and rage would have made his claws come out by now.

He'd been speaking to himself, but Jay answered. "Duvessa reversed the curse, remember? You're in control of it now. If you want to change, you're going to have to will it. Try humming."

Even though his friend Gert lay writhing on the floor, the security guard hadn't let go of Arlan's arm. Now he smiled. "He can't shift into a lion with his hands bound like this. None of you can do shit. We're gonna lock your dumb Warrior of the Light asses up."

Arlan laughed. "What does my being tied up have to do with shifting?"

"You'll still be bound, were-lion. You won't break free of those magic ropes."

From behind him, Arlan heard feminine humming. He turned in astonishment to see flames flickering at the ends of August's fingertips. Pure horror contorted her features.

Fear shone in the eyes of all the security guards too. One thug smacked his hand against the wall. "That bitch has finally come into her mother's fire-fae power."

"How could she do that?" one of the guards asked. "We should be the ones with that kind of power from draining the kids."

The first guard sniffed. "He mother was the daughter of a fae princess. Hardly surprising."

"Did you hear the way Gert was talking before?" Another man glared at Gert. "I don't think we're getting shit. No money. Nothing more than our wages. It's all about him and Silvara, not the Network." On saying that, the man hauled off and kicked Gert right where Arlan had kicked him. Gert's scream of pain might have made Arlan's blood run cold if it wasn't so deserved.

Arlan swallowed bile. "So where's Silvara now?

Gert panted hard, his words coming in short bursts. "Her...mother...died. Her parents are Americans. She's in Montana, sorting...the will."

"More money for you, eh, you prick? And none for us." The outraged employee gave Gert another kick.

August carefully rolled another ball of fire in her palms. She'd gotten over her shock and was gaining confidence.

Gert managed to blurt out more words around his pain. "We need...to stop her...before...hurts with fire. Get...knife." Though he still writhed in pain on the floor, his whispered words had the desired effect. One of the men bent to get the knife and lunged for August.

The beast inside Arlan gave an almighty roar. His lion leaped, battling to fully emerge. Claws burst through his hands. Fur raced up his arms.

Chapter Twenty-Nine

Don't be afraid.

Her first instinct had been terror. Childhood memories of her mother's use of fire magic had filled her mind. Duvessa had used fire to frighten her, to punish her, in so many of the memories she actively repressed.

But really when she thought about it, she knew why her power was coming back to her now. Love was making her whole. Making her who she was meant to be. Increasing her self-esteem, the lack of which had suppressed her magic. She clenched her fists, forcing herself to concentrate and take control. She rolled the flames erupting from her fingertips into balls.

Humming and concentrating carefully, she sent the fire to burn the ropes binding Arlan and Jay, willing with every shred of concentration she had that it wouldn't burn her lovers. The ropes sizzled around Arlan's bound paws. Then she willed the fire to die before it could touch his fur. Free at last, Arlan pounced on the man with the knife, sinking his fangs into the arm holding the blade. Perhaps the brassy taste of the man's blood was too much for him, or perhaps it made him want to feast. Whatever the reason, he dropped the screaming man on the floor.

One of the men, obviously terrified of the combination of fire and lions, pulled the door open and ran into the stairwell. Another man followed him.

August thought she might as well try asking the professor what he knew. "Hendrik, did you see anything more with your scrying? Do you know where exactly the children are?"

"No. Unfortunately not."

She rolled her eyes. Kruger had addressed her breasts again. He might have had a change of heart about where he stood on issues of good and evil, but he was still a pervert.

"You'll never find it, bitch." Gert struggled to get up.

Kruger hauled off and kicked Gert several more times. He couldn't get at the man's nuts now, but he got a few good kicks in the kidneys until Gert sprawled on the floor again.

Jay put his foot on head of the man with the bleeding arm. "Tell us where the kids are, or I'm going to stomp you."

"I...I don't know."

Jay put more pressure on the man's head.

"I *don't*. They don't share it with us. Mufaro must be right. Gert and Silvara were planning to keep all that power for themselves."

Jay kept pressing on the man's head until he said, "All right, it's fucking connected to this room somehow. I just don't know how. There's a secret doorway in here. That wheel of spinning light over there. It's something Gert rigged up. It drains magic power from the kids. I don't understand it all. I'm only a quarter fae. I have no power. Let me up."

But Jay didn't take his foot off the guy's skull. Instead, he began twirling his fingers, focusing hard, humming like a vacuum cleaner. To her astonishment, instead of light, a mini tornado appeared, floating in the air above his hands, along with the indigo light she'd seen him create when he cooked. His air-fae magic.

"August," he said, "roll up some more of those flames for me, would you, sweetness?"

She had no idea what he was planning, but she was getting the hang of this fire thing, and it was actually *fun*. She made a strong humming sound in her throat, letting the flames arise from her hands.

"Close the door behind the cowards, Kruger. We need an enclosed space here."

Kruger did as asked. Jay focused on the flame in her hands and shot the mini tornado right into the ball of flames. Smoke billowed up in the air, filling the room until everyone was hacking and coughing.

August blinked, her eyes watering from the smoke. Arlan let out a roar.

"What in God's name are you doing, Jay?" Kruger shouted. "I'm getting out of here."

"Help me!" shouted the man under Jay's foot.

"Don't even think of opening that, door, Kruger."

"I'm not letting you kill me with fire, you crazy mother—"

"*Look.*"

August and Hendrik stared where Jay pointed. The smoke seeped into cracks along the wall, outlining a doorway. Jay put his hands to his mouth and called, "Watch out, children. I'm breaking the door down. Move out of the way. Move any little ones out of the way."

August could only pray that the children heard and could understand English. "Wait. Jay, what if they get hurt?"

"I don't see any other way to do this, August.

"I don't either."

Arlan tapped on the outlined door. They called to the children several more times, urging them back. Finally, Jay strode to the door and began kicking it. August ran to join him and kicked too. Wood splintered, and a loud cracking noise rent the air. Light on the other side filled the dark room.

August took in the sight—toddlers, babies, preschoolers, school-age children, teddy bears, dolls, a train set, and beds stretching off seemingly forever, in a huge nursery.

A nursery-rhyme mural covered the walls. She wondered who among the evil kidnappers had had enough heart to do up the room in such a way. Most of the children huddled against the opposite wall, and they all turned to stare. One frightened child held a splinter of the broken door in his tiny hand.

Epilogue

Three Months Later.

"Have you felt the change yet, August?"

August took a sip of the dry nonalcoholic champagne that Nhamo had poured into her crystal flute. She smiled at her new friend, whose belly was swollen. She must be seven months or so along in her pregnancy.

"Well, yeah... Many changes. Fatigue, mostly."

Nhamo laughed. "That's not what I meant. The were-lion, Arlan. He is your mate, yes?"

August nodded, unsure what Nhamo knew about magic and were-lions, and where she stood on such issues as threesomes and fated mates.

"He told me that he really is the magic were-lion. He got me this job with the catering company," Nhamo said proudly.

August smiled. She was so glad Arlan and Jay had been able to get her a job with the catering company hosting the lunchtime feast.

"Your other boyfriend is very good-looking too." Nhamo nodded toward the podium in the lodge's spacious dining hall. They'd invited all the villagers to a catered lunch to discuss the situation with the witch doctors now that the danger had passed. "They are both half-fae your men, yes?"

"Yes."

Easier than explaining Arlan's only a quarter fae.

Jay stood at the podium, flawlessly handsome in a charcoal suit. He tapped twice on the mike, getting everyone's attention before speaking. "Good evening, everyone. I just wanted to say a few words about why Arlan and I decided to host this party." He took a deep breath. "Firstly, we wanted to celebrate the defeat of the group of men and women from the Half-Fae Network who have plagued this area for so long."

A wild cheer rose from the crowd.

"Another cause for celebration is the birth of three new lion cubs that have been born in the area, thanks to the tireless work of Professor Kruger from Long Island University and his gorgeous and accomplished assistant, my lovely wife, August Peak."

Loud clapping filled the dining hall.

"Most importantly, this party is to celebrate the successful return of fifty-five children to their parents, children who were stolen by the Half-Fae Network."

The applause reached a crescendo.

Clapping the loudest was Runo, his eyes filled with happy tears, Mukuru sat in his lap, playing with the orange and yellow beads around his neck and laughing. The little boy's head was shaved close. He looked so adorable with his chubby cheeks, big smile and little hands clapping hard. Mukuru's older brother, Pili, sat beside his mother, Nhamo, clasping her hand.

"But this is not the only good news concerning children I have today. For me personally, I've had the news I'm to be a father. My wife is due to give birth next July."

The applause from Jay and Arlan's friends was almost deafening. August looked down at the large diamond in her ring, surrounded by five smaller diamonds. It caught the sunlight and shone prisms of rainbow light in her lap.

Conservative Jay had had to buy her the biggest and the best, had had to marry her right away when he'd found out she was carrying a child. And he was convinced the child was his, despite the high likelihood to the contrary. She giggled. Oh well. One day she would have his child too.

August's smile widened when Arlan came up behind her. He slid his hand across her tummy, stroking the slight bulge that signaled the little miracle growing inside her.

"So much for fae condoms," she whispered

"Hey, now, human condoms break too. And I was going pretty hard at it."

"Shh." She put her finger to her lips, indicating all the people around him. Arlan only laughed. There were enough children in the dining hall that the low hum of noise ensured no one heard his words.

"Hey, Jay," Kruger shouted, "the news is about to come on."

Jay nodded toward the huge flat screen TV they'd set up earlier next to the podium. "Turn it on."

The crowd gathered in front of the television to watch. August knew they all wanted to see the same show they'd seen snippets of for the past three days on the news. The documentary began with a montage of images of mothers and fathers crying with happiness and hugging children of various ages. Then it shifted to pictures of the storm tower.

The Zimbabwean news reporter spoke with awe in his voice. "Many families have made some difficult claims about this mysterious tower. They claim this tower was not previously here and that some kind of magic was involved. Some blame witch doctors, others the so-called Half-Fae Network. What we can confirm, however, is that many children once imprisoned here have been returned to their ecstatic parents, and that two people involved with the Half-Fae Network have been arrested. However odd their stories about this occurrence, the fact remains that many missing children have been found."

More happy faces of parents and children showed on the screen. Pride at what she and her two lovers had achieved made August grin.

Then the reporter's smile faded. "But it is not a happy ending for every child. Some of these children are orphans, their parents not having survived while they were missing, and some no longer have homes. For this group of children, financial aid is desperately needed."

August squeezed Arlan's hand. Lately, when he wasn't with her or the lions, he was on the phone trying to arrange care for the orphans. He squeezed back then whispered, "Come outside with me."

The party was in full swing and had become so crowded that no one would notice them leaving for a while, so she let him take her hand and lead her outside.

They picked their way through the crowd of people. She looked behind her for Jay, wanting him to come outside with them, but he was busy talking to the caterers, probably about their pay.

Outside, the yellow grass swayed in the hot breeze, cicadas hummed, and far away, she could hear an elephant. "You got Nhamo a job with the new catering company. That's awesome."

"Her husband was earning next to nothing. They were barely surviving. Anyway, she's a fast learner."

"So this new catering company you and Jay invested in, you think it's going to provide a lot of jobs?

He leaned back against an acacia tree. "Yeah, finally gonna close down every one of my dad's hunting lodges, replace jobs with the catering company."

"That sounds like a lot of work."

Arlan grinned. "Not for us, baby. I still don't think you get how much money we have." He sighed. "I don't know how much evil my dad did to get all this money we have, though."

"Yeah, I know the feeling. Lucky I didn't inherit anything, huh?"

"We could fight that."

She gave him a cheeky grin. "Why bother when my men are both billionaires? Let June and April have it. I could care less."

"It makes me so mad, though. Those bastards..."

"Shhh." She put her hand on his arm. "I don't care, baby, really."

They walked on, holding hands for some time, until he pulled her behind another acacia tree and took her in his arms. "How are you feeling otherwise?"

"Me? I'm fine."

He frowned.

"If you're talking about the baby, Arlan, I feel great. Morning sickness now and then, but not too bad."

"August," he whispered. "I'm asking have you felt the change yet?"

"What? What change?"

He glanced up at the sky. "I don't know if it's true, and if it is, it's pretty rare, but I read that if you become pregnant by a were-lion, you may become one yourself. I'm so sorry about the burst condom. And it looks to me like you... Well, you seem different."

Her heart stopped. She could actually hear the thunder of it click off and the swishing sensation of her blood draining.

He put a hand on her shoulder, obviously noticing the shock on her face. "Baby girl, you okay? Don't be scared. Whatever happens, Jay and I will help and support you. If you have trouble controlling the shifting, we'll find someone else with magic like Duvessa's to fix it for you. We'll search far and wide."

She gave a gulp so loud they could both hear it. "I never expected to get pregnant, you know? I never even thought of it. I wouldn't mind being a were-lion, I guess, as long as I could change back."

"Whatever happens, we'll make sure to find a way you can change back. We'll find someone as clever and powerful as your mother was to help us." He pulled her into his arms. "Remember that day at the market, when we saw Mukuru and he threw his arms around you?"

She nodded.

"You were so gentle and sweet with him. When I saw that, all I could think of was you with a big round belly, swollen with my child. And one day, you'll have Jay's child too."

Her skin itched in the heat, itched so bad it hurt. Her nipples were tight buds, chafed by the material of her thin cotton dress. She had a fuzzy feeling in her head. Her muscles were twitching, then stretching. Every sinew ached. For a few moments, terror gripped her. Gradually, her fear faded, and sensuality took hold. A velvety, sexy sensation replaced terror. Fur sprouted from her pores and began to cover her body.

Arlan shifted into his own beautiful male form, and she rubbed her head across his flanks, full of affection, full of the deepest love she had ever felt. She smelled a dozen new scents and heard a dozen sounds she'd never heard before.

Together, they stalked across the dusty plain, and she truly felt she was the queen of this land and that he was her king. He began to chase her, and she ran swiftly. Never had she felt so wild and free.

On and on they raced across the veldt, until he caught her, pounced on her and pinned her to the ground. Without any kind of signal to each other, they both shifted simultaneously back into human form.

As she regained her human fear, worry and guilt rushed her mind. Along with a dawning horror that she might have harmed her precious baby.

He saw her expression and grasped her shoulders. "Sweetheart, sweetheart it's okay. It's okay." He pulled her into his arms, stroking her back. "Baby you know how much I read. I researched this. The fetus shifts with your own movements, from cub, to human, human to cub. I really thought this very unlikely to happen from what I read, or I would have warned you. I was torn between warning you and needlessly scaring you. I made a mistake. I'm sorry."

Arlan kissed her neck and throat, a great depth of love in his expression, intensity and devotion in those hazel eyes. "Do you have any idea how much I love you? How proud I am to have a woman like you bear my child?"

She could feel herself blushing. But she felt proud too, proud of herself and all she had accomplished in Zimbabwe. And so proud of her men.

"My becoming a were-lion is going to make it even more difficult to leave Africa. I'm going to want to run free on these plains in my animal form. Wow, I had no idea it was so much *fun*."

"We don't ever have to leave."

"Jay wants to, because of how gay and bisexual men are treated in Zimbabwe. He's been using a lot of magic to protect the two of you from being arrested all these years. I think it tires him out and stresses him. If we spent some time in New York, it would be relaxing for him, I think. It would be nice for him to see how much more accepted alternative sexualities are there."

Arlan kissed her. "Then we'll visit New York soon."

"I can't leave my sister to feed my cats forever."

"We can ship them over here, if you want."

He tilted her head so she faced him, capturing her mouth with his and holding her tight. As always, his kiss was sweet, powerful and intoxicating, like lighter fluid to her libido. But he broke the kiss before she could deepen it, and held her gently cradled against his chest.

"Hey, lovebirds. Aren't you forgetting someone?" She turned to see Jay and held out her arms to him. He picked her up, swung her around, braced her back against the tree.

"You used your new scrying talent to find us? I knew you would."

"Yeah, your grandmother's journal has a lot of great info. You should read it."

She shuddered. "I'll pass."

Jay kissed her, soft and quiet, until his warmth sparked licks of heat inside her, arousing her again. He broke the kiss and laughed when her own kiss became too passionate, and set her back down on her feet. "Baby it's too hot out here for more than a kiss. That'll have to wait till we get home."

Jay brought her hand to the lump beneath his trousers so she could stroke his firm length against her palm.

"Do I get a kiss?" Jay met Arlan's eyes, and heat shimmered between them. He grabbed Arlan's ponytail and traced the seam of his mouth, parting his lips. August imagined the dark taste Arlan was experiencing and gave out her own moan.

Watching Jay run his hands over Arlan's strong, muscular body never got old. He pushed Arlan's shirt up, and his lips mapped each ridge of muscle.

Jay dropped to his knees, but he laughed and stood again. "No, I'm not doing this in this suit. Let's go home." Putting his arms around both of them, he squeezed their shoulders. "I love you two."

His simple sentence hit her hard, just as hard as the first time he'd ever said it. Her throat knotted with emotion as it always did.

"I love both of you too." Emotion filled Arlan's voice. For the were-lion, it had always been easy to say. He'd always been brave and confident in his love. She knew, because of what she'd been through with her mother, it would never be as easy for her. Both her men understood that.

"I don't deserve either of you." Jay squeezed their shoulders again. "But you know, I'm afraid I can never let you go."

"Do you promise?" she managed to whisper.

"With everything I have. I promise."

Arlan grinned at her. "We both promise you, August. Forever and always."

About the Author

Since she came of age Lisa Whitefern has embarrassed people by talking about sex. Now she writes the hottest of erotic romance and erotica.

Lisa has a life-long passion for fairy tales and fantasy. Ever since her teacher read *The Lion, the Witch and the Wardrobe* to her class when she was six, Lisa's been looking for ways to visit Narnia. Lisa thinks it immensely unfair she can't wiggle her nose to clean her house like Samantha in the TV show *Bewitched*.

She has a master's degree with honors in English Literature, reads tarot cards and tutors children of all ages in English after school. Although born in New York City to American parents Lisa has lived most of her life in New Zealand. She now lives in the foothills of the beautiful Waitakere Ranges of Auckland with her husband and her two gorgeous sons.

Don't forget to follow Lisa on Twitter and like her on Facebook!

http://lisawhitefern.wordpress.com

It's a lovely night for a sleigh ride—until something evil takes the reins.

Wicked Wonderland
© *2013 Lisa Whitefern*

When Nick and Kris, the half-fae sons of human mothers, aren't using Santa's sleigh in the off-season to make deliveries for their booming sex toy business, they're setting off sensual fireworks in the bedroom.

Yet they dream of a feminine third to complete their lives. There's only one woman they can picture filling that role: Lilly, the girl they both dated in college.

Lilly thought earning extra money stripping was a good plan, until she's left battered, bruised, and stuffed in a back-alley trash can. He rescuers turn out to be the dark, brooding dom and the golden-haired sub whose faces—and shockingly entwined bodies—are still the stuff of her most searing fantasies.

While she's more than willing to take them up on their offer of one perfect night of magic, she questions whether anyone can break into Nick and Kris's powerful bond. But there's someone who's been waiting for this moment all Lilly's life. An evil psychopath who holds the secrets of her past—unless Nick and Kris can unravel them in time to save her from a fate worse than death.

Warning: Explicit ménage a trois, hot m/f/m scenes, hot male/male scenes, a ruthless stalker who torments the heroine, sex toys, sex on roof tops, spankings, BDSM, Dark Fae, birdmen, orphans, strippers, centaurs, a violent battle between good and evil creatures on board a ship, true love, and sex in Santa's sleigh.

Available now in ebook and print from Samhain Publishing.

Love can be a powerful ally...or a lethal weapon.

Blood for Blood
© 2015 Darcy Abriel
Zytarri, Book 1

The Past...

Leora Saguna has become what her kind fear most—a blood huntress. Fueled by a lust for revenge for the assassination of her Alpha, she has violated every Sangorrian law to track the murderers down. And one day return to her infant daughter, Katriel.

Each time Noah Chisca watches his mark take macabre delight in her task, he is one dead bandit closer to earning the highest bounty of his career. Yet he can't deny the desire that twists his gut. He takes her captive; she takes him as her mate.

The Present...

Katriel knows bonding with the mate her mother has chosen will ensure her future as heir. But the memory of the forbidden warrior monk who stole her heart haunts her, and she rebels.

Valyn's identity is hidden until he's proven himself worthy of Katriel. But fighting a deadly dragon is only the beginning of their nightmare, as sinister forces conspire to shake the foundations of Sangorrian society and unleash a reign of blood that may destroy them all.

Warning: Contains red-hot flashbacks, white-hot Sangorrian mating rituals, blood and gore, a villain into torture, and no-holds-barred erotic passion.

Available now in ebook and print from Samhain Publishing.

SAMHAIN
PUBLISHING

It's all about the story...

Romance

HORROR

www.samhainpublishing.com

CPSIA information can be obtained at www.ICGtesting.com
Printed in the USA
BVOW08s0848110716

455110BV00004B/70/P